PRAISE FOR M...
AND *TH...*

MATERIAL

"Mary SanGiovanni is one of my favorite authors. Her work is cause for celebration, and always a fun read! I'm a big fan!"
— Brian Keene, Bram Stoker Award-winning Author of *Dead Sea*

"With *The Hollower,* Mary SanGiovanni makes the kind of debut most horror writers dream about; this superbly-written novel is filled to the brim with mounting terror, shocking set pieces, some of the richest characterization you'll encounter anywhere this year, and a central figure of undeniable dread. It's got it all: scares, poignancy, people you know as well as your own family, and an unrelenting tension that will have your hands shaking by the time you reach its nerve-wracking finale."
— Gary A. Braunbeck, Bram Stoker Award-winning Author of *Mr. Hands*

"Mary SanGiovanni writes with all the skill of a neurosurgeon and all the passion of a Shakespearian actor on a roll. *The Hollower* is a fast building, high tension ride, with a solid mystery peopled with realistic characters thrown into a nightmare situation that grows darker by the minute. One hell of a novel by a writer everyone should keep their eyes on. I think we have a rising star on our hands."
— James A. Moore, Author of *Under the Overtree*

THE INTRUDER

Then Cheryl spied it. A chill like ice water down her back caused her body to shudder.

The poster. The Carmen Electra poster. A beer floated above the wrist, across a paperless chasm where Carmen's hand used to be. Both eyes had been cut out as well as the mouth, and a tiny strip to either side of her head where her ears would have been, if not covered by her hair.

Her hands—don't forget, her hands are missing, too.

Didn't killers remove hands to prevent police from identifying bodies?

Oh God. Someone—someone else really is in here.

Cheryl barely felt her arm yank the door open or her feet carry her to her car. It was like she was watching what she was doing rather than doing things herself. The "out-of-body" Cheryl saw herself scrabble to fit the car key in the lock, and fumble with the handle.

She backed out into the street and straightened the wheel, then looked up to the rearview. Suddenly, everything became vividly clear.

The outline of a head and upper torso stood several feet behind her car, its black clothes blending with the night around it, a hat perched on top of its head. Something was wrong with its face. No, not the face, not exactly. The lack—*yes,* the lack of features that made a face.

No eyes. No mouth, no ears….

THE
HOLLOWER

Mary SanGiovanni

LEISURE BOOKS NEW YORK CITY

This book is dedicated to Laura Mazzarone.
The person you are is not the person you stay,
but a true friend sees the core of you
through the changes and still cares.

A LEISURE BOOK®

September 2007

Published by

Dorchester Publishing Co., Inc.
200 Madison Avenue
New York, NY 10016

ISBN-10: 0-8439-5974-6
ISBN-13: 978-0-8439-5974-1

The name "Leisure Books" and the stylized "L" with design are trademarks of Dorchester Publishing Co., Inc.

Printed in the United States of America.

Visit us on the web at www.dorchesterpub.com.

ACKNOWLEDGMENTS

A warm and heartfelt thank-you to Heidi Miller, Christopher Paul Carey, Gary Braunbeck, Steven Piziks, and Seton Hill University's Masters in Writing Popular Fiction Program. Without you, this book literally wouldn't be here, and it is a far better book for your help.

Thanks to Brian Keene, James A. Moore, and again, Gary Braunbeck for the kind words about the book, and for their advice.

Thanks also to Chris Golden, Tom Monteleone, and Doug Winter for their advice.

Thanks to Frank Weimann and Yvonne Woon, and thanks to Don D'Auria for the chance to do what I've always wanted.

Thanks also to the GSHW folks, Meghan Knierim, MJ Euringer, and Paul Zema for the endless support.

All my love and gratitude to Adam SanGiovanni, Michael and Suzanne SanGiovanni, Michele San-Giovanni, and Christy SanGiovanni, who dealt with many late nights and absences so I could finish the book.

THE
HOLLOWER

Introduction
by
Brian Keene

What is fear?

Seriously. Can you define it? Perhaps. You can look it up in a dictionary. Talk about the emotional and physical responses it inspires. Toss around some big words and wrap it up with a pretty bow. But do you really *know* fear? I mean intimately. Has fear ever changed you? Have you shaken fear's hand; bought it a drink or slept with it for a night?

If you're reading this, then chances are you enjoy being scared. I do, too. I was a horror fan long before I made my living writing horror novels. But think about this for a moment. When was the last time you were really, truly scared by a horror novel or film? I'm not talking about jumping in your seat or sleeping with the bathroom light on. No. That's not fear. I'm talking about that sweating, pulse-rate-increasing sensation when your ears ring and your head pounds and your butt clenches and the room seems to spin. You can't breathe, can't think, and all you want to do is cry, scream, throw up, and laugh all at once. When was the last time a book or movie made you feel that way?

Once, when I tried to define fear, I wrote the following: "Fear is getting ready to go to a surprise fiftieth anniversary party for your parents, and then receiving a phone call informing you that they were killed in a head-on collision with a drunken driver while on their way to the party. Fear is when you find a lump in your testicles or breast. It's watching a loved one's mind be eradicated by the slow rot of Alzheimer's. It's learning that your newborn infant has cancer. That the bank is foreclosing on your home. The sudden screech of tires a second before impact. The 'Breaking News' alert on your television. The Emergency Broadcast System when it's not only a test. The knock on your door at three in the morning when your child isn't home. The realization that you've been working in a factory since high school, and that you're forty, and that you will *never* leave there. . . ."

I still believe this to be true. But I'm older now, and I realize that these are only symptoms of fear. They are not fear itself. It is our reaction to these things—how they impact our life—that causes fear.

But what *is* fear?

If you want to really know fear, then you have to look inside yourself. That isn't easy for most people to do. Oh, we might pretend to do it. We might hold hands with our support group or counselor and sing "Kumbaya" and read self-help books and look inside our hearts—but deep down inside, we're just bullshitting. Nobody likes to look deep inside themselves, because they know what's lurking in those dark corners of the heart. Remember Nietzsche's adage about staring into the Abyss? Each of us has our own Abyss. That's where true fear resides. No matter who you are, you've got some darkness inside you. You don't like to go there, so you hide it. You don't think about it. And that Abyss? It's a place where angels fear to tread.

Mary SanGiovanni is no angel. She's talented, beautiful, intelligent, clever, loyal, appreciative of good video games, fond of champagne, and possesses a wonderful sense of humor, but she is no angel. And unlike the angels, she is not afraid to walk the Abyss. She peers deep into that darkness and pulls things out, exposing them to the light. I can say this with some confidence because I've known Mary for many years now. I am her friend, and I am a fan. I've had the pleasure of watching her writing grow and develop—from her first short story collection, *Under Cover of the Night* (long out of print but worth the hunt online), to the novel you hold in your hands. And though I've written a number of introductions over the years, I can't remember being prouder to do so than I am for this one. I've never forgotten the first time I read her work, and I can guarantee that you won't forget either. Like most authors of our generation, she was first inspired by Stephen King. But if you look closely, you'll also see hints of Richard Matheson, Jack Ketchum, Peter Straub, John Carpenter, and others. Don't misunderstand me. Her work isn't simply a hodgepodge pastiche of those authors. Not at all. Her voice is strong and uniquely her own. But the influences are there, and they are a wonderful mix—a fantastic, tantalizing cocktail that is sure to please any horror fan.

The Hollower may seem like just another monster novel. And there's no shame in that, because we all love a good monster novel—and this one is indeed good. But the monster in this book can see inside you. It can delve into the Abyss. It destroys its victims from the inside out. It's not the bogeyman. Not again. You're far too old for that and there's no such thing besides. No, it's not the bogeyman. It's something much worse. Something primal. This monster *knows* fear.

So does Mary SanGiovanni, and she's about to share it with you. True fear; not that stuff we tell ourselves is scary. Her characters seem real because they are us—warts and all. Mary knows how you see yourself and how the world sees you. She knows that these are two very different perceptions, and that we aren't always aware of this. But more importantly, she knows what's inside us, what lies beneath the mind and spirit, beyond the doors of perception—that dark matter of the soul. That fear.

What is fear?

Turn the page and find out.

Brian Keene
Heart of Darkness, Pennsylvania

Prologue

A man could only take so much. Max had had enough.

The insomnia, that had been there all along (*They aren't nightmares if you're awake, Gladys*, but that had only made things worse). Then, after the first year, he'd slipped back into the stuttering. And he'd always had a bit of a nervous stomach, so the ulcer was no surprise. But the way his hands shook sometimes—like an old man's—he was too young to have hands that shook like that, wasn't he? Wasn't forty-eight too old an age to stutter and too young an age to shake? Sometimes, when he looked in the mirror, he wasn't so sure.

But not today. Today, he stared at his reflection with approval. The face that stared back at him was older, yes, but content. Almost the kind of content he'd been back before Gladys left him.

He looked good, he thought. *Well, maybe not good, but better*. A dress shirt hugged his build, and he still managed to fill out the pressed jacket. Auburn hair threaded with gray, neatly combed, covered a good portion of his head. His mustache and beard were trimmed. His lips were a bit dry and cracked yet, but he'd managed to kick the nervous habit of constantly licking them. And so what if his eyes had sunken into bags? They had stopped twitching, and shone with the kind of conviction he hadn't felt since his first days with the Group.

A twinge of guilt flickered just long enough for Max to notice it, then blew out. The Group. He'd miss that damp little basement room with the swinging lightbulb and the folding chairs that never warmed beneath the heat of his backside. He smiled to himself. The memory-scent of hospitality's coffee and Entenmann's cookies on the card table lingered, still fresh in his nose.

His friends from the Group were the only ones who hadn't abandoned him. He wondered if they would see this decision as his abandoning them. He didn't think so, though. They understood each card in his deck, one loser hand after another. Getting laid off from a job he'd held for twenty-three long years. The physical ailments that kept him from sleeping. Gladys leaving last fall. The throaty winds at night that made wind chimes out of barely audible words. The bills. The Group understood those things.

And if they were the only problems, he might have felt simple comfort in the understanding of his friends. But they weren't. The far worse problems (*Gladys, they aren't really* nightmares, *per se*), they didn't understand. Well, Dr. Stevens certainly didn't. None of them did. Except Sally Kohlar. And she had assured Max that her brother understood, too. They knew about the faceless thing that haunted him in every facet of his life. And he couldn't bear to confront it one more time. Not even once more. Nobody who *understood*, nobody who *knew*—could ever hold that against him.

The blue tie with the black S-hook pattern was Gladys's favorite. He tied it carefully, smoothing it over his chest.

He felt calm. It was the first time he'd felt that calm in years. He'd even managed to work up an appetite that morning and had cooked himself up a damn good plate of bacon and eggs, if he did say so himself.

After the video, it was like an albatross had dropped from his neck and gravity had dissolved in the cosmos. He was alone with his thoughts, and relieved that he could find that calm again, to hold on to.

The Group members rematerialized before his mind's eye again, but this time no guilt followed. Their mouths moved without sound and they offered encouraging smiles. They were shouting to him, shouting approval. They knew. Understood, all of them.

He had polished the shotgun the night before. Now, fully dressed, he sat on the edge of the bed next to it, suddenly shy. He felt like he was fifteen again and looking to slip an arm around his girl. The gun would make no protest when he picked it up. The metal felt good in his hands—cool, smooth, like skin on a chilly spring night before the goose bumps rise. His old girl.

With slow and deliberate movements he opened the night table drawer, took out the box of twenty-gauge shotgun shells, and loaded her. The letter to Gladys he produced from his shirt pocket with a flourish aimed to please no one but himself, and he propped it neatly against the lamp base on the night table.

Then Max wrapped his lips around the gun (*metallic taste, like blood, but cold*) and was surprised how natural it felt. He'd expected it to be clumsy, oversized somehow. But his old girl's lips were smooth and the barrel slid right in, just as deep as he was comfortable.

The phone jerked him from his reverie and his finger twitched on the trigger. His heart shifted gears suddenly and pounded triple-time to the shrill little bell. He waited, counting off the rings, eyes closed and tongue tasting the sour metal that pressed against it.

Three, four, five . . . The phone stopped after eleven rings. Eleven rings and then a rush of soundlessness that dampened even the cheerful warbling of birds outside.

Impulse drew his eyes to the window on the left wall. Dark treetops speckled the bottom half of the sky right above the sill. Exhaust-pipe wisps of racing clouds stretched pleasantly around them. From his place on the bed, Max couldn't see the street. He didn't have to. He knew *it* was watching, waiting, a pallid oval of nothingness tilted quizzically to one side and up toward the bedroom.

Not even one more time. This was it.

It took very little pressure to squeeze the trigger. It was almost as if another finger pressed against his own, guiding him.

Had Gladys, or anyone else for that matter, still been in the house, she might have heard dry chuckling and the hollow sound of footsteps echoing up from the street below, followed by the soft, drawn-out creak of the front door opening.

One

Sean opened his eyes and then immediately wished he hadn't, because the strange shape in the window that both was and wasn't a face scared the hell out of him.

It's not the bogeyman. Not again. You're too old for that and there's no such thing besides. No such thing, Seanny. Don't be a sissy.

And Sean didn't think he was. He didn't cry when he got shots at the doctor's, or when he'd fallen off those railroad ties behind Chris's house and broken his arm, or when he'd taken that tumble down Schooley's Mountain and sprained his ankle. Sean was smart for his age—"unusually inquisitive," he'd heard Mrs. Appleman, who had been his second grade teacher, tell his mom once. And he was brave. He hadn't met a dare he wouldn't take. He didn't have time for bogeymen. At eleven years old, he was the man of the house, with a mother and big sister to look out for. He couldn't afford to be a sissy.

But that glowing white oval peering in through

the window (*oh my God, it's coming into the room, it's coming right for me*) opened a door somewhere inside him, and a weighty dread came through and took over his limbs.

Not in the room—in the mirror. The face is in the mirror.

Sean wasn't even sure it could be called a face. Nothing about it was face-like. There were no eyes, no mouth, not even any indents where the features would be. But on top of its head sat a dark hat like the men wore in those old black-and-white detective movies his mom loved so much. And the way it tilted made it look kind of . . . well, thoughtful, somehow. Like it was watching him, thinking deep thoughts about what it was going to do to him.

He closed his eyes and opened them. No one was at the window. Nothing, he noticed, in the mirror, either. The glass stood across from his bed, capturing in reverse the closet door, a battlefield of strewn action-figure bodies by his dresser, the foot of his bed encased in navy sheets and blanket, and a band of the window that looked out over the front yard from the second floor. The empty window.

Sean settled down beneath his sheets, a chill brushing along the hairs of his neck and down his spine. Until that moment, he hadn't been aware of the thudding of his heart. *Moon, it had to be some type of reflection of the moon or—*

A scraping that he felt more than heard brought his gaze back to the window. His breath shrank terrified into the deep recesses of his lungs.

The heavy storm pane skittered up along the frame. By itself.

By itself.

A scream died silent in his throat. *Ohmigod, ohmigod . . .*

The screen followed in stiff jerks. A cool breeze blew in. Sean heard the low whine of the wind as it banged the garbage cans out on the curb.

And into the bedroom floated a red balloon—stately, as if the noises on the street below had heralded its arrival. Its string fluttered behind it like a royal train. The balloon bumped lightly along the ceiling, its course set, its purpose decided.

The balloon came to rest dead-center above his bed, bobbing lightly to and fro with the late September night breeze. It was then that Sean really noticed the chirp of friction against rubber and the tiny writhing that stretched the confines of the red bulb.

Something—some things—are in there.

He felt the revulsion as a tingling in his extremities, originating from that single realization in his brain. Something was in that balloon, trying to get out.

"Mom." The whisper was drowned out by the sound of (*what, legs? Claws?*) things stretching, expanding . . .

The balloon burst with a pop that thundered through the little room like an explosion. A black rain fell from it onto his blanket. The drops dispersed with a din of angry chatter, spreading outward like fallout and spilling off the bed in wave after wave.

It took only a moment for Sean's mind to wrap around what was happening. Hundreds of spindly legs and barbed stingers dug into the blanket for purchase, propelling bloated black bodies forward in the race toward Sean.

The chirp of the bugs' skittering legs over legs sounded loud in his ears. Just as they crossed the border between blanket and pajamas, Sean dislodged the scream from his chest. Flinging the blanket off, he leaped from the bed and flew to the door. His feet landed once on several crunching obsidian shells before he launched through the doorway.

The light in his mother's room flicked on before he even reached it. Her legs kicked off the blankets and she swept toward him.

"Sean!" She cupped his chin in her hands. "My God, baby, are you all right? You're shaking—"

"Bugs," he whispered, the word dry and hard in his throat. "Millions."

She searched his face for several seconds, concern and confusion in her eyes. Then she led the way back to his room. Sean, hanging a safe distance behind, ran a pale hand through his bed-fluffed brown hair. When her arm reached around the door frame for the light, he had a terrible vision of a writhing black wall of insect bodies swarming from the switch plate down her arm. He could see it, a black sleeve of their polished backs and needle-legs. He opened his mouth to say something to stop her.

The switch clicked, flooding the room with light. His mother didn't scream. She crossed her arms—her bare arms—over her chest, then drew them tighter around her body as she stepped through the door.

"Sean, it's cold in here. Why did you open a window?"

Sean peeked around the door frame, his eyes panning the room. The blanket hung crumpled off the side of the bed. His pillow still supported the dent where his head had pressed it in. Nothing chattered, nothing scrambled over the wrinkled sheets toward the headboard. Nothing on the floor, either. No bug carcasses crushed into the carpet by flying feet, no smears of bug guts or blood. Nothing on the walls. Swiveling around, he examined the light switch. Bug-free. The whole room looked bug-free.

And there was no sign, as far as he could tell, that they'd been there at all.

His mother grunted lightly as she fought with the window. "How did you even get this open, honey? Crowbar?" It stuck. It always had. Sean had never been able to open and close it by himself. It used to take him and Mom and his big sister, Ruthie, to budge it past a certain point.

"I didn't." His voice cracked.

"What?"

"Nothing. Will you . . . check the sheets?"

With a sudden bang, the storm window finally gave and crashed onto the sill. His mother yanked her fingers out of the way just as the wood splintered beneath them. She glanced at him, a dry-faced sort of look that meant she was tired or irritated. In this case, he figured, probably both.

"I think you must have had a nightmare. Maybe something buzzed into the room through the window—"

"Please, Mom, just check the sheets."

She seemed to consider his request a moment, then crossed to the bed and yanked off the blanket. The sheet followed. She shook both out thoroughly.

A tiny pelting of black rain on the floor made him flinch. Bugs—dead spiders the size of half dollars, it looked like. His mom looked down at them, then back up at Sean. "Sweetheart, I'm sorry. These look like some kind of jumping spiders. Maybe they're coming up out of the basement. How about we change your sheets," she said, pulling off the offending linens, "and I'll call the exterminator in the morning?"

Sean nodded slowly, swallowing several times. He wasn't quite convinced the bugs were all dead. He imagined that once the door closed behind her, more would flood the ceiling and drop down on top of him like shiny black paratroopers.

Sean's mom unrolled some toilet paper from the bathroom and used it to sweep up the little black corpses on the floor, then chucked the whole thing in the garbage can by his door. She changed the sheets and pillowcases, smoothed a hand over the mattress, even got down on her knees and looked under the bed.

"I think we got them all. You okay?" She pulled back the clean sheets and nodded for him to hop in. Staring at the cool linen, smooth and flat and utterly unmoving, Sean felt better. Much better.

She hugged him good night and her nightgown was soft, smelled vaguely of her perfume and her deodorant. "We'll take care of it, Sean. It was probably all this rain. Brings them up out of the ground, I think."

He briefly considered mentioning the balloon to her, but decided against it. "Okay," came a resigned, if not altogether hearty, response muffled by the nightgown. She let him go. Sean's eyes shifted hesitantly around the room again.

"Good night, tiger." She left the door open a crack behind her, as she had since he was seven years old.

When the retreating footsteps in the hall faded,

Sean pulled back the sheets, slipped out of bed, and crept over to the garbage can. Inside, half curled, lay red rubber fragments of balloon where the carcasses of those bugs should have been. A flash of nervous heat pulsed across his skin and drew sweat out under his arms. His fingers closed over one of the balloon fragments and he lifted it up. It was cool and smooth in a way that turned his stomach, a greasy and almost insubstantial kind of smooth, the way gum got if it was left in the sun. He fingered it uneasily, repulsed and fascinated.

It melted in his hand and he jumped as if he'd been bitten, shaking the dripping liquid rubber from his fingertips into the round bin. He squeezed his eyes shut (*it's not, not blood, not my blood*) and when he opened them again, his hand was unblemished. He peered around it into the garbage can.

No trace whatsoever of the balloon.

The nagging voice in Erik's head echoed one solitary word that he'd grown to loathe. "Loser." He hadn't realized he'd said it aloud until Casey turned her head toward him, her eyes wide and brown and throbbing with hurt feelings.

"What?" she said.

"Nothing, baby. Just thinking out loud, I guess."

"Erik, are you mad at me or something?"

He turned on his side to face her, propping his head up with his hand. Her eyes immediately searched his for an answer.

"Of course not, baby. Why would I be?"

"Then I don't understand." Casey turned her head away from him, the moon gliding over her hair in a gleaming halo. Tea-and-milk-colored hair, his mom had once called it, though it was coffee-brown in the dimness of their bedroom. Soft sheaths of it fell over her bare breasts as she lay on her back, her arms wrapped around her waist in a hug of self-pity. As he stared at her, an unexplainable surge of love welled up from his gut, followed by a wave of guilt.

She was a pretty girl. If he'd ever had occasion to forget how pretty she was, some friend of his was right there to remind him. Great body, nice breasts, long legs. She always complained that she had no hips and no ass, but Erik thought those looked great, too. Even when she was dating that skinny little jerk-off What'shisname and he was with Tanya, Casey had turned his head more than once. It was a sex appeal of contradicting forces, a way that she had about her that was both innocent and seductive. Big, bright eyes and tiny features, a kind of pretty the way those girls in perfume and fabric softener commercials were pretty, picking flowers out in sun-soaked Spring Fresh fields. She carried herself as if she were both surprised and fascinated by men, and the mystical, mysterious, forbidden concept of sex.

Of course he wanted her—who wouldn't? Yet lately . . .

His fingertips stroked her shoulder lightly. "I'm sorry," he repeated for the fifth or sixth time. He didn't know what else to say, so he pulled away. The bed creaked as he swung his feet over the side. She didn't move.

"I . . . I'll be right back." He slipped on boxers, then made his way to the adjoining bathroom and closed the door on the heavy air of disappointment behind him.

"Loser," he sucked in a breath. Damn it, what was

wrong with him lately? The nagging voice in his head came back louder, more insistent. *C'mere, you little shit. Didn't I tell you you'd never be anything but a stupid loser good-fer-nothin' son of a—*

His eyes squeezed shut, he concentrated on the feel of the cool bathroom tiles on his bare soles (*one, two, three, four*) and the breeze swirling around his shoulders from the open window (*five, six, seven*) and the sound of crickets. The disparaging voice ebbed away like the retreating of a cramp in a muscle, and he opened his eyes.

From the window, Schooley's Mountain stood almost black against the muddied charcoal of early morning. An irregular hairline of treetops separated mountain from sky.

Below lay a sullen empty street. The garbage cans lined the curb to the right of the driveway. A tiny luminous Chemlawn sign stood amidst the dark patch of lawn. The low rumble of cars from the cross-street provided an arrhythmic heartbeat to the neighborhood that was not altogether unsoothing in its way.

A densely wooded lake area of serenity and tranquillity, with Quick Checks and Wal-Marts few and far between, Lakehaven had served as a vacation community for New Jersey's more prominent citizens until the fifties. As the years passed, Morris County, with its new upper middle class New York-commuter families moving in, grew more expensive. Many younger people like Erik and Casey found that the only affordable housing was out north or west. So they'd laid claim to places like Lakehaven and made it their own. He and Casey—they'd built a home together.

She could have had a hundred men but she stayed

with him—just about six years come May. They'd survived a layoff (hers), a breakdown (his), a break-up with coke (his again), and the death of his father. Six years was a long time. And he loved her—at least, believed wholeheartedly, with little basis of comparison, that he loved her. But lately, things got fouled up when it came to sex, or those deep talks she felt compelled to have once in a while. It wasn't that he didn't want to try. He just didn't seem to have it in him anymore to try hard enough.

Why? The wind rattled the garbage cans, carrying their metallic voices up to him. *Why?*

"I don't know why," he whispered back.

Turning to the sink, he splashed some water on his face—an okay-looking face, he'd always thought, but not one he wanted to look at in the mirror right now. He leaned over the sink basin, droplets dripping off the stubble of a mustache and goatee that stippled his jaw and chin. A slightly trembling hand yanked dark blond locks from his eyes and off his shoulders, then let them fall back into place. He was scruffy-looking, he had no doubts about that. But his eyes were a soft and honest blue that had worked in his favor many times, and his build, now that he was off the drugs, was on its way back to lean and muscular as it had once been. Erik had no reason *not* to look at the reflection in the mirror. So what was the problem?

Not tonight, he thought. *No more thinking for tonight. Thinking only ever leads to*—He turned back to the window, and his heart shot into his throat.

In the silvery blue glow of the moonlight, it stood watching him.

No, no, not again, not now. At the foot of the driveway, a figure in a black trench coat, black pants and shoes, and a black hat not unlike Humphrey Bogart's stood with legs slightly apart, arms resting at its sides. With a stance both predatory and confident, the thing bided its time in the camouflage of the driveway behind it, as if waiting for a sure kill to strike. The surface where the figure's face should have been was white, round, and featureless, tilted up in his direction. It reminded Erik a little of fencing masks. His guidance counselor in high school thought joining a club would keep Erik out of trouble, and he'd suggested fencing. But Erik had to drop out of it. He never would have admitted it, but he couldn't stand the mask. It made his skin crawl. Something about it, about any white mask, struck him as so emotionless and utterly alien, and the thought of it pressed to his own face bothered him.

You are not there, he told it silently. *Not there at all.*

A sharp pain in his head caused him to wince. *Oh yes. Yes, I am.* Not Erik's thought, but a silent invasion into the most personal of territories.

He blinked several times but the figure remained. The wind stirred leaves and papers behind the black trench with a low whine. The figure remained silent, quizzical, watching him. He wasn't sure how he knew that with such certainty, but he did. Even without eyes, it stared right at him.

He squeezed his eyes shut again, so tightly that kaleidoscope shadows whirled behind his eyelids. His fists clenched, too, as he willed the figure to go away. He concentrated on the floor tiles, the breeze, the crickets.

Wanna get high, Erik?

The voice, soundless but commanding in his

mind, made him think of Escher art—it had a quality like that, impossible but breathtakingly there all the same.

He saw the figure behind his eyelids, clothes blacker than a vortex, face as luminous as the Chemlawn sign. Better still, though, than the awful possibility that if he opened his eyes, the figure would be closer, hovering right outside the window, inches from the screen.

Wanna get really high?

"Stop it." Something wet and heavy turned over in his stomach with a gurgle. He opened his eyes.

The street below lay empty, except for the garbage cans, the Chemlawn sign, the chirping of crickets.

No one was there.

Two

Dave Kohlar shivered, pulled his trench coat tighter across his stocky frame, and quickened his stride. He cast a suspicious glance skyward and frowned. Above, the insipid gray blended like an overwet watercolor with the clouds. The Weather Channel had threatened rain, but so far it was little more than cold, overcast, and windy. Cool drafts lifted his blond hair, tugging it from his forehead with little jerks that matched his steps.

The funeral-goers stood out like a black inkspot against the pale colors of the cemetery, flanked by two mounds of coffee-colored dirt.

So Max won't be the only new kid on the block, Dave thought, and glanced at his sister, standing over by the other Group therapy members. Sally had taken Max's death hard. She'd been with another Group member, Alice Vance, when they went to Max's house, concerned that he hadn't shown up for the last two meetings. She and Alice both found the body. Dr. Stevens hadn't been with them. For that, Dave would never forgive the doctor, or the Group.

But Sally loved every one of the Group members, especially Max. She'd tried so hard to get through to him and make him feel safe and cared for. She insisted her brother meet him, and Dave had put it off every time, partially because of a discomfort and mild distrust of the Group. Too many secrets, too many shared hurts and knowing glances, too much guilt. Dave wanted no real part of any of them. But even that wasn't the real reason he'd put off meeting Max.

Mostly, it bugged him that Sally claimed Max saw the figure in the black "detective hat," too. The very idea that he and Max Feinstein shared a—what? Hallucination? Vision?—stirred up far more hypotheticals about Dave's own state of mind than he was ready to speculate on.

At a tombstone several feet from the funeral gathering, he hesitated. A woman Dave assumed to be Max's ex-wife stood in front of the casket. Sourdough woman, Sally once called her, and judging by her short, round frame and pasty, puffy skin, Dave guessed it suited her. Gladys looked up briefly at the sound of Dave's feet crunching on the dry grass and frowned, her wispy eyebrows knitting over eyes as dark and severe as her dress. He nodded a hello, but her gaze was already fixed again on Max's casket.

Sally's small hand waved from the far side of the funeral-goers. Dave skirted the circumference of the ensemble to join them.

"Glad you finally made it," she whispered, her breath warm on his ear.

"I was . . . held up." He could feel Sally's eyes on

his face but made the pretense of surveying the green-and-wheat-colored patchwork plots of the cemetery, broken by the widely placed stone or monument or memorial bench.

"You saw it, didn't you?" An almost accusatory hiss. Her intuition was dead-on.

He said nothing. His little sister was sensitive— always had been, particularly after their father died. But finding a counselor to provide the right diagnosis as to why had been harder than the family expected. The first blamed Mrs. Kohlar's child-rearing techniques. Their mother dropped him after the second visit. The second wanted to consider institutionalization, with a strict regimen of dosages and milligrams. Mrs. Kohlar politely bowed out of his services, thank you very much. The third blamed the disorder on the late Mr. Kohlar, whose death had left a great many things unsaid and a lot of unarticulated thoughts to gather dust in the quiet, shadowed corners of their minds. None of them liked that therapist at all.

The fourth couldn't quite say for sure what was wrong with Sally, but he recognized many of the symptoms. He suggested outpatient therapy as a first step, with light and regulated medication to follow should her condition worsen. That seemed doable for his mother. She could handle that. They all could.

Dave was young, not much more than fifteen, when his mother sat him down to break the news to him. She wouldn't use the medical term for what was wrong with Sally, but she conveyed its effects neatly and efficiently. Mrs. Kohlar had always con-

structed precise bridges over unpleasantness, and
trod lightly across them. This situation required no
different sort of action, in her mind.

Sally is like the clock in the downstairs hall, she told
him. *Sometimes the gears slow down and sometimes the
metal keys wind her up too tight. The pills help her regu-
late her clockwork. Do you understand?* And part of his
brain did understand—Sally was sick. But the part
that was at times still nine (*David, watch your sister*)
and thirteen (*David, you can't go unless you take her
with you*) couldn't help but get angry. Angry that he,
as big brother and man of the house, was responsible for looking out for her.

And guilty that no matter what he did, he couldn't
ever really protect her.

Yet another smaller and simpler part of him simply feared his sister—feared someday hearing her
voice sink in timbre and wind down gradually, like a
robot whose power supply had been cut. No matter
how often he told himself that *people don't really* do
that, he half expected the light to suddenly die in her
eyes before they shot from the sockets and bobbed
cheek-level on silver springs, while gears and wheels
and cogs exploded from her in a fireworks display
of metal.

"It was nothing, Sally. Just traffic."

But she knew. Even with the pendulum swinging
the wrong way, so to speak, she had a sense about
him, and about when trouble bought him a drink
and told him to stay awhile. She idolized him, and
depended on him. Her world revolved around his
being okay enough to protect her, and so she tuned
herself to his frequencies of discomfort or stress or

anger. He never liked her to worry about him but she did, and ceaselessly. And that was his fault, too.

Once, in a moment of weakness, a stupid drunken moment of selfish need to connect on her level, he'd told her about how sometimes he dreamed of a figure. It stood out in crisp black clothes and one of those old-fashioned hats that men used to wear in the forties. But he'd never quite managed to get a good look at its face. Some primal instinct in the dream told him it was better that way, not knowing, not getting too close. Dave found its very posture menacing, the curious tilt of the head and easy wave of the gloved hand sinister in their lightness.

In the dream, he'd be walking down a shadowy alley, between two impossibly tall buildings whose upper floors dissipated like smoke high in the sky. He'd become aware of something close at his heels, its rancid breath (did it breathe?) an almost tangible force that propelled him into a run. He never turned around, but he could feel the thing that swam through the darkness only inches from his back almost as surely as if he saw it. A luminescent face, maybe, blank but radiating a hatred that splashed cold waves of pain across his spine. The hard skittering of its metallic claws reverberated in his skull, even when his eyes first opened in the morning.

Stress of the job, was all it was. That's what he'd told her. That's what he'd told himself to block out the idea that maybe Sally wasn't the only one whose gears were slipping. But the dreams brought on a nebulous kind of terror difficult to shake, a sense of impending . . . what? Something hard to put a finger on. Something bad, like the beginnings of a tornado about to swirl up and out of control. Whatever it was, it wanted to close in on him until it bridged the gap between the shelter of daylight and whatever nameless, shapeless, faceless horrors were caught up in its maelstrom.

"Traffic." She said the word as if it tasted bitter on her tongue. Sally knew he was lying. She knew that sometimes he saw the figure in black when he was awake, too—on assignment, across a busy street whose traffic in the next moment whisked it away from view, or in the shadows between two houses on his way home from the bar down the road. On the latter occasions he'd stare at it, forcing the panic down with the drunken logic that monsters would break apart if he could just get it together and focus his eyes. Whatever was left would be real and no more intimidating than a mailbox or garbage can or hell, maybe even a lawn gnome.

She knew because he told her. And he told her because sometimes the figure wouldn't disappear right away. Sometimes the tequila shots still sloshing around in his head dulled his vision like bad reception on a TV and he'd think—this was crazy, he told her—that the figure's eyes and nose and mouth had been rubbed out. Erased like smudges of graphite on a paper. Before the perception could fully swim through the tequila and take hold, the figure as a whole would, indeed, recede into the dark. But he told her because sometimes it scared the shit out of him anyway and just once, he wanted someone to tell *him* it would be okay.

He told her and then immediately regretted it. She was sensitive. She had a tendency to internalize— another phrase her therapist liked to throw around.

She'd internalized his little problem as her own. She even claimed some others in her therapy Group saw the same thing.

Like Max. Sally believed that Max took off the back of his own head because of the figure in the fedora that Dave sometimes thought he saw on street corners. It was simple Sally-logic (often not at all discernible to him as *being* logic), but she believed it wholeheartedly, forever and ever, amen.

Dave glanced at her. Her eyes were fixed intently on the minister. Her bottom lip rolled beneath the gentle chew of her teeth, pale skin cast in a bluish hue as a cloud passed over the sun.

". . . soul finally find peace in heaven with God, with the multitude of angels, the saints . . ."

She cast a reproachful glance in his direction. She knew he didn't want to talk about it, and she didn't normally push it, but that look in her eyes remained. *You can't take care of me because you can't even take care of yourself. . . .*

He suddenly wished for a drink, and checked his watch: 2:13. Three hours more, tops. Another half an hour or so at the cemetery, and then he'd take Sally home. He'd stay for a bit, make some chat, then drive out to the bar. He could be there by quarter after five, easy, and could busily set about forgetting the day had ever happened.

He turned back to the heart of the funeral. The minister closed the book and stepped aside. Gladys took a carnation from the bundle in the funeral director's arms and tossed it onto the coffin. She then let herself be led away by a younger man, probably a nephew—Dave didn't think Gladys and Max had any children. The other mourners followed suit, each taking a flower doled out by the severe-looking funeral director and pausing for a moment to drop it onto Max's coffin. Their fingers lightly grazed the wood as a final good-bye passed from the mind of the living to the container of the dead. Dave shifted uncomfortably as a fresh wellspring of tears erupted from a nearby aunt.

After many of the family and friends had dispersed, Dave relieved himself both of the carnation and the awkward obligation to say good-bye to a man he really didn't know. As he turned toward the car, Sally caught his arm, the pressure of her fingers light like a child's.

"David. You saw it, didn't you? You saw the monster?"

"Sally, really, I don't th—"

But the word died in his throat when he saw something half hidden by an immense oak several yards away. The sleeve of a black trench coat and the leg-line of pants leaned away from the trunk in familiar silhouette. The hat was tilted down against a wind that had built without his notice and now whistled low around the stone monuments. As if Dave had called out a greeting to it, the figure's head rose slowly, a vacant canvas of white beneath a black brimmed hat. Without the slightest movement or smallest wrinkle of the face, Dave felt it smile at him. He pulled the coat tighter, but the chill got under the cloth—under the skin, even. A leather glove, dark as the sleeve from which it protruded, rose slowly to tip the hat.

"You're seeing it now, aren't you?"

Sally's voice, barely above a whisper in his ear, made him jump. He swallowed several times to keep his heart from pounding its way out his throat. "Yeah. How did you—"

"Because I can see it, too."

It had definitely turned into a drinking night.

Lakehaven's best local bar came up over the crest of the road, warm against the cool backdrop of dusk. The neon tubing of the sign glowed with a diffused halo of red, bent into shapes that pressed the words OLDE MILL TAVERN into the sky. Simply designed, the solid wooden oblong emanated a kind of reliability that transcended the problems of its patrons, as if it could stand the test of weathering and time. It was Dave's second home. He parked in his usual spot and made his way across the parking lot.

"*I can, Dave. I can see it.*" Sally's voice, terrified and small, echoed in his thoughts. He wanted to believe she was internalizing again. It was easier to accept that he hallucinated alone, rather than shared that thing as a reality with anyone, least of all Sally. But she had spoken with such conviction that it was hard not to believe her. And not just by the conviction in her voice, but the things she said, for Chrissakes. "*I can see it, Davey. It's waving at you right now. And it's saying the most terrible, beautiful things.*" When she said the last part, her eyelids shrank away and one trembling hand brushed a thin strand of blond hair off her face. She lurched forward toward the thing as if tugged by some unseen cable. An icy panic crystallized in Dave's lungs.

Because if she could see it, it could probably see *her*, too. An insane thought, possibly, but it scared the hell out of him. He'd taken off after the streaming blond hair, the flurry of feet, both of them clos-

ing the distance within seconds between the grave
site and the oak. They made several laps around the
trunk, scouring the panorama of tombstones. No
sign of the figure—except for on the tree. A long
crude heart had been scratched into the bark. Inside
the heart, it had carved

DK

+

SK

+

ME

4-EVER

Dave had felt a little sick.

He pushed open the bar's wooden door and
stepped in from the iciness of his thoughts, breaking
the barrier between the stretch of virtually carless
road and the inviting world of the Tavern. As he
crossed the threshold, the last vestiges of that afternoon's nausea subsided. Classic rock floated down
from overhead speakers set to the local rock station,
tripping lightly across the merry clinking of shot
glasses and beer bottles, laughter and small talk. The
interior was dimly lit, more cozy than seedy. A bar
ran along an 'L' shape, the shorter leg crossing in
front of the door while the longer ran the length of
the left wall. To the right the bar area opened up into
a room for tables and chairs, mostly empty. A few of
the regulars occupied stools at the bar, bent intimately over their drinks. An older guy with a balding head and a spreading gut—Arty, a retired
salesman and widower—waved and smiled. Another regular, a long-haired kid he saw mostly on

the weekends, offered a faint, halfhearted smile. Erik, he thought the boy's name was, or Evan, Dave couldn't remember which. He smiled back with the same enthusiasm as he took a stool at the bar. Kid was probably having a day like he was.

"Hi there, Dave. What can I get for you?" Cheryl, the bartender, swiped the counter in front of him, her brown hair swinging off her shoulder to brush her tan cleavage, and he flushed warm beneath his jacket. Dave thought she was beautiful enough to be a model—high cheekbones, full lips, brown eyes fringed with long lashes. And she had a body to rival the *Sports Illustrated* swimsuit pinups. In Dave's opinion, she was too good for this place or the countless guys that ogled and stammered and clamored to the bar to be near her. Including him.

She dropped the rag under the counter and swept a shot glass onto the bar in front of him in one motion. Her hand hovered around the neck of the tequila bottle. "Usual?"

"Hey." He smiled again, this time a genuine, brighter kind than he'd managed for Erik-Evan. "You know me too well."

"So, how're you doing?" She poured an expert shot whose surface was flush with the top of the glass.

Dave knocked back the tequila before answering. It blazed a hot liquid-lava trail down his throat. "I've been better."

Her arched brows tented and she frowned. "How come?"

"Ehhh, long story. But thanks for asking." He dismissed her question with a halfhearted wave. "Could I have a Killian's, please?"

"No problem. Hey, I hope everything works out, huh?" Genuine concern stared back at him from brown eyes, touching him with a tingly kind of warmth.

He smiled back. "Sure, thanks."

She paused a moment as if considering something, nodded, and produced the beer from the cooler beneath the bar. He watched as she filled a glass with Pepsi and brought it to Erik-Evan. Then Dave turned his attention to the refracted slips of light that rocked along the bottom of his bottle.

"*I can, Dave. I can see it.*" Sally's voice tinkled like broken glass in his head.

Why Sally, of all people? Dave had been seeing the figure in black for about four months. Its haunt brought with it a foreboding, an unshakable sense of vague but terrifying things to come. He hadn't dealt too well with it, but Sally wouldn't be strong enough. A few weeks of head games with Dave's man in black might very well prove the solid *whack!* that knocked her last few gears out of place. She might as well pull up a patch of dirt next to Max, for all the good her Group therapy would do in the face (or conspicuous lack thereof) of that thing.

He drained the Killian's bottle within minutes, and another one met its doom shortly thereafter, followed by a third, a fourth, a fifth. He barely noticed the bar clearing out—did not, in fact, notice it until he drained the seventh beer bottle. The overhead radio station snapped off and the emptiness of the place seemed to clear its throat and tap him on the shoulder. His head swiveled slowly as he took in the vacant bar stools, the mug- and glass-strewn tables, and Cheryl, wiping down the bar.

"You okay, Dave?" she asked. "I mean, you gonna be okay going home and all?"

Dave nodded slowly, aware of the sensation of the cool metal-rimmed bar stool beneath him, holding him up. He slipped off the stool and moved toward the door, peripherally aware of Cheryl's gaze following his shuffling steps. She stopped wiping up and crossed around to open the door for him. When he passed her, he caught a faint scent of vanilla.

"Cheryl?" He stopped outside the door and wheeled around on clumsy feet.

"Yes?"

Date. The word pulsated, purple on a black background, a visual prompter behind his eyelids. Dinner. A movie. A wild roll in the hay. Dave wanted to ask her out. The moon lit her soft hair. A small smile played at her mouth as she leaned against the door frame. Her expectant eyes searched his, patiently waiting for his half-numb lips to form the question so she could go and lock up for the night.

Then the rare but radiant light of drunken self-awareness dawned. He realized that anything he managed to slur at her would sound pretty pathetic, even to him. The prompter faded.

He smiled. "Nothing. It, uh, it can wait. Take care, huh?"

She smiled back. "Yeah, you too, Dave. Take care."

The door swung closed behind her. He studied its wood grain for several moments before he finally turned to leave. Brain to foot, connections restored.

An afterglow of that drunken insight glimmered still in his head, telling him to walk home and leave the car until tomorrow. He nodded slowly to himself and slipped the keys back into his pocket. Dave con-

tinued on past the car and down along the tree-lined
road. It was a silent trip except for the slap of his
shoes against asphalt and the occasional rustle of a
rabbit or deer in the surrounding wood. The air felt
cool and good, smelled good after the lingering scent
of spilt beer and stale cigarettes from before the smoking ban that he'd breathed for the last few hours.

For that half hour or so while he walked, peace
reigned, and all thoughts of Sally and the faceless
thing got lost in the blissful fog of inebriation.

"Cheryl . . ."

She jumped at the sound of her name spoken over
her shoulder, her hand paused on the lock. Her heart
sped up in her chest as she turned from the door.
The echo of the voice, unsettling and surreal, overlapped the original, giving its otherwise flimsy and
insubstantial tone some depth. Cheryl couldn't be
sure whether the man's voice overlapped the
woman's voice or vice versa, but two distinct gen-
ders spilled across each other in a singsongish kind
of wave. Her eyes panned the room.

Cheryl thought she was alone. Dave had been the
last, hadn't he?

The bottles stood sentinel on the shelves behind
the bar, winking into the moon shining down
through the skylights. The mirrored Jeigermeister
plaque reflected the bent neon ribbons of the $1
DRAFTS FRIDAY! sign in the front window. The only
face in the Tavern besides her own was that of Carmen Electra, smiling seductively down from the old
"Queen of Halloween" promo poster on the far wall
that was such a popular favorite with the longtime
regulars.

"Hello?"

"*Che-ryl . . .*"

A sudden panic bottomed out in her stomach. "Who's there?" Creeping back to the bar's edge, she checked the alley lined with ice buckets, coolers, extra bar sips, and menus. Aside from the occasional straw wrapper and a shining nickel, the alley was empty.

"*I'm not behind the bar, Cheryl. But I'm very close.*" The whisper drifted hazy over her head like cigarette smoke.

Heavy, plodding footsteps (*stalker-killer boots*) unconnected to any pair of feet that she could see moved away from the bar. She heard the dull thud of them on the hardwood floor retreating around the corner to the sit-down restaurant area.

She reached over the bar and, with trembling fingers, grabbed the gun.

Bob Mercer, proprietor of the Olde Mill Tavern, had sternly informed his employees that his "beaut of a .22" Luger automatic handgun should only be used under the most extreme of circumstances (*Basically*, he'd remarked, *if a psycho has a knife to your throat*) and only with the utmost care. He'd given each of the girls and his two busboys a crash course in gun basics—where the safety was, how to hold the gun to keep the force of a bullet's discharge from snapping the wrist backward. Cheryl felt fairly sure that even if her aim was off, a deafening shot in the general direction of the intruder would be enough to scare (*him, her, it?*) away.

It? Where had that *thought come from?*

The gun barrel shook as it navigated the shadows ahead of her. At the end of the wall before the restaurant area, she took several deep breaths. Lifting the gun, she spun around the corner.

The forest of chair legs, sticky with overturned drinks and the dusty atmosphere of a working man's night of drinking, spread out before her. Maybe some poor dummy had passed out under one of the tables and was only now just coming to . . . But she found no fetal form curled up against the cool hardness of the floor, either.

"I have a gun." She felt silly saying the words aloud even before she was finished with them. Clearly, no one was there. Not in the back booths, not by the dark screen of the *Outrun* video-arcade game or the light-tube arches of the four-foot juke-box. Both stood silent, their electronic noise turned off for the night. The thought of checking the bath-rooms and kitchen ground unpleasantly against her insides, but she was, after all, the one with the gun.

Still, Cheryl figured she should probably just leave. Bob would have told her to haul her little ass right on out of the bar. Whoever had been calling to her had split—that was obvious. No sense in stick-ing around, right?

And . . . if whoever it was hadn't left, what then? It wasn't too hard to imagine the swift and silent feet of a crazed killer creeping up on her and stabbing her. Outside, though, even if he was hiding in the bushes, she had a shot. She could run, run all the way to town, if she had to. But if she wasn't alone in-side, she wouldn't have much time to cover the space between her and the bar door.

Against the sheer face of logic, she crossed the restaurant area to the ladies' bathroom and pushed open the door.

The room fit two stalls and a window, and the window wasn't even big enough for someone to escape through. She knocked open the stall doors. Nothing out of order there except a lipstick-smudged wad of toilet paper sitting on one of the seats. She swept through the men's room next, followed by the kitchen, and found both just as empty.

Good, she thought. *Now I can go—*

She saw one of the knives from the kitchen, handle embossed with the Tavern logo, lying casually on the otherwise empty bar she'd wiped down minutes ago. The blade glinted in a patch of moonlight that filtered in through the window. Cheryl sucked in a breath. Her heart fluttered like a caged bird beneath her chest.

Along the serrated edge of the blade were small chunks of (*oh my God, what the hell is that?*) . . .

Paper. Cheryl squinted. Minuscule bits of paper were caught on the jagged ends. Tiny crumpled nibblets of white lay scattered around the blade. She frowned. Why paper? What did that mean?

Then she spied it. A chill like ice water down her back caused her body to shudder. The gun hung limp at her side.

The poster. The Carmen Electra poster. A beer floated above the wrist, across a paperless chasm where Carmen's hand used to be. Both eyes had been cut out as well as the mouth, and a tiny strip to either side of her head where her ears would have been, if not covered by her hair.

The adage about evil and the three monkeys popped into Cheryl's head, except the monkeys gave way to the three Budweiser frogs. The implication hung over her mind like a threatening cloud.

Her hands—don't forget, her hands are missing, too.

Didn't killers remove hands to prevent police from identifying bodies?

Oh God. Someone—someone else really is *in here.*

As she inched around it, Cheryl gave the knife on the bar a wide berth, as if it might leap up and stab her. Or do to her what it had done to the poster. She barely felt her arm yank the door open or her feet carry her to her car. That threatening cloud had condensed into a miasma of fear. It was like she was watching what she was doing rather than doing things herself. The "out-of-body" Cheryl saw herself scrabble to fit the car key in the lock, fumble with the handle, then fling the gun on the passenger seat.

She backed out into the street and then straightened the wheel, then looked up to the rearview. Suddenly, everything became vividly clear.

The outline of a head and upper torso stood several feet behind her car, its black clothes blending with the night around it, a hat perched on top of its head. Something was wrong with its face. No, not the face, not exactly. The lack—*yes*, the lack of features that made a face.

No eyes. No mouth, no ears.

See no evil, hear no evil, speak no evil. The connection between the poster and the thing standing behind her car singsonged like some childish chant in her mind.

The figure raised a black glove in an almost jaunty wave, and Cheryl had the terrifying notion that the glove floated empty above the sleeve.

A scream welled up in her throat and lodged there, threatening to choke her. Her head snapped around to the front. She shifted the car into Drive, her eyes straying up to the rearview mirror.

The figure was gone. Cheryl didn't wait to find out where it went. With a puff of exhaust and a chirp of tires, she sped off in the car.

It wasn't until she'd put several miles between her and the bar that she felt her heart slow in her chest. She took several deep breaths. She didn't scream, but she didn't look behind her again, either.

Three

The icy shrillness of the phone pierced through the fog of hangover sleep. Dave rolled over into a sharp headache that ticked off each ring with a painful jab.

"Hello?" he croaked into the receiver from a tight, dry throat. The bad-taste coating on his tongue felt thick in his mouth.

"Mr. Kohlar? This is Dr. Stevens."

Dave sat up straight in bed. His insides took a moment to follow.

"What's the matter? Is something wrong with Sally? What happened?"

"Mr. Kohlar, Sally had an episode. I'm afraid it caused quite an unpleasant stir. Her employers called me and asked me to come and get her." A pause. "She requested that I call you. We're at the hospital now."

Dave couldn't be sure, but he thought he detected a hint of disapproval in the doctor's voice. "I'll be there in thirty minutes."

"I'll see you then, Mr. Kohlar."

He arrived at Sisters of the Holy Rosary Hospital

some twenty minutes later, breezing through the open motion doors of the psych ward with a half-hearted wave to the nurse at the station.

"Room 406, Dave," she called down the hall, and he tossed back a hurried "Thanks" as he swept by.

Both Sally and Dr. Stevens looked up as Dave swung through the doorway and into her room, a neat cube of generic articles of pleasantry like silk flowers in a nondescript vase, clean white linens, tidy right angles of wall and window. Sally had spent time in dozens of rooms like this one, emotionlessly tasteful and simple.

A reproachful frown twitched across the doctor's thick lips as he hurried to meet Dave. "A word, Mr. Kohlar." Taking his elbow, the doctor led Dave back out into the hall, a continuation of the tidy green floor tiles and linen-white walls.

"Is everything—"

"I wanted to go on record as saying," Dr. Stevens interrupted in a tight, forced whisper, "that I understand and respect family business as family business, and I certainly encourage a relationship between you and your sister."

"What? What are you—"

"Please, keep your voice down. I thought I was making a good deal of progress with her, but frankly, it took us two hours to calm her down at her office. Her employer—a Mr. Dibbs, is it?—said that she'd been brooding all morning. 'Pensive,' was the word he used. Then, out of nowhere, she started screaming and she fell out of her chair and crawled under her desk. Anytime anyone came near her, she lashed out with her fingernails. Gave this Dibbs quite a nasty scratch. A coworker finally found my name and number in Sally's Rolodex, and I came as soon as I could."

Dave stared at the doctor's shiny shoes. Tiny twin distorted Dave-reflections stared back.

"Mr. Kohlar, do you have any idea what she told us?"

Please, Dave thought. *Please, oh please, God, don't let it be what I think it is, please don't—*

"She claimed that this figure you told her about— she calls it the Hollower—was standing out on the sidewalk, watching her. Waiting for her."

Dave reached a shaky hand out to the door frame to keep the brightly lit hospital hallway from dissolving in a gray dizzy haze. "Dr. Stevens, I . . . I don't know what to say."

"I'm sure Maxwell Feinstein's funeral served as a catalyst. But I hope you'll pardon my saying that stories about ghosts and monsters do her a disservice. This afternoon, she spoke to me of ghosts, Mr. Kohlar. Ghosts now, in addition to monsters. Which indicates to me a regressive step in her therapy." The doctor's voice never rose above a "shouted" whisper, but Dave flinched just the same. Dave's impression of the doctor was that the man wielded quiet authority to demand the necessary attention from patients, family members, and staff alike. His cultured—even sculpted—voice conveyed the disapproval or understanding as he saw fit.

"Ghosts?" Dave spoke more to fill the space than to question. He knew, already, who the doctor meant and the idea lifted the hairs of his arms and the back of his neck with an unpleasant chilliness.

"She was referring to Feinstein. She believes she has spoken to him since his funeral yesterday."

Dave pinched the bridge of his nose. His head pounded lightly. "Can I see her now?"

Dr. Stevens returned a narrow-eyed glare. Glancing back once at Sally, he answered with his usual decorum, "She's been heavily sedated. Mr. Kohlar, I feel I should tell you that outbursts like those may better be curbed by admitting her to a facility. If she becomes a danger—"

"She hasn't," Dave broke in. "Really. Please, just . . . just let me talk to her."

Dr. Stevens let out a long, slow breath. Dave felt it indicated not so much a sigh as a dramatic pause. "Fine."

Dave slid in past him and approached Sally's bed. Her head lay turned away from him, her hair cascading like a flaxen waterfall over the pillow and down the side of the bed. Under the hospital light, her pale skin had taken on an almost translucent quality, the faintest hint of spidering blue veins beneath the smooth cheek. At the sound of his footsteps, her eyelashes fluttered. She turned a soft smile on him.

He took her hand and gave it a small squeeze. "What happened?"

"I saw it. The thing that follows you around." She sounded tiny, weak, her body drained of the energy or will to fill out her voice.

"I'm sure it wasn't—"

"It *was*, Dave." Her insistence shot outward from her mouth like a little arrow, hitting him painfully someplace right between the lungs. A dull ache rippled outward from the spot.

"I'm so sorry," he whispered miserably. "I never should have told you."

Her eyes closed and opened slowly in a drawn-out blink, her dry lips peeling apart to speak again. "It hurt me. In the noggin. That's where it goes after you." She shook her head slowly, her eyes fixed on the ceiling. "It knows things. It knows what to show you to make you hurt. To make you afraid."

Dave glanced back at Dr. Stevens, who stood in the doorway with his arms folded, his mouth pushed up in that same frown. "Listen to me."

She gave a petulant tug at the restraints on her wrists. Dave squeezed Sally's hand again. It felt so cold and small in his.

"This—this whatever, this Hollower is my problem, not yours. I can handle this thing on my own. I can get rid of it, make sure it doesn't bother you anymore. But you have to forget about it for me."

Her eyes sought his again. "Can you? Can you really make it leave us alone?"

"Sure. But you have to forget it exists. That's what makes it go away." Dave forced his lips to form what he hoped was a convincingly confident smile.

"That's not what Max says."

His smile faded. "What does Max say?"

Sally turned her head. "He says you can't kill it. He's seen it from the other side. It's ageless, and it won't die. . . ."

"Max is dead. He can't talk to you now. And even if he could, that isn't true. Everything dies." Dave fought to keep his voice even, but Sally jerked upward, straining against the restraints, searching his face.

"Am I going to die, Dave?"

"Sweetie, don't talk like—"

"It wants me to, you know. The Hollower wants us both to die."

"This is absolutely—" Dave caught himself before the word "insane" slipped from his mouth, but her brow furrowed and her blue eyes filled with tears. She settled back onto the pillow.

"Promise me, David Michael Kohlar. Promise me you'll get it. Go to the house and get it."

"Get what?"

"Promise me. Please." Her eyelids closed, forcing the tears from the rims of her eyes down her cheeks. "In Max's front closet. Please, you have to get it. You'll know what it is when you see it."

When Dave glanced back, the doctor made an impatient tap on the face of his watch.

Turning back to Sally, Dave ran a dry tongue over drier lips and said, "Okay. Okay, Sally. I'll look, all right? If Gladys will let me, I'll—"

"No!" Her eyes snapped open. "No! Gladys will never understand. You have to just go and get it. Please, Davey."

Davey. When was the last time she'd called him that? When she was six years old? Seven? He frowned. "Okay."

"Promise?"

"Promise."

"On bones and stones?" It was something they used to say as children, but to Dave, it carried the weight it had back then. The ultimate swear. It sent a prickly twinge of inexplicable fear across his neck and shoulders.

"Bones and stones," he mumbled.

Sally's eyelids sank closed again. "Thanks, Davey."

Dave left without looking at the doctor or at his sister, who was asleep before he even crossed the threshold.

Erik reached the corner of Main Street and Hokokam Avenue. He pulled the flaps of his jacket closer to his body, but he wasn't really cold. The morning sun smoothed the rough edges of mid-autumn, pressing warmly against his back and shoulders as he headed away from the rec center. In spite of the communal atmosphere of N.A. meetings, particularly on Saturdays, a loneliness had swirled out of the air above as others spoke around him and it settled deep into his meat and bones. A heavy kind of feeling, it vaguely reminded him of the blurred days of his solitary past before he'd ever discovered cocaine. As he put more and more distance between the rec center and himself, the sensation got stronger. That was a bad sign.

Five years, eight months, nineteen days, and six hours clean and cocaine-free, Erik thought. Hell, if it came to splitting hairs, then twenty-nine minutes, too . . . but who was really counting?

He was.

His sponsor always said sobriety was a bitch, but better than addiction. He and the others at N.A. encouraged recovering addicts to focus solely on being sober one day at a time. Erik couldn't imagine that anyone *didn't* think about it all the time, or a lot of the time, at least. Sobriety certainly was a bitch, yessiree, and a whore at that, and he fought with her every day to keep her around. He fought with her because his life depended on it.

Erik turned left onto the long wooded road that bisected his street. The muscles in his legs burned from the pace he kept, but that felt good, at least—a grounded reality to focus on.

His thoughts, however, etched a scowl into his brow.

The first four months out of the Sober-Living Apartments by far had been the toughest. Just under a year since he'd last used cocaine at that point, but even with detox and rehab behind him, still a yearning to get high often crept into his thoughts.

The group advised—they never demanded, only suggested—that recovering addicts wait at least a year before becoming involved in romantic relationships. Sobriety—that bitch—was his new mistress, and a demanding one at that.

But he'd just gotten involved with Casey before rehab and he'd gotten better partly for her—yeah, yeah, for himself, of course, but for himself so he could be with her and make her happy. The whirlwind of pent-up attraction to her proved a high all its own, and she got caught up in it. She agreed to go out with him again.

There were crashes, too—ominous moods of jealousy or paranoia, tough to shake.

There were the phone calls, and the late nights out with her friends. She wanted to take things slow. She wanted to hold on to her freedom, she said. And most of the time that was okay. But sometimes it was downright fucking lonely. That was the jealousy.

Not nearly as bad as the paranoia, though.

At first, Erik thought his new girl might be trying to sabotage his recovery. *He* certainly wasn't planting the bags of coke around the house, but he saw them there all the same. The bags disappeared as his tentative, outstretched fingers brushed against them, providing his first indication that the girlfriend conspiracy theory had gaping holes in it. The shrink at the rec center thought Erik was experiencing some kind of concentrated form of wishful thinking. That, at least, was easier to swallow than the other options.

Like he was losing his mind.

Like he had no willpower.

Like deep down, he wanted the coke more than Casey.

Sometimes, out on the street, walking to or from the N.A. meetings at the rec center, he'd catch from the corner of his eye a face that wasn't a face staring at him, always just far enough away from Erik that its features (*if it had any*) were unclear. It never spoke, but it *thought* things at him. Terrible, terrible things.

His shrink called that a manifestation of his guilt, the Jones personified. To make it go away, all Erik had to do was squeeze his eyes shut and count backward from ten or concentrate on the sensation of the floor beneath his feet. Refocused, he'd open his eyes and the figure would be gone.

Erik could buy that it was a figment of his imagination. He could believe that wholeheartedly with stubborn resolve, if that's what it would take to make it go away. But the problem was, the figure didn't go away. Not at first. It took sheer willful blindness to stop the hallucinations.

No, Erik thought angrily, *that's not true. It took one tiny little relapse, none before and none since. But after that one time . . .*

The hallucinations stopped after the night he'd

done some coke. He'd scored it from Jimmy Du-
monte at the usual haunt around the corner from the
Quick Check. Beneath a canopy of stars who'd
turned their gaze the other way, amidst the shadows
drawn like curtains across the wooded lot behind
the local high school, he'd gotten good and high.
And in his delirium, he'd seen the faceless figure
one last time, standing above him, thinking down on
him, urging him to get lost in the high and bleed into
the shadows and never come back.

Except, it was the faceless Jones that hadn't come
back. It vacated the weird waypoint where Erik's reality skewed, and with it left a great deal of pressure
as well. Things with Casey fell back into place. He'd
found a decent job in landscaping and masonry that
kept him working hard and staying out of trouble.
He hadn't touched coke, nor wanted to, since.

But now he felt . . . different. Regressed. He suspected maybe he wasn't quite okay enough with sobriety yet to have someone depend on him to be clean.
At the meeting, the realization had hit him full force.
In its wake, the old-time insecurities found their way
back into his thoughts—like weeds, they kept sprout-
ing up just when he thought he'd killed the last of
them. And to be insecure, the way Erik saw it, was to
be inadequate. Weak. A worthless good-fer-nothin'—

"Stop." He said it out loud, soft under his breath.

But he'd felt it the other night, when the middle-
of-the-night romp in bed had gone wrong. He'd felt
inadequate. He still wanted to get high, and it must
have sent out some signal somewhere before he'd
even realized it, because the figure had come back.
The Jones in a black hat was back.

Erik turned up his empty driveway and made it

practically onto the porch before he realized the front door stood slightly open beyond the screen. He cast a puzzled glance at the driveway.

Casey's car wasn't there. Too early for her to be home, anyway. Frowning, he opened the screen door. The creak of the hinge sounded magnified in the empty hall.

"Hello?" No answer. Peering into each room as he passed, he made his way down the hall to the kitchen.

"Casey? Baby, you home?" She'd left after him to go to work—maybe she'd forgotten to lock the door in a rush to get out this morning. Maybe she hadn't closed the door all the way, and the wind had pushed it in.

Sure, maybe, Erik thought, *but that isn't like her. She doesn't just—*

"Back here, Erik!" Casey's voice carried through the open kitchen window from the backyard. So she *was* home, then. Erik crossed to the back door and swung it open. Casey sat on a patio bench, turned away from him, her head bent over something at the table. Strands of her hair hung in front of her face. Without looking up, she curled her fingers in a half wave.

Erik crossed the backyard toward her. "Hey, baby, what're you doing home so early? And where's your car? I didn't—" He gestured toward the front of the house but stopped, his gaze falling on Casey's head as she inhaled sharply.

"Casey? Whatcha doin'?" A crazy thought occurred to him. *Please let her be sniffing flowers or perfume or Crazy Glue for all I care, but not . . .*

"Coke," she said lightly, snorting again. "Want some?"

Erik swallowed the thick, sandpapery lump in his throat. "Huh?"

She giggled.

"Casey, stop messing around, okay?"

Sniff. "It's only a little coke, Erik. Isn't it bad enough that you're a kill-buzz in bed? Do you have to take away all my fun?"

"What did you say?" Heat radiated across his face and threatened to force tears.

"I'm saying," Casey replied in a voice not quite hers but several androgynous voices harmonizing at once, "that you're a loser, Erik. A stupid loser good-fer-nothin' son of a bitch."

She looked up. Erik's knees buckled where he stood as he stared at her face.

Her lack of face.

The honey-framed oval was a stark white contrast to the pale neck upon which it rested. Where Casey's eyes and mouth had been were burnt holes stuffed with ashes, which blew away on some otherwise unfelt wind. Her nose, as well, was a crater of blackened fillings. Erik squeezed his eyes shut *(ten-nine-eight-seven-six-five-four-three-two-one . . .)*, hoping it was only a hallucination. But when he opened his eyes, the figure from the other night sat in Casey's place, a black-gloved hand raised in a wave. It was close to him, closer than it had ever been, a mere arm's length away, there but somehow not there, an alien image imposed on a natural, familiar landscape. Bile rose in Erik's throat.

"Don't you love me anymore, Erik?" Casey's voice again, coming from that thing, Casey's mannerisms so clearly recognizable in the way it crossed its legs and tilted its head. The fabric of its hat and clothes looked cold—almost frosted, and utterly unreflective of the sun's rays. Erik was somehow sure that one touch could cause frostbite. Maybe even death.

Erik's voice failed in his throat. "Go away."

A rumble deep in the meat of the blank visage pushed him involuntarily backward with a real, physical force of its own. Erik took it to be a laugh.

"Please," he whispered. "Please go away."

"Erik?" The screen door to the backyard slammed shut and Erik jumped, whirling around. Casey smiled at him and waved.

He didn't wave back. For a moment, the world threatened to slip away beneath the growing kaleidoscopic patterns before his eyes. He took several deep breaths and looked down at his hands. They were shaking and he shoved them in his pockets. When he looked back at the bench, he saw it empty. The figure was gone.

Casey's expression changed to one of concern when she saw his face. "Baby? Are you okay? What's wrong?" Her hand, cool and smooth and dry, touched his cheek lightly. He flinched, and gave her a narrow-eyed once-over. She frowned.

"What's wrong, Erik?" It sounded more to him like an accusation than a question. *Are you high, Erik? Are you messing around with that stuff again?*

"Casey." He searched her eyes for something familiar and undeniable to hold on to, but his vision blurred with tears. "Casey?"

"What? What's wrong?"

He grabbed her hand suddenly and dragged her around to the front of the house. Her car was parked in the driveway. He touched the hood. Still warm.

"Erik, what happened?"

"I . . . I don't know. I'm just glad you're home." He pulled her into a hug so tight she winced. "I love you, baby."

"I love you, too, Erik. Are you sure you're okay?"

"I am now."

Cheryl saw the Lakehaven police office as little more than a converted log cabin set a little ways off the main road. The white-walled interior of its reception area included a few important town notices hanging from corkboards, a framed picture of the department softball team, and a brass clock that ticked the minutes out with a lazy sound like air leaking from a tire. Even in the low hum of early morning under way, the place stood empty except for a handful of visitors crossing and uncrossing their legs along the pine benches. Cheryl approached the policeman at the front desk. After looking Cheryl up and down, he asked for her name and the type of crime she wished to report.

"Breaking and entering," Cheryl said between deep breaths, "and maybe threatening behavior, too."

The policeman raised an eyebrow at her. "Do you need medical attention?"

"No, no, nothing like that, but . . ." Her voice trailed off.

The man paused a moment, eyeing her in the space between her words, and then handed her a clipboard of papers to fill out. When Cheryl had written down as much as she could pick from her panic-jumbled thoughts, she handed the papers back to the policeman.

"Please take a seat," he said, more as a command than a request. "A detective will see you in a few minutes."

Ten said minutes later, the detective came out of the room behind the reception desk. She was the smallest woman Cheryl had ever seen, wiry, with a bony but not unpleasant face beneath a cloud of brown hair. She tilted her head to one side, nodded at Cheryl and asked, "You Cheryl Duffy?"

"Yes, that's me."

"Pleasure to meet you. I'm Detective DeMarco." The detective's grip was strong for such slender little hands, and she gave Cheryl a quick, confident shake. "Ms. Duffy, please follow me." They passed through a doorway into a brightly lit room that sharply contrasted with the waiting area. Cutting a swath through ringing phones, noisy detainees, and a few other cops scribbling away at notepads, she led Cheryl to a desk that dwarfed her size. Skyscraper stacks of papers and files created a miniature city of open cases on her desk. Cheryl's eyes surfed over the high-rises of file folders, papers, and Post-its. A few coffee rings and pens were scattered among the paperwork. The black name plaque across the front of the desk by the phone read in solid white lettering DET. ANITA DEMARCO.

DeMarco motioned for Cheryl to sit in the wooden chair to the side of the desk, and then sat down herself. She pulled Cheryl's report from amidst the stacks and drummed the nub of a pencil as she skimmed through it.

"So, tell me what happened again with the knife on the bar." *Tap, tap.*

Cheryl let out a shuddery sigh and said, "I came around from over by the bathrooms and I saw it lying on the bar. It wasn't there when I went into the bathroom."

"And you said you found"—she glanced down at the report—"little bits of paper stuck to the blade?"

Cheryl nodded.

"But no blood, nothing like that, is that correct?"

"Yes, Detective, that's correct."

"I see." *Tap, tap, tap, tap.* "What did you do then, ma'am?"

"I got the hell out of there. I didn't want to hang around and wait for the guy to walk up and order a drink, you know?"

"No, I don't suppose that would be wise on your part, ma'am." She smiled, and it seemed genuine to Cheryl. "Can you describe the intruder?"

"Well, it was dark . . ."

"But you did say you saw someone, is that correct?" She glanced down at the pages. "Someone in a coat and hat?"

Cheryl nodded hesitantly. "Yes, that's right. A black hat, you know—like Humphrey Bogart wore in those old movies. Black trench coat and shoes."

"Did you get a look at the intruder's face? Hair color, eye color, anything like that?"

An uncomfortable heat fanned out beneath Cheryl's skin. "No. No, I didn't." She cleared her throat. "It was dark, like I said, and—"

"Height? Build? Was it a man?"

"I—well, it—it was hard to tell. I mean, it was tall, broad like a man, but the way it moved . . . I honestly couldn't say what it was."

"It?"

"He or she. You know what I mean."

DeMarco studied her face. Cheryl figured the detective was assessing how much of the bar's fringe benefits she'd swallowed down before coming to the station.

DeMarco's gaze dropped again to the report, trailing the lines for the description of the intruder. "Says here that he—or she, as the case may be—wore gloves."

"Black gloves," Cheryl said. "No hands."

"Pardon?"

Cheryl felt a warm blush rise from between her breasts to redden her neck. She hadn't realized how that would sound out loud.

"I mean, I couldn't see hands. Or wrists. I guess with the darkness, and the gloves, and all . . ."

"Smart enough not to leave prints, I guess." DeMarco smiled into her paperwork. "Now, the poster especially is very strange. This figure scratched out the facial features, left the bits of paper stuck to the knife, and taunted you from various locations around the bar, but you didn't see it inside the premises?"

Cheryl paused. "No, I heard it, but I didn't see it."

"When you saw the figure outside the bar, did you notice if it had any kind of weapon then?"

"No, not that I saw." *See no evil*, she wanted to add, but didn't.

Somewhere in the back of Cheryl's brain it registered that Detective DeMarco had begun calling the figure "it," too, and although it was an underthought, it made Cheryl relax some. She hadn't gone to the police right away because she knew how crazy her account sounded. She'd taken the rest of the night to think (*to hide*). If she had gone in the state she was in the night before and the police found nothing to substantiate such a wild story, what would that say about her? So she'd waited and called Bob in the morning and he agreed she should go to the police right then and there. Based on Bob's tone over the phone, she still wasn't sure what it said about her.

DeMarco, though, seemed willing to give her a fair chance to explain. "Did this figure threaten you in any way? Come at you, or the car?"

"No, it just stood there. But . . . inside the bar, I—"

"*I'm not behind the bar, Cheryl. But I'm very close.*"

"—felt very threatened. I don't know if it meant to hurt me, but I firmly believe it meant to make me think it would. It meant to scare me into thinking it would kill me."

"Have you ever seen this figure before?"

And there it was. *Seen it? No, ma'am. But sometimes, at night . . .*

"It knows my name." This she said very softly, and the currents of talking and telephone rings and shuffled papers carried it away before DeMarco could catch it.

The detective leaned in. "Pardon, ma'am?"

"I hear it. In my house. Just like I heard it in the bar. It knows my name."

DeMarco paused, and Cheryl got the impression the detective was trying very hard not to dismiss her outright as a schizophrenic.

"A bar regular—someone following you, maybe?"

"It isn't a regular. It knows my name and I've never seen its face before in my life, because for Chrissakes, Detective, *it didn't have a face.*" Her voice grew high and strained but never rose in volume.

DeMarco stopped tapping. She no longer appeared to be sizing up Cheryl's possible mental disorder. Something in her expression had changed—a surprised arch of the eyebrows, a bright flash of the eyes, and a silent "uh" that parted her lips. Cheryl thought she saw recognition.

It was then that two officers walked into the room. The shorter of the two, a young, wiry, sandy-haired man, laughed loudly as he crossed the threshold. The taller came in behind, deep lines carved by annoyance into the features of his weathered face.

Panning the room, the officers spotted Detective DeMarco and made their way across to her, elbowing a cop here, cracking a joke with another there. The younger nodded at Cheryl as he approached, his eyes sweeping her up and down with subtle interest.

"Ms. Duffy, Officers Penn and Jenkins, our patrolmen. They'll be heading over to the bar to check things out." DeMarco gestured vaguely in their direction. "I think we have enough for now, Ms. Duffy. If you'd like, Penn and Jenkins can escort you home and give your house a once-over." The detective scribbled something on the report that Cheryl couldn't read from her angle, then closed the file.

"We'll get back to you and your employer with any findings. Not to worry, Ms. Duffy. We'll search the place from top to bottom." She leaned in and added in a low voice, "We'll find it."

For a moment, it seemed the detective wanted to ask her something, thought better of it, and offered a smile instead. Handing her a business card, DeMarco accompanied Cheryl back out to reception, with Penn and Jenkins in tow.

She waved the officers away, already feeling somewhat better in just having gotten the incident off her chest. She went home alone and did a careful search of her own, room by room. And naturally, she found nothing. The birds chirped outside and she could think of nothing she'd rather do more than take a nap. After she'd climbed into bed, though, sleep did not come quickly, in spite of the drain she felt and the weightiness in her limbs. Instead, she stared at the ceiling until the fuzzy patterns her tired eyes made on the surface expanded and melded into one black blanket of sleep.

She dreamed of alleyways, and a high-pitched skittering like nails scraping over glass.

The deserted street stretched a block before and behind Dave, lined to either side with basically the same design of house—bi-level, cold in the shadows of sunset, uninviting with their closed doors, inky windows, and smokeless chimneys. A shallow high-pitched wind skittered to the other end of the block.

Dave's car rolled to a gravel-crunching stop outside 68 River Falls Road, and he cut the ignition. Part of him couldn't believe he was even there. Another part fought to keep in check a vague fear that gnawed at the edges of his thoughts. Whatever was in that house, waiting for him, he wasn't too sure he wanted to find it.

In the blue twilight, splotches of gray clouds hung above the severe slate-colored roof. To either side, trees flanked the lawn, halfheartedly offered before the house itself. It struck Dave that, like its former inhabitants, the ex–Feinstein residence had just given up. It was dejected, empty not only in its overall exterior, but in the very wood and fiberglass itself.

Dave let out a long breath. With wary eyes panning the streets for witnesses, he got out of the car.

The front door would most likely be locked. Had to be, he reasoned. Gladys didn't seem the type to trust neighbors even in such a mild, suburban area. He could always tell Sally the door was locked, and he didn't want to break in through a window because, after all, trespassing was bad enough without tacking on breaking and entering charges.

But she would know. Some gut feeling inside told him if he lied, she would know, and for some reason this was important enough to her that a lie would be an outright betrayal.

Stones and bones. A guy couldn't go back on stones and bones.

With a final glance toward either end of the street and to the window whose curtain lay motionless against the frame, Dave headed toward the house. He wondered briefly what ghosts were in that house, memories let go, tears long dried, old pains left to fall apart like his surroundings.

Dave shook his head. He was, of course, being silly. There was nothing waiting inside for him but dust and old furniture. Gladys and the executor of Max's will no doubt had taken anything important from the place already. And Dave would make sure by seeing for himself. To put Sally's mind to rest, of course.

Dave's feet creaked beneath his weight on the first wooden step, and for a moment, he stopped, compelled to silence by the overcautious desire to slip in unnoticed. Back in his days of teenage escapades sneaking in and out of the house, a friend had told him that climbing the stairs with feet as far out toward the side edges of the steps as possible made for a quieter ascent. It didn't really work, but by instinct Dave reverted to the trick every time he wanted to sneak up stairs. His feet splayed toward the outermost edges, and he climbed the remainder of the steps. Taking hold of one of the posts to either side of the steps, he hoisted himself up onto the porch. It groaned as he crossed to the front door. The knob felt cold in his hand. As he turned it, it caught.

Locked, see, it's locked, thank God, and now I can just—

The door swung inward on silent hinges.

Damn.

Dave crossed into the shadowy front hall.

The house had simply ceased to be domestic. The hall held a grayish tinge of dust that made it appear grainy and secondhand, a replication of a real house assembled in a charade of hominess. An air of unuse hung heavy, almost humid. Dave went to turn on the light and thought better of it.

Nothing moved. Nothing settled or creaked or even ticked. He alone breathed. The house was dead.

Stairs rose upward into shadows from off to the left, a few feet before a living room, while the right offered a dining room. In those spaces, too, Dave couldn't help but feel that the spirit of the rooms had departed, and the empty shell, still as stone, lay open to other more terrible things occupying it.

Parallel from the stairs on the right side before the dining room, a rectangular portion of the wall jutted outward. Embedded too deeply into the surface of the outcropping stood a weather-worn old door with an old-fashioned brass handle.

Dave reached a hesitant hand out toward the handle, his fingers brushing the cold metal. *Please, God, let this one be locked, at least,* he thought as he gripped it. With a woody whisper the door arced open.

Damn again.

The boxy gloom of the interior molded into winter coats, and above them, an empty shelf. He peered on tiptoe, just to see what was back there. Nothing.

He crouched to peer under the coats. A pair of galoshes, a couple of pairs of winter boots, and some scarves littered the floor. Nothing Dave figured was meant for him.

With distaste that raised the hairs on the back of his neck, he reached gingerly into the pocket of a pea-green canvas jacket. Something about the sensation of the fabric on his skin gave him goose bumps, as if he were touching the dead flesh of the man who had once worn it.

The pocket was empty. He reached into the one on the far side. Empty. One by one, he delved into the pockets of a fur, a winter coat, a couple of spring jackets, and a few windbreakers, but his search turned up nothing. Unless Max had meant for him to be warm in the chill evening wind, there was nothing in that closet for him.

Dave sighed—a long, slow exhalation of both relief and disappointment. Sally was wrong. She was off. A gear was definitely and most clearly out of whack in her head, probably one of many. And that meant Dave could take back the Hollower as his own problem now, and not include Sally in the mess. She'd had a bad scare, but she could relax. It wasn't after her.

Her giggle floated down from the murkiness at the top of the stairs. Dave at first assumed it was a part of his thoughts, a wave in the flood of his relief.

Then it came again, louder, higher in pitch—more the way she'd giggled as a child than her laugh now. Dave frowned.

"Hello?" No one answered. "Uh, Gladys? Mrs. Feinstein, the uh, the door was, ah, open so I thought I'd come by to see if you needed—"

Fresh laughter, a full-force peal of glee from the top of the stairs, cut him off. Sally's laughter.

"Sally?" His feet carried him unwillingly back across the hall to the bottom of the stairs. A diminutive silhouette—a woman, maybe, or a child—sat cross-legged at the top of the stairs. The darkness swam thick around it and obscured any feature or detail.

"Sals?"

The giggle floated down to him again, a slow, dry chuckle that dropped in pitch to a sinister bass. *"Davey . . ."* It was Sally's intonation, but overlaid with another, manlier voice. The delicate outline of her hand rose like a shadow puppet on the wall behind her, waving. The waving became a clicking that grew to a metallic chatter and reverberated down the stairwell.

Dave bolted to the front door, yanked it open, and leaped across the porch and down the stairs in one catapult motion. It was only when he made it to the car, panting, his heart jackhammering in his chest, sweaty palms on the hood to steady him, that he dared look back at the house.

Against a backdrop already dotted with occasional stars, the ex–Feinstein residence stood quiet.

The front door was closed.

"Mister?"

Dave jumped, whirling around on a boy no more than eleven or twelve years old. The boy's fair-haired head was cocked to one side, his eyes squinting inquisitively over his freckled cheeks. He scratched at a scabbing scrape along the underside of one skinny forearm.

"You okay, mister? I saw you boltin' outta the ol' Feinstein place like a bat outta heck."

"I—I'm fine. Fine. Yes, I'm fine. Thanks." By degrees, the pounding in Dave's chest receded. "What are you doing out here?"

The boy jerked a thumb to the house across the street. "It's curfew now. Was on my way in. Boy, I've never seen a grown-up run so fast." He cast a wary eye at the upstairs window. "Look like you seen a ghost."

"Why do you say that?" Dave snapped.

The boy shrugged. "Dunno. You know the guy that used to live there? Guy that shot himself?"

Dave exhaled slowly. "Not well. He was . . . a friend of my sister's. You know him?"

"Not well, either. Friend of my mother's." The boy hesitated, as if a question hovered on the tip of his tongue, but he seemed to decide against asking it. "Well, I'm sorry all the same. For your sister, I mean. Her loss, and all. He said . . ."

"What?"

The boy looked at the upstairs window again. "Said he saw monsters or something."

Dave frowned, but said nothing.

The boy paused a moment before adding, "I dunno. I don't think a person's crazy, just for seeing monsters. Do you?"

Dave searched his face. "No, kid, I guess I don't."

"My dad didn't think it was crazy, neither. When I was little and my dad was still alive, I was afraid of these bug monsters under my bed—baby stuff, but I was little then. Anyways, my dad showed me this thing he called a Warding Ritual—"

"Sean!" A woman leaned from the doorway in the house across the street, waving the boy inside.

Sean looked up at Dave sheepishly. "Well, I guess I oughta go, mister. That's my mom. See ya around." The boy turned and jogged off toward the soft glow of his house's interior. He cast one final glance back at Dave and another at the house across the street before he and his mother disappeared inside.

Dave stared at the closed door for several long seconds afterward. If that kid had seen what he had seen—if he'd seen the Hollower—what did that mean? What could it possibly mean?

Reason, cold and clear, splashed Dave in the face. He was reading way too much into an innocent, harmless conversation. Opening the car door, he slipped inside and pulled away from the house.

Sean watched the man's car drive away until it was out of his line of sight from the bedroom window. He didn't know monsters went after grown-ups, too, but he was sure the man had seen the thing that had sent over the balloon (Sean shivered inwardly, the sensation of bug legs on his blanket raising goose bumps on his skin). It had been the way the man tore out of the house and the look on his face when he'd stopped by the car—like he was a little sick around the edges, and scared in the middle—that made Sean sure enough to cross the street. Sean knew better than to talk to strangers, but they shared an enemy; no one the monster would go after could possibly be a bad kind of stranger.

Sean had seen it himself that morning, at first a glowing orb hovering just beyond the curtains in an upstairs corner window across the street.

"That was Max's bedroom, honey," his mother had told him when he'd asked. "Why?"

Sean shrugged it off, unsure how to answer. Okay, so that was the bedroom where old Max Feinstein had shot himself. Nothing to be a sissy about. It wasn't like there were such things as ghosts. But he'd seen something in that bedroom window, all right. Sean was pretty sure it wasn't a ghost, but it was something. And Sean had started to wonder if Max maybe had seen it, too.

He didn't think the thing was always there in the master bedroom of the house across the street. In fact, Sean was sure, although he couldn't say why, that it only visited there to keep an eye on him. To scare him. To watch him, and wait for the perfect chance to—

"Sean, into bed."

Jolted from his thoughts, Sean turned from the window. His mother stood in the doorway, arms folded beneath her chest. He glanced once more at the house across the street. Dark, empty windows. The curtains hung still.

"Okay." He hopped into bed, and let his mother tuck him in and kiss him good night (even though he was really getting to be too old for those things). Then she turned out the light.

Alone in the room, eyes glued suspiciously on the window, Sean went through the series of gestures his father had shown him to keep the bug monsters away. His father hadn't thought seeing monsters was crazy at all. His dad taught him the Ritual with total seriousness. Three circles around the face, an X, a reverse X, and a spit off the side of the bed. Worked every time. Not a bug monster to be found ever after. And that faceless monster could hide out across the street and wave all it wanted, but the Warding Ritual would keep it at bay. It had to. Sean refused to believe otherwise. Three circles around the face, an X, a reverse X, and a spit off the side of the bed.

That done, he settled into the pillow.

Too bad, Sean thought before sleep overtook him, that he didn't get the chance to show the man the Ritual. It looked like the guy would probably need it.

Four

"You are not there."

Erik spoke the words aloud to himself as he stood in the bathroom with the lights off. His heart pulsed a resounding unease that stuck to his ribs. The thinnest slivers of moonlight sliced through the blinds and lined his bare chest, but for all intents and purposes, the view of the street below remained obscured. Erik stared at the blinds and reasoned to himself that there was no harm in peeking outside. After all, there was only so much a guy could be expected to take, wasn't there? And a quick peek would satisfy that little nagging voice that so stubbornly needed to know.

Erik's sponsor had told him he'd recover faster if he'd only realize that no one always has control over every situation, and that sometimes a person needs to trust a Higher Power. Erik found the concept difficult to understand, that a person could trust anyone or anything blindly. He wasn't sure he'd ever put much stock in a Higher Power. His mother had

been a flat-out nonpracticing Catholic and his father
was an atheist who never brought up God unless it
was to call him a goddamned son of a bitch. But
Erik was willing to entertain the possibility that
there was probably Something up there looking out
over the universe, and he didn't think that the
Something was malicious—indifferent, maybe, but
not outright mean-spirited. Erik wanted to believe
that this Higher Power, God or whatever It was,
could protect him from the Jones. But he'd wanted
to believe It could have protected him from his dad
and It hadn't. He wanted to believe It would save
him from himself, and It hadn't done that, either.

Erik figured he could handle the occasional desire
to get high. He'd resigned himself to the fact that
cravings came and went—for food, drugs, sex.
Sometimes a person could satisfy those cravings.
Sometimes a person couldn't, and it sucked all
around, sure. Sometimes a person jerked off or
chewed gum or bummed a smoke and sat down
somewhere to wait it out. He called it the religion of
Shit Happens. He could accept its doctrines, and
didn't think a Higher Power wasted time getting in
the way of it. Erik could not, however, accept that the
Jones was part of the natural order of Shit Happens.

So that night at their regular N.A. meeting, he'd
had a talk with Gary, his sponsor.

"Sometimes, you just gotta let go, my friend."
Slouching under the orange glow of the rec center
porch light with his toughened hands thrust into
worn denim pockets, Gary had squinted at him as
the smoke rose into his eyes from the cigarette eter-
nally clamped in his mouth. He'd always struck Erik
in general as being the perfect man to wear the

shirt—Shit Happens—and when enough of it had happened to Gary, he'd picked himself up out of the waste he'd made for himself and gotten clean. He'd taken on that bitch sobriety and when she threatened to leave him from time to time, he weathered the threats. That wasn't ever going to go away.

"It's more than that. Different. Weird shit, Gary, that I don't think is supposed to happen."

Gary raised an eyebrow at that, but Erik ducked his gaze and hurried on. "It's hard to explain. I'm having more trouble, I think, than I ought to be."

"Want to talk about what's been going on?"

Erik considered it, then shook his head. "Not . . . yet. I don't think I can yet."

"Well," Gary replied with a barely perceptible shrug, "I'm sure it's nothing you can't handle." He glanced down at his Dunkin' Donuts coffee cup, then back at Erik.

Gary sighed, suddenly looking very tired. "Sometimes the old feelings come back. You know, like nostalgia. Then they go, simple as that. Sometimes shit happens, but hey, that's healin' for ya. You have to remember to see it for what it is." He paused. "It isn't some untamable beast, Erik. You've seen its true face, and it has no power over you."

Surprise flopped like a cold fish in Erik's gut. Its true face? Had he really seen its true face? It was such an odd choice of words. Did Gary see the Jones, too? Did all recovering addicts see it?

He'd been tempted to tell Gary then about the Jones, but others had started filing out of the rec center and he lost his nerve. Along the walk home, it occurred to him that he'd never understood how lonely he really was until the possibility had surfaced that maybe he wasn't alone. Well, at least not alone with the Jones.

Erik reached tentatively toward one of the slats. He had to know if the Jones was out there. Actually, he corrected himself, he had to know it *wasn't* out there.

And yet, his fingers refused to touch the string to draw the blinds. They hovered so close to the window he could feel the cool night air seeping in beneath the slightly open pane, but he couldn't will them any closer. Dust had settled in symmetric rows along each of the slats. A dead bug carcass lay bottoms-up in a corner against the lower-most slat. The paint had worn thin where Casey had accidentally dripped nail polish remover on the sill, then tried to rub it off. Erik took in each detail, close enough to notice every chip, mark, and dent. He breathed in a musty smell, like old clothes. *Like old costumes*, he thought, *and dead actors awaiting their curtain call with their feet in the air on the paint-worn stage. And once the curtain is drawn, the tragedy and the comedy masks will be hovering outside the window.*

He blinked, swallowed the dry patch in his throat, and wiped sweaty palms onto the thighs of his pants. Those didn't feel entirely like his thoughts. What the hell did he know about the theater? It was the Jones's thought.

But it wasn't going to be out there. Wouldn't, couldn't, no way in hell.

And what if it is?

Erik's stomach tightened as he forced his fingers to pinch an edge of the blinds. Gently, as if disturbing the dust would bring the Jones into being, Erik bent down a slat to peer out the window.

For a moment—just a single moment—a dark

mass loomed at the end of the driveway, and something unpleasantly hot and tingly ricocheted around his rib cage.

Damn, oh, damn, it's really—

The mass took on the form of a garbage can. Erik released the breath that had locked in his throat and yanked the cord to pull up the blinds, his eyes scanning the street below for any signs of the Jones. Several other garbage cans lined the curbs, ready for the next morning's pickup. His car, parked in front of the house, cut a hulking, quiet shape in the shadows. Aside from some debris that the wind urged down the street, all else remained still, everything as it should be.

Erik turned to splash some water on his face, the thudding in his chest growing steady. Then, patting his face with a nearby towel, he turned back to the window.

Still nothing there. Nothing—thank the big H.P., wherever, whatever—was there.

"Erik?"

His skin leaped before his body had a chance to follow. He wheeled around, his heart picking up where it had left off. Casey stood in the doorway, hands on her hips, a confused frown on her face.

"Jeezus, Case, you scared the hell outta me."

"What are you doing in here?"

Erik found it hard to look her in the eye, and so focused on her nipples, tenting the tank top she wore, and the string of her bikini underwear resting gently on her hips above the waistline of her pajama pants.

"Nothing. Just—just splashing some water on my face."

"You don't look so good."

"Well, you nearly gave me a heart attack." He looked up at her.

Her thin arched brows had connected in a crinkle. She shook a lock of hair from her eyes and sighed. "What's going on with you lately?"

"What do you mean?"

"Can't you feel it? Tell me you can actually recognize that something is wrong here. You're differently lately. Distant. Angry. Sometimes . . ." She slumped against the door frame, her eyes wet with tears. Her voice dropped to a whisper. "Sometimes you look so scared. Sometimes I think—"

Erik knew—or thought he knew—what she was going to say. *High, Erik. That's right, you've been acting straight-out* high. Instead she switched gears. "I just don't understand what's going on. Are you mad at me?"

"What?" Erik frowned. "No, no, of course not, I just—"

"Don't you love me anymore?"

"That's not it either. I—"

"Are you seeing someone else?"

Erik's eyes narrowed. "You really think I'm seeing someone else? Thanks for the fuckin' trust there, Casey." He threw his hands up and shouldered past her into the bedroom, but she was on him.

"What the hell do you expect me to think? For Chrissakes, I'm not the enemy here! If you're not mad at me and you're not seeing anyone else, then what *are* you doing?" Her words, thick with accusation, hung heavily between them.

Erik turned on her, eyes blazing with anger, mouth twisted into a snarl. "You have one hell of a nerve," he forced through gritted teeth. "If I was using again, then I sure as hell wouldn't be here listening to you."

That hit a nerve. The color drained from Casey's face, and with a slightly trembling hand, she brushed a loose piece of hair from her eye. For a moment it looked as if she were going to say something, her pink lips parting a little and working toward a word. But then they clamped shut again, and she brushed past him out the bedroom door. *Damn.* Her footsteps, heavy on the stairs, drummed up a headache in his skull. *Damn, damn, damn.*

He grabbed his jacket from where it lay flung over a corner of the bed and stormed out into the hall and down the stairs. Soft, broken sniffles carried from behind the closed door of the spare room, off to the right. They used it as a guest bedroom when Casey's parents came to visit. Erik paused a moment, hovering uncertainly at the bottom of the stairs outside the spare room's door. He hated to make her cry. The sniffling dissolved into tiny sobbing. He yanked the front door open and swung out into the night.

"Cheryl . . ."

A whisper of labored breath close to her ear made her jump. Lukewarm bathwater, milky from dissipating bubbles that foamed around the glistening peaks of her knees, splashed loudly against the side of the tub. Immediately, the terror from the night before resurfaced. She opened her eyes.

"Hello?" Her voice lingered in the stillness of the empty house. She lived alone in the place on Cerver Street, and didn't expect anyone to answer—hoped, in fact, that no one would.

Several seconds passed as she listened to the dripping of the water from her fingertips onto the floor tiles before she finally opened the drain.

What few noises permeated Cheryl's suburban rental were usually the products of groaning pipes and creaking wood, or the occasional thump and bump of her neighbor tooling with his muscle car across the street. At its worst, it made for far less noise than a house with six older brothers and two tightly wound terriers had. The objective had been to find her own space—sweet blessed privacy and a quiet place to think. She liked that in her own place, she could take a bubble bath or walk around in a bra and panties without fear of intrusion. She decorated the apartment to her taste alone. She could watch the movie on the Lifetime for Women channel rather than concede to *Monday Night Football*, and always got first dibs on the best piece of KFC chicken or the last Hershey bar. If she felt so inclined, she could even leave boxes of tampons sprawled out over the bathroom.

But despite the perks, it was an adjustment. After the last few days she'd been having, Cheryl missed times when she'd had the security and the comforting presence of other human beings close by. Her brothers were classic beer-belching, mess-making, knuckle-scraping bruiser men, but they were warmly and reassuringly *there*.

As she'd gotten up from her nap that afternoon with the remnants of strange dreams still clinging to her, she felt the distinct lack of their company. She couldn't seem to hold on to the relief she'd initially felt after talking to Detective DeMarco. Why?

Because the detective had gotten Cheryl to admit that it wasn't the first time she'd heard that voice from the bar. That was part of it. Over the last few weeks, when she was in bed or crashed out on the couch or when she was in the tub, she'd hear—

"Cheryl . . ."

She rose quickly—too quickly. A wave of white dizziness threatened to bring her crashing down. The towel rack steadied her. Once the spell had passed, she took the blue terry cloth from its bar and wrapped it around her body. "Hey, hello?"

No one answered, but that didn't mean no one was there.

At the door she hesitated with hand poised on the knob, considering whether there really was someone on the far side of the door. She imagined the freak that she'd seen outside the bar. The man in the white mask, the man (*c'mon, Cheryl, you know it wasn't a man*) behind her car.

You're being silly. You know that. She did know that. The doors were locked, the windows shut tight. No bogeymen here. No slumber party slasher movie trench-coated killers, either.

The sound of footsteps—were they footsteps? She couldn't be sure—retreated down the hall. Her stomach lurched, a surge of sudden panic like she was losing her footing. She saw the figure in her mind's eye, its hulking form graceful, almost intangible, a blur of black on black in the shadows.

Of course, she couldn't stay in the bathroom all night, either. She counted off seconds, then minutes in her head, waiting and listening for that voice or for the sound of footsteps.

Maybe it was waiting for her in the bedroom. Maybe it was hiding in her closet or on her bed, ready to pounce on her as soon as she entered the room. Maybe it would rip off her towel and—

Cheryl shook her head, shivering now all over from being wet and cold (yes, *yes*, just from the cold). *There is no one out there.*

She eased open the door.

And she found the hallway empty, bathed in golden light from a covered bulb overhead.

Some part of Cheryl thought it better not to speak. She dripped on the tiles, acutely aware of the even colder air against her damp skin, and listened, but heard nothing. She padded to her bedroom, glancing into the guest room as she passed. No one.

As she slipped into underwear and then pulled on a pair of roomy sweatpants and a tank top, a part of her wished she was working that night. She'd rather be in the company of the Tuesday after-work regulars than alone—*mostly* alone, which seemed somehow worse—in that house. A sudden quiet pervaded the upstairs rooms, but a heavy quiet, charged with the crackle of bad things to come.

She had seen a documentary once about Devil's Island, a brutal segment flashing scenes of gaunt, baggy-eyed faces with prickling gray stubble and spindly hair. The outlines of their bones appeared as shadows beneath their skin. They looked positively haunted, starving and beaten and left alone to their own minds, to their own grumblings and the constant chatter of deadly bugs inches from them in the darkness. They cowered, their eyes squinting when the warden finally opened the door and swinging-bulb light flooded in and they gazed up terrified and relieved at their jailers like they were looking on the face of God Himself.

But why—why had she thought of that just then?

Relativity, she realized. Evil was relative. It was a

matter of perception. And solitude and silence were only okay if you knew you were truly alone in the dark.

I should call the cops, she thought. *Or Mike or Teddy. I could just ask them to come check out the noises, or maybe I could—* Could what? Tell them what she told the detective? That a head without a face and a glove without a hand were trying to scare her? No, sir. No, thanks. Her brothers had enough reason to think that living on her own was a bad idea to begin with. She wasn't about to give them any further reinforcement.

"Cheryl . . ."

She whirled around. The voice tickled inside her ear as much as out, and that time she was sure she'd heard her name.

She couldn't see it. She felt it, though, when it left. A sudden change in the air, as if the house breathed a sigh of relief. Whatever it was, it was gone.

Five

"Saaa-leeee . . ."

Sally awoke to night, unsure for several seconds whether she had even opened her eyes. The sedative felt heavy inside her head, and made it hard for her to focus. Hazy charcoal clouds grew clearer by degrees and took on forms: machines, monitors, a small end table, the bathroom door, and the other bed. The hospital room. For two hours the old woman who slept there in the other bed had moaned into the night around her, then cried until sleep overtook her. Sally didn't like this hospital at all.

She looked over at the clock on the wall, but it ticked off five seconds . . . then took them back as the hand moved the other way. Then it stopped altogether.

She turned her head and squinted in the dark at the woman next to her, looking for the rise and fall of her chest. She saw no movement and heard no breathing. A kind of dusty inanimate quality had settled over both the woman and the room, and gave

Sally the impression that everything around her was a cardboard cutout of hospital scenery in some strange play.

She scratched her nose. It felt good—much needed and well deserved—

Wait a minute, she thought. *What about—*

The restraints? Slowly, she bent her head until her chin touched the hospital gown neckline. Someone had unbuckled the restraints on her wrists. Her wide-eyed gaze traveled downward along her legs to her bare feet. Someone had removed her covers as well. She frowned. Some crazy person had taken her blankets. The thought caused a sharp pain to strike her skull behind the eyelids, and she blinked several times to work it away.

"Saaa-leeeeee . . ."

She jumped at the sound of Dave's voice. *Dave's* voice? What was *he* doing here? It occurred to her vaguely somewhere in her mind that it was after the hospital's visiting hours, and that Dave probably shouldn't be in the women's wing.

"Dave?" she whispered. She didn't like the way her voice sounded—too loud in the utter stillness. Too much, she thought with distinct unease, like the sounds the boiler used to make in her childhood home. The sound memory came, unbidden and unwelcome, to her mind—a hissing of barely discernible words of steam that she caught every time she stood at the top of the basement stairs. A cold ripple of fear crawled across her skin. That boiler had always scared her as a child, and every time her mother asked her to get soup cans or a box of Ronzoni from the storage closet down there, she'd run to find Dave. The boiler never bothered her when Dave was around. And it never called *him* the way she just had (*shudder to think*), with the steam sticking to the sharpest sounds of the name. But when she was alone—when Dave wasn't around to protect her—it called to her then, with its scalding, scathing steam-words, threatening to boil the skin off her little bones. . . .

"Sally, come here. I need to talk to you."

She blinked a few times. It was hard to tell where the sound came from. It had a faint faraway kind of echo, but at the same time, it was soft, close to her ear.

"Please . . ." The voice came from the floor right beneath her bed. Sally frowned. Couldn't be—Dave couldn't fit there without his feet sticking out. . . .

"Dave? Where are you? Can't you come out of there? I don't think I should—"

"I need you to get up like a good girl." Dave's measured tones came from beyond the curtain that was pulled back between the two beds. His shadow was distorted by the folds of the curtain, but she thought by his silhouette that he was wearing a hat, maybe, and a long coat. "I need you to come out here."

"Out where?" The flutterbugs (that's what Dr. Stevens called them, but she thought it sounded stupid) flapped up a squall in her stomach.

"Out . . ." The voice passed from the bathroom to outside the room door. ". . . in the hallway."

"Okay. Okay, I'm coming." With deliberate slowness, she dangled her legs over the side of the bed. Her toes tingled, and the floor felt cool against the bottoms of her feet. The world around her lurched off-rhythm to her movements as she crouched to peer beneath the bed—just in case. Nothing but dust like a fine hair on the tiles of the floor there. No Dave.

She stood.

"Dave?" Her voice sounded small in her ears, tinged with childhood fear.

"Come out here." An infinitesimal skittering of metal across the hallway tiles like the wheels of gurneys drew her gaze immediately in that direction. The door stood slightly open.

"Dave?"

She made a few tentative baby steps toward the door. All around her the silence was deep, and she concentrated on nothing but the rectangle of weakly lit hallway and the buzz of her own internal workings in her ears.

The moment she crossed into the hallway, a cold wind sliced down the corridor like the backswing of a pendulum, cutting through the thin cotton of the hospital gown and sticking deeper into her flesh, nicking her bones. She wrapped her arms around herself in a tight hug. Her head swiveled back and forth for signs of Dave as she hopped from one foot to the other to generate some heat.

"Dave?" she whispered, eyeing the empty nurses' station warily. Where was he? And where were the night nurses? Her fingers and toes felt as if they'd been dipped in ice water. "Davey?"

A shiver racked her body. She hated the cold, always had. Reminded her all too well of that time she'd snuck out to retrieve a toy one winter night and the door had closed and locked behind her. She'd pounded and pounded on the front door for what felt like hours (Dave swore it was only a few minutes), her little purple-white fists two bundles of alternate numbness and shooting pain. The realization that she could freeze to death had drawn tears from her eyes that froze to her cheeks. Her skin felt like a sheath of cold separate from her body, pinching her toes in her slippers. She'd finally fallen into Dave's arms in the great, gold box of the house's interior warmth, blubbering uncontrollably, refusing from that point on to go out in the snow alone.

The hallway stood empty, a void of soundlessness. Shadows took on sinister shapes on the wall by the nurses' station, in the narrow doorways of the other rooms, beneath the gurneys (*is that frost on the metal there?*) parked against walls and forgotten about.

"Dave? I'm cold." Silence met her plaintive protest. Panic rumbled like hunger in her gut. "Where are you?"

She felt it before she saw it, long before she even heard it. Her head was turned to peer down one length of hallway, but she could feel its eyeless gaze on the back of her head, her shoulder, her waist. She turned slowly in its direction, and something flipped over in her mind. It was not Dave who had called her. Not Dave at all.

The Hollower.

Its footsteps made no sound on the gray-blue tiles—not a scuff, not a squeak, not an echo. Its stride was confident, determined. She could feel its hate; frigid waves of it radiated from the Hollower's body—not quite physical, but raw on the flesh inside the nose, like the harsh smell of winter.

It wanted her dead.

Her eyes grew wide, her feet frozen to the spot,

her leg muscles cramped, then weak and threatening to buckle beneath her.

"Leave me alone," she managed to whisper through chattering teeth.

The whiteness of its empty face grew taut near the bottom in what she knew without a doubt to be a grin.

She willed all the strength in her body into her legs, forcing stiff movement, urging them to run down the hall.

Behind her, a chirp like squeaky sneakers in a gymnasium rebounded in the hallway, echoing. She wouldn't look. Couldn't.

Sally concentrated on the neon EXIT sign to the left, letting her vision fill with the crimson glow. She'd take the fire staircase.

Sally reached the door and pushed it open. It scraped against the tiled floor, sticking a little. She whimpered, but the sound got lost beneath the drawn-out squeals of claws running furrows in the walls.

It wanted her dead. She felt the sentiment cut through the static of noise and chaos in her mind. It wanted her dead, dead, dead, dead, dead . . .

She flung herself onto the staircase and skidded down two at a time, the din behind her reverberating, magnified by the acoustics of the stairwell. It was coming closer, scraping paint from the walls. She felt the vibrations, the shudders of hate, beneath her palms.

As she reached the second or third landing, she heard it over her head. She stopped short, touching the wall to steady herself, and looked up.

All sound ceased. The ceiling above her head was

empty. Her gaze trailed to the staircase. The thing was gone.

She noticed the ragged sound of her own breathing. Nothing. Nothing there now. But where did it go?

"I haven't left you, Sally."

She let out a short yelp, and dove headlong down the stairs again, landing with a jump onto the marble pattern of the main floor. Dave! She'd have to find Dave. He'd know what to do. He'd know how to fix it.

She exploded through the side doorway, a tangle of wispy blond hair and flailing arms, into an unusually long alley between the hospital and the doctors' offices in the next building over. Bars of light and shadow sliced at odd, unnatural angles over the Dumpsters and garbage cans, melding into blackness.

Dave. She had to find Dave. . . .

"Saaaaaallleeee . . ." The hollow voice, close to her ear, zipped like a strong breeze around her head. The garbage cans trembled with metallic groans. Her head snapped around, her heart pounding against the fragile bones of her chest.

The Hollower stood at the far end of the alley, between her and the main street. The wind whipped at the tails of its coat, drawing them out like great black wings.

It tipped its hat. A low, guttural sound that Sally took to be a challenge bounced back through the urban valley to her. She shivered.

Then she ran toward the opposite end of the alley. Behind her, the noise like nails on a chalkboard spurred her on.

Please, please, God, don't let it be a dead end, oh please, oh please, oh please. . . . If she made it that far to run up against a brick wall, she knew the Hollower would do horrible things to her—invade her thoughts and bring the bad voices and pictures and hurt her.

Sally maneuvered around Dumpsters and stiff-looking lumps of rags as she navigated the long, long passage between the two buildings. She jumped to avoid a wire-mesh crate with several uneven, extended spokes, but a sharp end snagged the skin behind her ankle and opened a jagged rip. Caught off balance, she landed sideways on the ankle. She cried out in panic as pain shot up her leg. *God, it could be sprained, maybe broken, infected even, and it hurts, it hurts, it hurts* . . . She got up, panting heavily.

The sounds of pursuit behind her ceased.

Extending two wary hands into the gloom, she limped down what could only be another alley. She felt for but touched nothing. Her eyes adjusted only enough to see vague outlines of forms nearly transparent. Some moved out of her way.

Where was she? How would she ever find Dave?

Her hands scraped suddenly against rough brick, drawing cool pain across her palms to match the throbbing in her ankle.

"Sally." It was Dave's voice behind her.

Sally stopped. "I'm scared," she said to it, finally turning.

"You should be."

"So, Cherry, I heard you had a break-in last night."

Cheryl wiped the bar down in front of the man, a middle-aged regular in a dirty red baseball hat and flannel shirt. Ray Gravelin, the Olde Mill Tavern's somewhat seedier answer to Norm Pederson and the Bloomwood Police Department's local station handyman. He ran a grease-stained finger beneath his nose as he eyed her up and down, about a sheet away from being six to the wind. Mostly, he was harmless, but when he drank he sometimes gave her a look that could strip whatever dignity she had right off her body like a flimsy dress. At times like that, she took to avoiding him altogether.

She frowned, returned a single "Um-hmm," and scooped up a tip as she made her way down the bar to the hippie. He looked up gratefully as she approached.

"Hey, there. Can I have a Coke?" His eyes looked red, strained, as if maybe he'd been crying.

"Everything okay?" she asked, offering a smile.

He molded his lips into a lopsided grin. "Yeah. Yeah, I'm okay."

She knew the boy came in here against his own better judgment, against the advice of his N.A. group, and probably against the will of the girl-friend he'd shown her a picture of once. He didn't drink, but rather soaked up the atmosphere like a sponge, watching people indulge in vices forever out of his reach. Maybe he wanted to live vicariously. Maybe it was a form of self-punishment. Cheryl wasn't sure. But he was a sweet guy, with sad eyes and a warm smile, and if he chose to spend his time under her semiprotective eye drinking Cokes all night, that was fine with her. There were far worse things he could be up to on a Saturday night, in Cheryl's opinion.

"Okay, one Coke it is, sweetie." She smiled at him.

A drunken slur punched into her thoughts.

"Cherry, c'mon! Tell us about this break-in last night! What happened?" Ray swayed ever so slightly on the bar stool. The door opened behind him and Dave Kohlar walked in, taking a seat next to Erik and smiling vaguely at them both.

"Nothing happened, Ray," Cheryl replied more pointedly than she meant to. "Just some nut messing around." She forced a smile that felt fake and over-sized on her face. "Nothing the police thought—"

"Police?" Dave interrupted, suddenly concerned. "What happened?"

"Cherry had a break-in," Ray explained, heavy lids blinking several times to bring his eyes into focus. "Some nut with a knife."

"God, are you all right?"

She laughed uneasily as she filled a chilled glass of ice with soda and dropped a wrapped straw next to it in front of Erik. "I'm fine, boys, really." Without asking, she filled a shot glass with tequila and put it in front of Dave. He waved away the change from his money, and, tossing him a smile of thanks, she continued. "I thought I heard someone in here, saw his knife on the bar, but I made it just fine out to the car and over to the station. The police checked the bar out and found no trace of the guy. No knife, no nothing." Her gaze traveled to the empty square of wall where the Carmen Electra poster had been. The police had rolled it up and taken it with them. Other than that, there hadn't been any evidence to collect. She hoped to God no one noticed.

"No big deal!" Ray shouted, punctuating his comment with an overly boisterous laugh. "If I din' know Cherry better, I'd say she was pulling their legs."

"Someone breaking in here with a knife doesn't sound like much of a joke," Erik mumbled over his Coke.

"Na-na-no," Ray replied, shaking his head. "You doan gettit. She"—he pointed a clumsy finger at Cheryl—"told th' police that some freak—black hat, gloves, trench, the works—talked to her an' shit, but the man din' have no mouth. That's what Jenks and Penn told me. No face, right, Cherry?"

Dave coughed, spraying the tequila in front of him. Erik put down his glass slowly, but the glass tipped once, sloshing soda on the bar, before he caught and righted it.

Ray didn't notice anything amiss. He kept babbling on about the police report. But Cheryl noticed. She saw pure and utter panic in the men's eyes. Dave's hand visibly shook as he put the shot glass back down on the bar, and Erik kept wiping his palms on his jeans, as if trying to rub off evidence. For a moment, the noise of the bar faded out, the picture out of focus everywhere but where Erik and Dave stood.

They know something. They know.

But how could they possibly? Do they know the guy? Or is one of them the knife-wielding freak with the mask?

Erik tried to sop up the spilled soda with bar napkins. "I—I'm sorry, Cheryl, I . . . I'm just—" He offered a tentative look of recognition to Dave, but Dave avoided his gaze and busied himself with fishing his keys out of his pocket. She reached over the bar and put a hand on each of their arms. Suddenly, she felt hot, her mouth dry.

"You know," she said to Dave, beneath the din of Ray's story. "You know who I saw."

His bottom jaw sagged, then worked out a word, soundless. It looked to Cheryl like "I . . ."

"What's wif you guys?" Ray's voice carried over through the haze, and the bustle of the bar suddenly burst to life again. As he leaned toward them, his body tilted at a crazy angle off the stool, and his foot came down suddenly in a knee-jerk reaction to keep from falling. Erik flinched.

"Miss? Miss, I'd like a beer. . . ." Some GQ-dressed thirty-something and a crowd of his friends huddled around a single empty bar stool near Ray took the break in the conversation as a chance to order drinks. Cheryl only half registered their order.

Dave stared at the door.

"Dave?" When she felt Dave flinch and resist her touch, the breath caught in her chest.

He turned slowly to face her, his eyes vacant, his mouth hanging limply open.

"Who is he?" Genuine fear brushed her neck, her shoulders, a promise of bad things to come. She felt his helplessness. It sank like a chill beneath her own skin and spread outward.

"I—I don't know. It . . . it's not—"

"Please tell me."

"Miss? Hello? Earth to the bartender! We'd like some beers here!"

She turned a fiery glare on them and they collectively shrank back. "I'll be with you in a minute," she replied through clenched teeth, then turning back to Dave, "You've seen the guy? Tell me."

"I—I'm sorry. It's my fault, I guess. It . . . it's not . . . it's not what you think." He pulled gently from her grasp and shouldered past a crowd of college coeds coming in on his way to the door.

"Dave, wait! What is it, then? Dave!" She felt tears crest her lashes, blurring his retreating form.

He paused at the door, meeting the gaze of several curious patrons before meeting hers. His mouth was twisted in a grimace, and guilt shone painfully bright in his eyes.

"I don't know," he said. His words were nearly drowned out by the sudden blare of classic rock from the juke box. "I don't know what it is." And he slipped out into the night.

Cheryl turned to Erik, but he was already making his way through the crowd to follow Dave.

Dave stumbled away from the bar and toward his car. Behind him, he heard a rise and fall of noisy drunken sound. Someone had followed him out. He didn't turn around.

"Hey! Hey, stop a minute, will ya?"

Dave kept walking to the car. His hands shook and he had trouble getting the key in the lock. He managed to get the door open and fell into the driver's seat. Only then did he glance up.

A figure stood by his window and he jumped.

It was the kid from the bar. He tapped on the glass. "Please. I wanna talk to you for a minute. Just a minute." The voice, muffled by the glass and probably by the tequila in Dave's head, sounded laced with desperation. With *need*. So much so that for a minute, it reminded Dave of Sally. He rolled down the window.

"Dave, right? I'm Erik. I figured—I mean, we were never really introduced, and, well . . . I'm Erik."

"Nice to meet you." The words tasted stale in his mouth.

"So much for pleasantries," Erik said, and thrust his hands in his pockets. "Look, I'm not sure how to say this, but . . . if you've seen that thing, whatever it is, please tell me. I'm not asking for details—whatever your vice is, man, that's all you, and it's none of my business. But I need to know. I need to know it isn't just me."

"Vice?"

Erik gave him a sheepish grin. "Mine was coke. Been sober five years, eight months. Almost nine." In the moonlight, his cheeks grew ruddy. "I call that thing Jones, 'cause every time I see it, it makes me want to get high again."

Dave exhaled slowly. "My sister calls it the Hollower."

There was a pause as Erik shifted his weight. "So it's real, then? I mean, a real thing? What the fuck is it?"

"I don't know—I meant it when I said that I didn't know." Dave glanced at the door. "I thought it was only me—well, me and Sally, my sister. And only her because of me. And maybe Cheryl because of me."

This time, Dave heard that desperation creep into his own voice. "I can't let it do to Cheryl what it's doing to me. Or to Sally. I can't be responsible for one more. It kills people. It tortures them in their heads and it kills them."

Erik nodded solemnly and shifted his weight to his other foot. "What do we do?"

"Stay out of its way. Stay alive. Maybe stay away from each other." Dave turned the key in the ignition and they both jumped at the volume of the radio. He smacked at the knob and turned it off.

Erik leaned in the window. He smelled like Right Guard. His face was flushed despite the cold night air. "What if that's what it wants? Divide and conquer, man. You and I, at least that's something, some comfort in knowing we're not crazy. But Cheryl, man—she's alone."

"It's better that way."

"Yeah? You think so? I don't know about you, dude, but I don't think being alone is better at all."

"I'm sorry," Dave told him, and he was. He wanted to spare this kid and Cheryl any further pain, but he couldn't do anything about it. He couldn't take on any more broken clocks in his life. He couldn't live with failing anyone else.

"I'm sorry," he repeated, and drove away.

Sean stood in an alley, but he wasn't himself. He was taller, with delicate hands, like a girl's, and wisps of blond hair that kept drifting out of place into his eyes. He looked down, aware of breasts and the desire to giggle over them, and at the same time, not surprised they were there.

The sensation of cold came on suddenly, and he shivered.

The sharp wintry breath of the alley whispered a name he couldn't understand. It chilled his blood.

He was afraid, but he wasn't sure why. Help, he needed help with something, but what? He sprinted off down the alley and the sound of his footsteps—light girl-footsteps—echoed between the buildings.

In response, the high-pitched chatter of a thousand bug legs closed in around him, the stink of

trash and bug-meat heavy in the thick darkness collected in the corners between the garbage cans.

*They sound like they did when they were in that
balloon. . . .*

Sweat trickled from his pores and turned cold, but
he ran as fast as those skinny little girl legs would
carry him. The chirp of the bugs grew louder, closer,
more insistent. A crunching from the ground behind
him grated across his nerves, and he imagined the
bigger bugs surging up over the littler ones, crush-
ing them in their wild frenzy to push forward.

He opened his mouth to scream, but the voice was
not his—weak and afraid, it was lost in the noise
around him. He dove into a boxy corridor of shadow,
and turned just in time to see (*oh, shit, oh no, oh no*)
the thing from across the street bearing down on
him full force, only there was no trench coat, no hat,
no semblance of anything human at all. Just a mess
of tentacles and claws glinting in the moonlight and
a crinkling of the white, featureless head into a snarl
of hatred. . . .

It pulled above him, drowning out the feeble light,
and Sean screamed in the girl's voice again. The
Hollower (*the girl knows it, knows what it is*) crashed
like a wave into the wall before them, breaking up
over Sean's (the girl's) body in a shiny insectoid rain.

The dream-him (her) sank to the ground beneath
the oppressive weight of the bugs' sheer numbers.
Needle legs sank into the soft, skinny girl arms, the
breasts, the thighs, the stomach, cheeks, forehead,
over the lips, inside the mouth, the tongue, which
promptly swelled. They stole the air. Their chattering rose and melded into a wail like a teakettle. He
clawed beneath them, fighting to pull them away, to

pull them off, to breathe even the heavy rot-choked air of the alley, to breathe anything at all but them.

With a sharp breath he woke up. The remnant scream leaked from his lungs in little huffing whimpers, the stipple of a thousand spindly legs fresh on his skin.

Wiping sweat from his forehead with the cuff of his pajama sleeve, he listened. Silence, unbroken, reigned from the other side of his door. No bug chatter, no scrabble of legs on the floor or the walls.

His head sank back to the pillow.

"Fuck." He whispered it, a word still too reverently adult and powerful to be spoken aloud yet. He didn't use that kind of language often, but saved it for occasions where no other word would do. It made him think of his dad. While his mother never allowed either of "her boys" to use that kind of language in the house, Sean often thought words like that were shared between grown-ups. Men, especially. And maybe if his dad had lived to see Sean become a man, they could have drunk beers and watched football and swore about those "fucking Giants" and their chance at making it to the "fucking Super Bowl."

In the wake of his thoughts, he heard a faint strain of whistling from outside. Sean frowned. The storm window was closed and usually blocked out all sound. He sat upright in bed and looked at the window. He recognized the song vaguely somewhere in the back of his head, attached to memories of the front yard at tricycle-height. A male voice broke occasionally from the whistling to sing lyrics:

"I love you, and you love me, and I'll tell ya the way it's gonna be. . . ."

He could almost smell the scent of fresh-cut summer lawn clippings and the organic rot of kitchen garbage leftovers stuffed tightly into Hefty bags on their way out to the curb. That song . . .

"I know we were meant to be, 'cause no one knows you quite like me. . . ."

It's Dad's song. That was unmistakably his father's voice. It had been five, almost six years since he'd heard it, but Sean remembered that voice, and that song. Sean's father used to sing it when he took out the garbage, mostly, or when he worked on something in the garage or the shed. He had always thought his father might have made up some of the words, because they changed from time to time, but the melody was always the same. The very melody he could hear clear as day now from outside.

"Dad?" The tentative whisper hung in the foreground of his room while the whistling continued lightly out of view.

The silent pounding in his chest sent a pulse he could feel all the way up in his head.

Dad. It had been so long. A lump of pain stuck fast in his throat, threatening to choke off all air to his lungs. Dad. It couldn't be . . . could it?

His father's death had been sudden—a heart attack—and Sean missed him fiercely. He thought he was mostly okay with it now; he was a brave boy, and tough, like his dad had been. He'd accepted early on without any real concrete understanding of death that he had to take over as man of the house. But sometimes, more so since the thing across the street first reared its vacant head, Sean wished he didn't have to be so tough. He was scared. And sometimes he wanted to be scared and be able to go to someone braver and tougher to tell him everything would be okay. It was then that he missed his dad the most.

The thought of facing his dad as a ghost scared the hell out of him. And it had to be a ghost whistling and singing after all, because as much as Sean sometimes wanted to believe otherwise, he knew it wasn't possible his father was alive. That faint hope had been put to rest when he was seven, and Eddie Myers, the town mortician's kid, told him and a few of the guys what he'd seen his dad do to bodies that were brought in to the funeral parlor. Even if the hospital had made a mistake, Sean's father would never have survived the whole embalming thing. It had turned Sean's stomach to think of anyone doing that to his dad, but it ended the worrying and waiting at the window for his father to maybe return.

"Don't say it begins where it ends. . . ."

Sean blinked and shook his head.

"Lovers can't end up as friends. . . ."

The words deteriorated into whistling and then into humming. Sean peeled the covers away from himself and the air of the room chilled the damp, sweaty skin of his underarms and the back of his neck. Dangling his feet off the side of the bed, he inched his backside to the edge of the mattress, then met the cool floor with the soles of his bare feet.

The whistling abruptly broke off.

Sean's brow crinkled, something inside tearing away, leaving a mild pang of loss.

"Dad?" he croaked into the night. "Dad?" *If it is you, don't go,* pleeeease *don't go yet. . . .*

He crossed hurriedly to the window and peered out.

His father stood on the sidewalk by the curb, near the garbage cans. Mostly obscured in shadow, the details of his face and body were difficult to make out, but Sean knew it was him. The build, the shape, the way he stood—Sean knew. Just like old times, down to the Hefty bag dangling from one massive hand.

"Dad?" The word condensed on the cold pane of glass. He refused to let the tears blur his view of his dad.

Why didn't he come inside? What was he staring at?

His father gestured for him to open the window. Sean pointed to the pane and shrugged, mouthing the words "It sticks" with exaggerated clarity. His father motioned more insistently for him to push up the pane. Sean reached out to touch the cool wood. Then, sucking in a sharp breath, he braced himself and pushed upward with all his strength. With a loud scrape of wood against wood, it flew upward and a cold gust of air smacked Sean in the face. He blinked several times into the wind, affirming that he was truly awake. Awake, with his father, however impossible that seemed, standing on the street below.

They stared at each other for several long seconds in silence before Sean managed, "Why are you here?" He wasn't sure he'd spoken above a whisper, but his father tilted his head and waved.

"Hi, son." He spoke in a low voice, too, but it carried clearly up to Sean's room. No puff of breath came from his lips when he talked, but Sean figured that was probably normal for ghosts.

"Why are you here?" Sean repeated dumbly.

"I wanted to check on you and your mother."

Something in Sean's throat twisted painfully, forcing the tears to the corners of his eyes again. "I miss you. Are—are you a ghost?"

A smile on his father's face. "Something like that."

He studied the outline of his father's form. The moonlight skewed around it, as if afraid of coming in contact with it. Sean's gaze shifted to the garbage cans near his father. They caught glints of moonlight, as did his mother's car in the street in front of them. His father looked like a cutout pasted to the wrong background. Sean frowned, turning his attention to the Hefty bag in his father's hand. A pool of something spread out beneath it slowly, toward his father's shoe, fed by droplets that leaked from beneath the bag.

"Taking out the trash?" Sean asked softly. The overripe smell of garbage carried on a night breeze to his nose.

"Yeah. Wanna come out here and help me?"

Sean frowned. "Don't you think Mom will—"

"Your mother won't mind. C'mon out, son, and let me get a good look at you. It's been so long . . . you must be a giant by now."

Sean hovered uncertainly at the window. A part of him was tempted to bolt down the stairs and out the door and fling himself into his father's arms. But something was wrong. People didn't just come back from the dead to take out the trash. If that was, in fact, his dad, Sean thought he should have been overjoyed at the second chance to see him and talk to him again. But was it his dad? How could that be? And why was he hanging back outside? Why didn't he just come in, if he'd come all the way from the Great Whatever to check on them?

"Does Mom know you're here? Should I go get her, too?"

His dad stepped backward off the curb and into the street. "How about you and I spend some father-son time first, before waking your mother? Whadda ya say?"

Sean's eyes narrowed. If his father had the chance to come back to his family one more time, nothing would have kept James Merchand from barreling through that front door and scooping up both his mom and him in those muscular arms and holding them tight. Sean was sure of that.

"Let me see your face."

"What?" His father sounded startled.

"I want to see your face—to see if it's really you."

"It *is* me."

"I wanna see."

His father took several steps forward from the shadows and moved full force into the moonlight.

And James Merchand ceased to have a face.

Sean bit down hard on a scream and leaped away from the window like the sill was on fire. *Fuck.* His heart thumped in his chest. He was acutely aware of it. For a moment, no sound reached Sean's ears except that of the blood pumping in his head. He tottered, then leaned against the side of the bed for support, squeezing his eyes tightly shut.

The thing from across the street, good Christ, the thing she called the Hollower . . .

The Hollower. It was trying to trick him, to lure him outside. *That motherlicker,* Sean thought fiercely. *Pretending to be Dad . . .*

The soft strains of whistling, mournful against the background noise of the wind in the thinning trees, floated up to him through the still-open window. *Don't say it begins where it ends. . . .*

Sean sat on his bed.

With shaking hands, he made three circles around his face, drew an X into the air, followed by a reverse X, and a spit off the side of the comforter.

The whistling stopped. Sean sat a long time without moving, silencing even the sound of his own breathing.

No whistling, no singing, no humming—nothing. He tiptoed to the window and peered out. Nothing down below on the curb but the garbage cans. His mom's car sat in the shadows of the street alone, reflecting moonlight off the windshield. He raised his eyes slowly to the window across the street. It was dark and vacant. The Hollower was gone.

A loud crash from downstairs thundered through the house, and Sean jumped, his heart pumping with a new shot of adrenalized speed.

"Jeezus H. Christ!" he muttered into the empty room, and ran to the top of the steps.

"Damn it!" his mother's voice carried up from downstairs.

"Mom? Are you okay?"

"Oh yeah, sweetie, I'm fine. You can go back to bed. I dropped a lamp—ow! There are some sharp pieces, and I want to get them up off the floor."

"Need any help?"

"Are you wide awake now?" She sounded frustrated. He could imagine her standing there amidst the broken pieces, frowning at them the way she frowned at him when he and Chris got "too rowdy."

"Yeah, pretty much." Some of the tension in his

thin frame eased, and he smiled. "You got a flash-light down there?"

"Got one right here." A narrow beacon of light waved from the living room.

Sean jogged down the steps, and as the living room came into view over the side of the railing, he saw his mom's bathrobed, fuzzy-slippered form crouched on the floor. Her head was bent over a pile of curved pieces of ceramic, her face obscured by strands of her hair. A cold feeling slid sickly down the back of his throat and into his stomach. *Can it pretend to be anyone? How would I ever . . .*

She looked up as he reached the floor and Sean breathed a sigh of relief. No, it was her, definitely—her face, her eyes, her smile. "Clumsy me. I went to turn it on and I don't know, the sleeve of my robe must've caught something and . . . crash!"

Sean crossed the room to where his mother stood. "What do you want me to do?"

"Well, I figure at least if I get the big pieces off the floor, we can Dust-Buster the rest tomorrow morn-ing. I'm going to hand the big ones to you—but be very careful, okay? Don't cut yourself."

"I know, I know. I'm always careful." He cupped his hands in front of him as his mother collected five or six big pieces and some medium-sized ones. "Hey, Mom, what were you doing down here so late, anyway?"

His mother dropped the ceramic pieces into his hand so they landed heavily in his palm.

And she laughed with someone else's voice.

Sean felt a tickle on his palm and looked down. The pieces were wiggling around—writhing, actu-ally, and changing. The shine of the porcelain took on a sickly pale cast, like blind newborn things spawned by the lamp that had held them, and the grinding movement of fired clay against itself took on a new tone entirely as the pieces raised themselves up from his palm on hairy, spindly white legs.

Bugs, oh my God, they're bugs, but . . . but Mom knows, *she knows I . . .*

Sean shook his hand like he'd been burned, and the pieces of lamp fell, skittered across the floor, and disappeared into the dining room across the hall. He looked up at the thing pretending to be his mother.

The faceless head hovered above the neckline of his mother's robe, just beneath her hair. The Hollower.

He ducked past it and ran up the stairs. Behind him, the front door opened and closed, but the light laughter of the Hollower followed him all the way to his mother's room. She lay sleeping in bed. How hadn't he noticed when he'd passed her room on the way down? It was like his mom's bedroom hadn't even been there.

He shuddered, then crept quietly to the window by her bed and peered out. The Hollower waved at him from the street.

And if it was out there, then the sleeping figure—the figure with his mother's face, his mother's scent, his mother's heat and solid *realness* in this world—was really his mom. He climbed into bed next to her and pulled the covers over him. In her sleep, she stroked his head and mumbled something he didn't quite catch.

He shut his eyes. It was a long time before he fell asleep.

Six

Everything about the newspaper office where Dave worked was a study in "organized clutter." That's what his boss, Crinchek, said of business: the most efficient ones ran on the fuel of organized clutter. Along the eggshell-white walls of the office hung random articles clipped and framed, collages of the paper's biggest news stories, and an award or two, generally hanging in a prominent spot above the cubicle of the recipient. The cubes themselves, a static-colored gray, were chest-high and afforded the casual observer a glimpse of computers and printers, the tops of stacked paper, half-eaten working-lunches, the occasional houseplant or picture frame crowded by file folders and binders, and telephones. The phones added their own irregular rhythm to the din of the office, and the excited murmur of journalists following leads filled the remaining space.

All this was in the background of Dave's mind, the way strangers in crowded elevators or on the subway remained in the periphery of thought. His primary concern was elsewhere.

Dave wanted to write off seeing that god-awful figure as a hallucination—work stress, a bad enchilada, whatever. Sally seeing it . . . well, that was just her nerves, her disorder talking there. But Erik and Cheryl seeing it—that was almost beyond comprehension. Maybe it meant he wasn't crazy, thank you very much, no gears slipping in his future, but then what *did* it mean?

It means you've screwed them all.

"No, it doesn't," he said. His own words, spoken out loud with a volume that inner voice didn't have, gave him back some control of himself.

He remembered Cheryl's face, her beautiful brown eyes, the outline of her pleading lips, and he wanted to protect her. But his only thought had been to get away, to distance himself from her, and by doing so, distance her from the Hollower.

I don't know. I don't know what it is. That, at least, had been the truth. He didn't know what it was, or where it came from, or why it was stalking him or anyone else.

Maybe, the internal voice broke in, *it's time to find out.*

Dave thought about what Erik had said about being alone and considered going back to the bar to talk to Cheryl. He also entertained the possibility of getting a CAT scan and ruling out tumors or whatever else might be causing visits from strange beings who clearly wanted him de—

"Dave?" Georgia's voice made him flinch.

A delicate hand flew to the silk valley between her breasts, and she let out a low whistle. "Tense?"

He grinned—tried to, at least, though it fell short.

"Sorry, Georgia. Rough night last night. You looking for my write-up on the Bobcats versus Ramblers home game?"

She nodded, and glanced at the clock on the wall across from him. "Crinchek wants the features bundled up and ready to go by eleven."

"I've got it right here somewhere. . . ." He shuffled through some papers without a clue as to where he'd put the article, or, in that moment, if he'd even written it at all. He discovered it beneath some scribbled notes, smoothed out the crinkled corner, and handed it to her.

She nodded. "You know, if you need to pass off your notes to someone else—"

"No, I'm fine. Really."

"Because Crinch, death, and taxes wait for no man."

"You're right, and—"

"And," she added with a small smile, "he'll kill you if you're late on another piece."

Dave regarded her with an even look. "I suppose he'll have to take a number and get in line."

Georgia offered him a weird smile but said nothing. She turned on her tiny pinpoint heels and clicked away. Dave watched her retreating form, swore at the inner voice under his breath, and then turned to his computer screen.

It was close to deadline, and he had an article to proofread and another on a different local college sporting event that he still needed to translate from his chicken-scratched notes to legible, press-ready inches of copy. He didn't want to do anything but go home and sleep off the remaining tequila in his system from the bottle he'd bought last night on the way home from the bar.

The monitor stared back at him mutely, its blank white Microsoft Word face awaiting his commands. He had nothing to tell it.

Dave jumped again as the bleating ring of the phone on his desk yanked him from his thoughts. He stared at it and it rang again, then a third time, before he clutched the receiver and brought it to his ear.

"Yeah, hello, *Bloomwood Ledger*. This is Dave Kohlar."

"Mr. Kohlar?"

"That would be me." He switched the receiver to the other ear with an impatient sweep.

"This is Dr. Stevens. I'm at Sisters of the Holy Rosary Hospital. We need you to come down here right away."

Dave sat up in the chair. "What's wrong? What's the matter?"

"Please come right away, Mr. Kohlar."

"God, is she hurt? What happened?"

Dr. Stevens cleared his throat. "She's missing."

Dave sank back into his chair, the air deflating from his lungs. "She's . . . gone? Like, gone from the hospital, gone?"

"I'm afraid so."

Gone. The idea gripped him that somehow, some way, the six-foot trench-coated tumor had broken into the hospital and done something awful to her.

"How could that have happened? Don't people watch them? How could she have gotten out without anyone seeing her?"

"We don't know. Believe me, I wish I could tell you. The last nurse to check said she looked in on Sally and her roommate right before the end of her shift, and saw them both asleep. When the night nurse made her rounds later that night, Sally was gone. Now, rest assured, this has the full attention of the psychiatric staff here at Sisters of Mercy, and the police arrived a while ago and are looking into everything. But they would like to ask you a few questions, so if you'll just—"

"But no one saw her go?"

A weighted pause hung across the phone line.

"Did someone see her leave the hospital?"

"It's nothing to concern yourself with at this—"

"Who saw her go? What aren't you telling me?" Dave was aware that the volume of his voice was rising steadily, threatening to crack. He glanced up and several curious pairs of eyes returned to their work as he met them.

A sigh came from the other end of the phone. "One of the patients, Mrs. Saltzman."

"What did she see, exactly?"

"Maybe the police—"

"Damn it, Stevens, *what did she see?*" The fringe of his hearing caught polite shuffling of papers from a desk nearby.

Dr. Stevens cleared his throat. "Mrs. Saltzman said that she awoke to see Sally sitting up in bed, free of restraints, talking to someone."

"Who was she talking to?"

"Mrs. Saltzman couldn't see anyone else in the room."

"And?"

"And she said Sally got up and walked out into the hallway. But, Mr. Kohlar—"

"That's all she saw?"

"It would be better if you came down here and let the police explain."

Dave waited out the pause that followed.

The doctor sighed. With reluctance, he added, "She said Sally saw something that must have frightened her, because she ran toward the fire stairs. Moments later, according to Mrs. Saltzman, 'the black doctor,' as she called him, glided past the doorway. But the nurses at the station not more than fifty feet away didn't see anyone in the hallway at all—including your sister."

Dave's arm began to ache from the trembling of his hand, and the effort of holding the receiver to his ear. "The black doctor?"

"It is under investigation. Currently, the staff at Sisters of Mercy is being interviewed."

Dave felt a wave of nausea and sat up again in his chair. A dull throbbing against his eyeballs made him squeeze his lids shut and pinch the bridge of his nose. "Maybe she meant his clothes. You know, doctors wear white coats. Maybe this man that took Sally—or scared Sally, or whatever—wore a black coat, black hat, maybe. Black gloves."

"I suppose that's possible, and something for the police to follow up on. Please come right away. The detective here may be able to give you more details."

"Right. Right, I'm—I'll be there as soon as I can," Dave answered, pulling up the document that needed proofreading on his computer. He clicked on the Print icon. "Dr. Stevens?"

"Yes?"

"Did Mrs. Saltzman say anything about the black doctor's . . . uh, face?"

"No. No, she didn't."

"Okay, thanks. I'll be there soon." Swiping his car keys off his desk, he also grabbed the legal pad of notes on the article that needed writing and practically yanked the drafted one out of the printer.

He found Georgia redlining an article, her glasses perched on the tip of her upturned nose. She looked up at his approach and, seeing the papers in his hand, frowned.

"Please, Georgia." He had always suspected Georgia was attracted to him—nothing serious, just enough of a crush that he could talk her into shoehorning him out of tight jams. He tilted his head and offered her a pleading puppy look. "Please, it's my sister. The hospital called and—"

"I can't keep doing this for you, Dave." She sounded annoyed but not quite angry—not yet.

"I wouldn't ask you if it wasn't an emergency."

She sighed, putting down her notes. "Fine. Tell me what needs to be done." Before he could speak, she pointed a long, red-painted acrylic nail at him accusingly. "Don't you dare blame me if Crinch throws your ass to the curb with your legal pad and pen behind you."

He let go of his breath. "You know I appreciate this, right?"

She let go of a small smile. "Yeah, yeah, I do. Now talk to me."

The entrance to the psych ward was, for all intents and purposes, blocked off. Turning the wheel, Dave cut a sharp right and maneuvered the car around several hospital and utility personnel. Some type of truck—heating and cooling, maybe, or electronics—was parked beneath the cement overhang. Several jumpsuited workers, some atop ladders, busied themselves with cables that ran along the inner

tracks of the automatic doors. Interspersed among
the workers, a couple of police officers stood by the
blue-red-blue-red of their patrol car lights and gestured to each other and at other cars. An older policeman with bushy gray eyebrows sewn over the
bridge of his nose waved him back toward the main
entrance.

Dave rolled down his window. "I'm here to see Dr.
Stevens. He called me."

An uninterested nod. "Visiting hours are tem-
porarily suspended, sir. If your visit is regarding a
patient, you'll have to speak to the officer at the front
desk. Go around front."

"Officer, I'm Dave Kohlar. I was told the police
wanted to question me about my sister's disappearance."

The cop strolled to the window, a don't-question-
me expression settled deep into the lines of his face.
Dave suspected it was an expression he practiced in
front of the mirror, and reveled in its very copness.
The tag on the policeman's uniform read OFFICER M.
L. JENKINS. Smacking a weighty hand on the cab of
the car, he loomed closer to the window and cast a
glance around the interior, his gaze coming to rest
on Dave's face.

Another meaty smack to the cab's roof made Dave
flinch. "Okay, then," Jenkins said as if coming to a
decision, "go in through that side entrance there,
Mr. Kohlar, and follow the signs. Ask for Detective
DeMarco."

"Thanks." Dave put the car in reverse. Backing
carefully around the workers, he parked in the nearest lot, then sprinted across the roadway to the side
entrance of Sisters of the Holy Rosary Hospital.

Inside, the antiseptic smell of the hospital tickled something unpleasant in his nose and in his mind. It was a smell that had always been with him, in his clothes, his hair, his skin, and it reminded him of childhood trips to see Sally when she had one of her "episodes."

The signs above the doors to various corridors read:

← FAMILY / SUBSTANCE ABUSE / OUTPATIENT
COUNSELING
CRISIS / PSYCHIATRY / PSYCHOLOGY →

He half walked, half jogged down the corridor to the right, his chest tightening to force out the hospital air, to dispel the nightmare of Sally's disappearance in a long sigh.

Gone. Just vanished into thin air. How could that be? How could it have happened?

"She wanted to go," a female voice replied, heavy with tears, and Dave stopped short, his attention turned to the source of the words. Fear skittered up Dave's chest like a leaf caught in a breeze.

In the room to his right, he noticed a pretty young nurse with shoulder-length curls of auburn hair. She shrugged at a doctor with a clipboard. "In the end, she wanted to go."

The doctor shook his head and patted the hand of a teenaged girl whose pale face looked slack. Strands of hair (blond, like Sally's, he noticed) lay fanned out on a pillow, and her hands—tiny, bony little things at the end of stick-figure wrists, lay folded and motionless on her fairly flat, unmoving chest.

"It's a tragedy, what some of these girls do to themselves nowadays."

Dave started down the hall again. Behind him, he heard the nurse's voice again, calm this time.

"She wanted to get away."

Quiet enough to get lost under the scuffle of shoes down the length of hall he'd put between himself and the room. Quiet, and confidential, as if meant only for Dave's ears.

"She wanted to get away from you, Dave."

He nearly tripped over his own feet trying to turn around.

No one behind him—no rushing nurses, no orderlies, no patients—no one and nothing at all but a gurney laid out across the width of the hallway. A sheet had been draped across it, and a dark wet stain pooled in its center. In that stain, spattered by red so deep it was almost black, clots of something soaked the fibers of the sheet. That's what Dave thought at first, that he was looking at blood clots, and the acidy fear in his gut gusted to an unpleasant squall. He walked back toward the gurney, his feet tingling. Each footfall caused a surreal echo too loud for the space. He thought he heard words in their reverberation, but couldn't quite make them out.

When he got within five feet or so of the gurney, he realized the stain was most certainly blood, but the contents on the sheet weren't clots at all. The smell of them was coppery, metallic like blood, but . . .

Stuck between the teeth of the gears and the coil of the springs, he could see wisps of blond hair and milky bits of flesh.

Clock parts.

For a moment, the gurney swam out of focus, and

Dave staggered to a nearby wall. His breath came in ragged clumps of air.

Clock parts, for Chrissakes. Clock parts. Clo—

From his periphery, he saw the wheels turn and the corner of the gurney squeaked out of view, but he couldn't look up.

He flinched when the voice behind him said, "She wanted to get away from you, and she found . . . me." The delighted, almost girlish giggle tinkled close to his ear.

Then the world was yanked like a rug out from under him, and he sank to one knee.

Don't you dare, you dumb bastard, don't you dare pass out, don't you—

The walls around him shimmered, and the air in his ears made a chuffing sound that blocked out all other noise.

Don't lose it, man, not now, not like this. Don't do it.

The tiles gained clarity first, followed by the wall on which he leaned. They felt cool, solid beneath his burning palm. The floor and walls were back. He chanced a look up. The nurse from the young girl's room was half jogging down the hall to him. He glanced around the empty hall. No gurney now.

"Sir, are you okay? I saw you go down and thought for sure you were going to pitch forward onto your face." The nurse offered him a smile, but he found he couldn't return it.

"I'm fine—fine, thanks. Just got a little dizzy for a moment."

"Would you like me to get a doctor? Wait there, and I'll grab someone on call—"

"No—no, really. Thanks, but I'm fine. I—I gotta go."

He rose with a shaky groan and pushed off from the wall, then turned away from her and continued down toward the bend in the corridor.

Behind him, canned laughter, like a cheap laugh track, followed until he turned the corner.

DeMarco had decided right off the bat that she didn't like Dr. Stevens, officious little asshole that he was. She nodded at everything the doctor told her, jotting a continuous stream of notes onto a small pad, but the more he talked, the less she liked him. Too quick to place blame, too much hot air of no real consequence. He told her what Mrs. Saltzman had claimed to see in a rather clipped and uninterested narration, and moved on from the standard protocols of the hospital (which he followed to the letter, of course) to Mr. Kohlar, the missing woman's brother, who could do no right in this man's eyes. DeMarco wanted to punch him in the mouth to get him to stop talking. She didn't care about blame; she just wanted resolutions.

"And Mrs. Saltzman wants to talk directly to Ms. Kohlar's brother, is that it?" DeMarco asked between words in a stream of fault-finding and accusation.

Stevens, nettled at having been interrupted midrant, replied, "Yes, yes," with an impatient wave. "She refuses to tell me more. She wants to speak with Dave Kohlar."

Something about his expression gave DeMarco the impression that his mind was not so much on Sally's well-being, but on potential complaints of negligence and lawsuits. She didn't know the man well and nothing about his body language suggested outwardly that this was true, but there were the subtler mannerisms of the body that told so much—the movements of the eye, the turn of the lips, the amazing power of the eyebrows to convey so much with so little. And in these quiet little ways, this man screamed *defensiveness* and *worry*.

"I'm sure Mr. Kohlar will appreciate your letting us talk to Mrs. Saltzman," she said.

Dr. Stevens's eyes would have rolled, she thought, if not for the possible interpretation of unprofessionalism. "For the purpose of exhausting every possible lead, I suppose. I've cleared the necessary paperwork with her family, but I have my reservations about this."

"Duly noted." DeMarco scribbled into her notebook, and offered him a bright smile.

Dave found them at the end of the hall. The detective, a tiny woman with a wild tumble of brown hair, looked up as he approached. She had a nice smile— an understanding smile. He noticed it before it faded to a quizzical turn of the mouth, and decided she might be okay.

"Are you all right, sir? You look a bit peaked."

"Fine, fine," he replied, then put out a hand to greet her. "Dave Kohlar."

"DeMarco," she said, gripping and shaking it firmly.

"Hello, Dr. Stevens," he said, and the doctor returned a polite nod. Dave turned back to the policewoman. "Any news?"

"Nothing so far, but please rest assured that we will do everything within our power to find your sister. Time is crucial in missing persons cases and I don't want to waste any. May I ask you a few questions?"

Dave nodded.

"Good." The officer flipped the notepad to a clean page. "I take it Ms. Kohlar hasn't tried to contact you, is that correct?"

Dave nodded again. "Not a word. I would think if she was in trouble—"

"Sometimes, in these cases, the missing person wants to be missing. Or at least isn't thinking clearly enough to know who to notify or why," Dr. Stevens broke in.

"I can assume, though, that you're close?" De-Marco continued. "She'd otherwise have no reason not to contact you?"

"No, no, of course not."

"And she hasn't made any attempt whatsoever to give you some signal of her whereabouts . . . ?"

"No." Dave's brow furrowed. "I'd tell you if she did."

"Of course you would. Just checking. Gotta be thorough and all." She smiled, and Dave met it straight-faced.

The officer continued. "Any other next of kin she might try to go to? Any other family? Friends, maybe?"

"No, none that I can think of. Our parents are dead, and she didn't have many friends other than the ones in that help group she used to go to."

"Anyone from there, maybe?"

Dr. Stevens shook his head. "I've called them all. No one's seen or heard from her."

"Any enemies?" DeMarco asked.

"No, no one. People liked Sally, she . . ." Dave fished for the words. "She was like a kitten. People think she's helpless and fragile. They want to take care of her."

"Any places she loved to go, then? Parks or something of that nature?"

Dave shook his head. "Nothing that I can think of offhand."

DeMarco nodded, sizing him up a moment before flipping the notepad closed and sliding it into her pants pocket. "I see. Well, if you think of anything, give me a call." She handed a business card to Dave. "It's got my pager, so call anytime. If you think of anything—anything at all, let me know."

Dave pocketed the card. "Of course."

"Great." The detective offered another bright smile. "So, shall we see the lovely and vivacious Mrs. Saltzman?"

DeMarco and Dave followed Dr. Stevens to the far end of the hall and waited as he punched in a code to open the first set of doors. Along the length of the hallway that followed, there were closed office doors, good solid oak affixed with gold plaques that bore the names of the doctors who used them. At the end of that hall, they passed through to a second set of doors into one of the main gathering areas of the psychiatric wing.

The air of the General Recreation Room was past its sell-by date all around—stale flesh and stale minds, and the faint hint of stale urine hung over the room like a fog. In spite of the pleasant pastelled hues of the walls and furniture, Dave saw washed-out faces and blank stares, pasty nightgowns and ragged slippers. Some watched the soaps without really seeing them. He heard someone whimper, "No-

no-no-nononono" from behind a potted plant that stood next to the Ping-Pong table. Others played checkers by a large window. A few stood staring through the thick panes of glass to an outside world they'd likely never see again.

Dave sidestepped a wandering old lady drooling and chattering nonsense words to herself. One young woman whose tangled strands of black hair hung in her face glared at them as they got closer. Her wild eyes, sunken deep in bluish sockets, darted with clear hostility from one face to another. Thin white scars crisscrossed her cheeks and neck.

Dave took all the patients in with that same grim and stoic discomfort which he felt every time he'd gone to see Sally anywhere. These people had been parents or siblings, children or lovers to someone once. Every one of them revenants, not uniformly old, but possessed of the same haggard dryness, like flowers pressed into books, preserved but lifeless shells of what they once were. He felt for them.

And part of him, the guilty part that had never forgiven Sally for being sick, hated every one of them.

Dave turned his head, waiting for Dr. Stevens to punch in an access code for yet another set of doors. Passing through quickly, the three continued down a long corridor.

"We've moved her to a new room so that your people can collect whatever evidence they need undisturbed," the doctor stated, then came to a halt about halfway down the hall. He rapped on a door to the right, then led them into a small room with a white slab of bed to either side of the wall. Between the beds, a tiny box window looking out over the grounds let a narrow wedge of sunlight fall across the white-and-

green-tiled floor. On one of the beds, a pale, withered woman in a blue and pink floral dress sat
hunched on the edge of the cotton coverlet. Her
hands were folded in her lap. Dave thought she
looked fit to fall apart, a pile of dust held together by
flaccid skin. Her hair, cobweb fine and whiter than
any sterilized part of the room, was bound in a loose
bun atop her head. She looked up as they entered,
and Dave noticed that one of her gray-blue eyes was
slightly cloudy with the onset of cataracts.

"This is Mrs. Saltzman," Dr. Stevens said. "Mrs.
Saltzman, this is David Kohlar, and this is Detective
DeMarco. They've come to talk about Sally."

"Hello." Her voice was tiny, dried up in her throat
so that it did little more than rattle around inside her.

"Hello, ma'am." DeMarco smiled at her, but the
old woman ignored the detective. Her gaze was
fixed on Dave.

He glanced back at DeMarco and Dr. Stevens, then
put on a smile for the old woman. "Ma'am, it's, um,
it's good to meet you. I was wondering if maybe you
could tell us what you know about Sally. Where she
went, I mean." He crouched down in front of her, his
face close to hers. She smelled vaguely minty, and
antiseptic.

"You're her brother?" Each word sounded like a
deliberate effort.

"Yes, I'm her brother. I'd very much like to find her."

"Awfully warm for June." She turned her head to
gaze out the window and sighed.

Dave tried again. "Did you see where Sally went?
Who she went with?"

"Yes, I did."

A pause followed, and Dave could see DeMarco

nodding her encouragement from the corner of his eye. He pressed on. "Sooo . . . can you tell me about it, Mrs. Saltzman?"

She turned back to face him. "Claudia."

Dave blinked. "I'm sorry?"

"My name is Claudia. Everyone around here calls me Mrs. Saltzman. I haven't been Mrs. Saltzman in thirty years, and yet, it's been almost as long since anyone has called me anything but."

"Claudia, then. What happened to my sister?"

"It came and took her away."

Dave felt his heart freeze up in his chest, and each beat sent out cold throbs of pain.

Mrs. Saltzman cast him a look that pinched her wrinkles into a frown of distaste before she addressed Dave. "Your sister was talking to it. I heard her. I could hear it, too, only not as well. I don't think it was using real words, only impressions of words."

"It? What do you mean?" DeMarco asked.

"I guess it told her to go into the hallway," Mrs. Saltzman continued, ignoring the detective. "She didn't seem afraid. She talked to it like she knew it." A tiny spasm racked her frail little body and she coughed. For a moment, she seemed distracted, her eyes following something none of them could see.

"What happened next?"

She started humming, her voice high and unwavering like a child's, stronger than the tiny death-rattle she'd spoken with.

"Claudia . . . ?"

The old woman suddenly found her fingers fascinating, turning them in the slice of dust-moted sunlight that streamed in from the window.

"Maybe Mrs. Saltzman needs her rest." An "I told you so" hung off the tip of Dr. Stevens's tongue.

"Not any place physical. In the noggin. That's where it hurts you."

Dave swallowed to work the freezing knot down his chest. "What did you say?"

For just a moment, Mrs. Saltzman looked up at him, and Dave would have sworn he saw no eyes at all, but instead twin sockets of ash that dusted her cheek when she blinked. The moment passed, though, with the blinking of his own eyes.

She offered Dave a smile. "You can't kill it. It's ageless, and it won't die."

A silent throbbing began in his temples, his own voice distant to him, muted by the cotton-hazy pulse in his ears. He knew what she meant. Those were Sally's words. And the voice that had spoken to him—*that was Sally's, too.*

Neither the doctor nor the detective seemed to notice.

Dave felt a sudden urge to reach out and touch her—no, *shake* her, to see if she was real. Instead, he said, "What won't die? The person that took Sally?"

Her eyes focused on him and her thin fingers shot out and wrapped around his forearm. Dave was surprised by the strength of her grip; her fingers looked brittle enough to snap off under the force she applied to his arm.

"I followed Sally as far as the door. She was in the hallway, shivering. Shivering. The frost . . . and the cold . . . and she had no shoes, you know. Her toes could have frozen and fallen off. That happened to my uncle Murray—"

"Sally was in the cold? Where?" Dave interrupted. The throbbing in his head had grown to a pain that stabbed repeatedly behind his eyes.

"The hallway, silly. The hallway was cold with frost and ice and Sally looked cold. No coat, no shoes. And she sighed and clouds came out of her mouth. Then she got scared, and she ran to the fire stairs." Mrs. Saltzman's voice dropped to a conspiratorial whisper, her milky eye darting once around the room. "It was coming, you see."

"What was?"

Mrs. Saltzman shook her head. "Not really a doctor. Thought it was at first—you know, with one of those face masks to keep the germs out? But it wasn't a doctor, no, no, no. . . ." She let go of Dave and hugged her arms around her frail little body. "No, it wasn't. You can bet your buns on that." Mrs. Saltzman nodded as if to confirm her own story. "Made things cold. It was something from someplace else, someplace far away. Someplace where they don't need faces."

From somewhere behind him came a soft cough—DeMarco's.

Mrs. Saltzman looked Dave dead in the eye. "You know what I mean about that, don't you, Sally's brother?"

Dave swallowed, his gaze locked with the filmy lens, the words dying in his throat. *What better place to admit to insanity than in a psych ward?* he thought. The air was heavy with an expectant pause.

"I—I'm sorry. I'm afraid I don't. The man—" He choked on the term, as loose as it was to him. "Do you remember anything else about him?"

"Its feet pretended to touch the floor, but they

didn't. I don't think any part of it really touched anything in this hospital. It made no footstep sounds that I could hear."

"I think this has been just about as productive as it can be." Dr. Stevens gave the old woman a full-blown patronizing smile. "Thank you so much, Claudia."

"Mrs. Saltzman, to you." The shriveled bottom lip extended in a pout, and the doctor's smile faded.

"Yes, well, come along, Mr. Kohlar, Detective. Mrs. Saltzman, enjoy your afternoon." The doctor moved for the door with the detective in tow.

Dave rose, but before he could turn, the woman grabbed the hem of his jacket and tugged it, looking up at him with a sad sort of smile. "You know something . . ."

"Yes?"

A tear rolled down her cheek, cupped in the deep lines of her face. "It wants to kill you both."

With some difficulty, Dave disentangled her fingers from his jacket and hurried to the door before she saw his expression. He was sure the grimace of pain from his pounding head wouldn't be enough to mask the mounting terror.

"Sally's brother, one more thing."

He stopped and turned to the woman who, if it was possible, had withered even further as she sat on the bed. "What is it?"

"Now that I think of it—now that I'm remembering clearly, you see—when it spoke to her, it stole a voice. Tricked her. It sounded just . . . just like . . ." She turned her head toward the window again, and finished her thoughts in a barely audible singsong. "Just like you. Mm-hmm. Mm-hmm. Just like you."

Seven

Dave thought that Detective DeMarco looked thoughtful, scribbling away in her notebook as they passed through the doors and halls back to where they'd come from, and for a fleeting moment, he wondered whether he should mention the Hollower to her. If Cheryl and Erik backed him up, if it would help DeMarco find Sally—

But it wouldn't. He knew that. DeMarco wouldn't believe that some kind of faceless apparition had rippled the reality around Sally's room just enough to sweep her up in its trench coat and spirit her away right under the nurses' noses. No one in his or her right mind would believe that. He'd sound as crazy as . . .

As Mrs. Saltzman? the inner voice accused him. *Is that where you were going with that? Because, wake up, buddy. Everything that woman said about Sally's disappearance is true and you know it. You know it because you know exactly how that damned thing operates.*

He couldn't tell DeMarco. She would never find

the Hollower. But the way she nodded distractedly when Stevens requested being kept in the loop, and her expression when she finally looked up, said something. Dave wasn't a detective, but he was trained to read people. It was a job skill journalists inevitably picked up if they wanted to get their story. Before moving into the sports department of the paper, he'd done interviews, covered stories at the municipal buildings and the courts, and followed up on news leads, and in that time, he'd learned to pick up on what *wasn't* being said. And DeMarco *wasn't* saying that she knew something. Maybe she wouldn't believe faceless monsters and bleeding clock parts and icy hallways, but she believed something, and whatever it was might lead her to Sally.

He hoped for that.

Otherwise, there wasn't much else for him to do. He agreed to go home and wait (going back to work was out of the question now), and DeMarco promised to call as soon as something turned up. Dave reluctantly returned to his car and pulled away from the hospital.

The Hollower had done something to Sally and that was his fault.

Except that Erik had seen it, and so had Cheryl. Sally had seen it, too—Dave was sure of that now. And if he could believe Sally, he could add Max Feinstein to the list. That thing was no stress hallucination, and no tumor, either. It was after them (*"something from someplace else, someplace far away"*), and although he wasn't sure what it was, exactly, there was some satisfaction in knowing what it *wasn't*.

But the knowledge brought with it a new kind of fear, something almost tangible, sour on the tongue, thick and coppery like blood dripping down the back of his throat. He swallowed with difficulty, his mind another world away from the Mitsubishi Eclipse as it sped homeward. What had that thing done to Sally? Where had it taken her (*someplace where they don't need faces, maybe*)? And when would it be coming for him? What would it do to him when it found him? Or Cheryl or Erik? Would it be different for each of them?

"It wants to kill you."

Based on what he'd seen so far, that seemed to be a pretty fair assessment.

Dave made a left turn onto Bayberry Street without looking, then cruised through a red light at the next intersection, oblivious of the angry honks in his wake. Mrs. Saltzman had been right—dead on, in fact. It wanted to kill them all. But why? Why them? And if it was so all-knowing, so all-powerful, and it wanted them dead, why bother with the cat-and-mouse game?

He didn't see the old man until he'd almost hit him. A bent, plaid-flanneled form topped with whipped-cream-white tufts of hair had shuffled out in front of the car about ten feet in front of him. Dave's foot dropped on the brake, bringing the car to a squealing halt. For a moment, the old man disappeared beneath the hood of the car. Heart pounding in time with his head, Dave flew from the driver's-side door around to the front of the car where the old man stooped over, an age-spotted hand with wiry-haired knuckles feeling along the ground for something.

"My God, are you okay?"

The old man met Dave's inquiry with the soft patting of flesh against pavement.

"Sir, are you okay?"

The old man straightened up and jumped when he saw Dave. "Oh, pardon me, son. You gave me a fright." A shaky hand waved it off, followed by a frightfully lopsided grin composed half of teeth, half of gums. "Dropped my lucky coin."

Flabbergasted, Dave gestured at the car behind him. "I almost hit you with my car! Didn't you see me coming?! Didn't you hear me?"

The old man shrugged. "Can't say that I did, son." He nodded, and with a wave, shuffled back onto the sidewalk, heading toward the corner. "Good thing, though," he added over his shoulder with a papery dry laugh. "Could've been wiped off the face of the earth, eh? Lucky for me."

"Well, okay, then," Dave called after, more for something to say. Shaking his head, he turned to the open door of the car.

"Too bad Sally couldn't have been as lucky as me."

Dave whirled around, eyes wide.

There was no one on the sidewalk.

Dave found the package leaning up against the door when he got home, a rectangular box one foot by half a foot in dimension and almost as thick as a shoe box. It was wrapped in brown paper and tied with twine. An affixed label displayed his name and address in bold type, an envelope taped alongside it. He picked up the package, puzzled. The envelope read, in scrolling script, "David Kohlar."

He unlocked the door, dropped his keys and

jacket on a table in the front hallway, and strode into the kitchen to get a pair of scissors to cut the twine.

Dave set the package down on the kitchen table, studying it a moment before reaching for the envelope and sliding out the formal letterhead inside.

BRINDMAN & SYMMES, ATTYS AT LAW was printed in bold across the top, and beneath that, an address in Morristown. The message, neatly typed, read:

> *Dear Mr. David Kohlar:*
> *We represent the estate of Mr. Maxwell Feinstein. We have been instructed, in the event of his passing, to immediately allocate certain effects from his house as designated in his Last Will and Testament. Please find enclosed one such effect. Mr. Feinstein adamantly insisted that it be given to you as is, and so we have sent it as unscathed as time and law allows.*
> *Thank you for your time.*
> *Sincerely, Martin H. Brindman, Esq., and Stanley R. Symmes, Esq.*

Dave frowned, skimming the lines over again for a clue as to the box's contents. He and Max Feinstein had never reached a bequeathing level of acquaintanceship. Maybe it was the package Sally had been talking about in the hospital. Dave supposed that maybe the lawyers had gotten it off the shelf of Max's closet before Dave had gotten there that day.

Dave's gaze trailed to the package again. If it had to do with the Hollower—and he suspected that it did—then he wasn't sure he really wanted to know what was inside. Yet something, maybe a glimmer of that old journalistic curiosity, drew his hand toward the package.

The sharp, shrill ring of the phone startled Dave. His hand snapped back and grabbed the cordless off the kitchen wall instead.

"Hello?"

"Dave?"

"Oh, hey, Georgia."

"What's going on?" She sounded concerned.

"My sister. She's—the hospital's having some trouble—" Dave eyed the package on the table.

"The articles were done and on Crinch's desk at ten after eleven. But he's angry that you left. I mean, I thought his skin would steam off his bones."

"Uh-oh . . ."

"I covered for you. But he wants you in his office tomorrow morning at eight."

"Georgia, you're a peach." When he said this, she usually giggled. Not this time, though.

"Don't be late. I don't want to have to miss that handsome face of yours around this office."

There might have been a smile in her voice that time—he thought he could hear it, although it was grudging.

"I'll be there. Promise."

"You better. See ya."

He hung up the phone, stricken by a sudden loneliness. Was the total of his life so easily summed up as two real jobs, one of which he was on the verge of losing, three serious relationships, none of which existed now, and one coworker in the place a real friend should occupy? One solitary member of his family remained (if she was, indeed, remaining, and he quickly reaffirmed to himself that she was). And that was all he had.

And, of course, one supernatural stalker. Couldn't forget that.

His body felt at that moment much heavier on his bones, a kind of drain he imagined to be the feeling of age catching up to him. Thirty-three years, even thirty-three guilt-ridden years, wasn't supposed to feel like that.

Then again, seventeen years of steady drinking might feel that way. A few years of fearing his mind was pickling in his skull and causing hallucinations, maybe. A couple of hours possessed of the knowledge that a monster from someplace where they didn't need faces had kidnapped his sister, most definitely.

His gaze came to rest on the box again. Had Max felt that kind of drain, too? Had it gotten to be too much for him?

Snatching scissors from the nearby drawer, he snipped the twine and it fell away onto the table. One hand slid over the package, the texture of the brown paper rough beneath his palm. He paused a moment longer to consider the possible contents before he ripped it open.

And he discovered them to be somewhat anticlimactic—a small mirror in a burnished brass frame and a videotape.

Dave frowned. Rising with the videotape in hand, he crossed into the den to his video/DVD player and popped in the tape.

He saw first the blue screen, followed by a flash of static, and then a huge hand shadowing the frame. When the hand pulled away, Dave could see Max sitting behind a desk, hands folded over a forest-green blotter blanketed in Post-it notes. On the tape, Max smiled.

"Uh, hi, David. Hi. Or maybe I should call you Dave. I hope you'll forgive me for taking the liberty of informality here, but I believe we share a common affliction." Max straightened his tie, reached out a hand as if to adjust the camera angle, then drew back, evidently deciding it was fine where it was.

"I hope you can see and hear me okay," he said, leaning into the lens and confirming Dave's supposition. "I have so much to tell you.

"Sally tells me you've seen the Hollower. Worse, the Hollower has seen you." He chuckled. "I suppose 'seen' isn't the right word. It doesn't see you the way you or I might see each other. No," he said, shaking a finger at the camera. "Oh no. It's a different beast entirely."

From off-camera, Max pulled up a bottle of scotch and a glass of ice, poured two fingers of it, and set the bottle down off-camera again. It was as he poured that Dave noticed Max's hands were shaking. He tipped the glass as if toasting to Dave's health, took a gulp, and swallowed loudly. "I'd offer you some, but obviously, I'm not in a position to do that. I'm not a drinking man—never have been. But this is a special occasion. Today . . ." His voice trailed off and he took another smaller sip.

"Today is the last day."

Oh, damn. Dave shifted uncomfortably on the faded tan love seat, his elbows resting on his open knees.

"Dave, let me see if I can explain this thing as I have come to understand it. See, the Hollower is an intangible being. Where our senses stop, its senses start, and continue above and beyond the range of even the most psychic of our kind. The Hollower is not quite physical here, but it seems able to act on this world. As far out as all that sounds, I think you know this much. This . . . being, this monster—it feeds on its victims' sense of unreality. On their surreality, if you will. People's confusions. Their insecurities. I know that's vague, but it's the best way to put it, believe me. The Hollower is sustained by impressions and perceptions and points of view. Its greatest protection is its anonymity and androgyny. How does it find you on such vague terms, you ask? By 'smelling'—on the video Max made fingerquotes around the Hollower's concept of smell— "your most skewed thoughts. By 'smelling' your irrational feelings. These evidently carry their own musk, their own meaty scent that clings to us. Think about it, about those wonderful, awful dating years, and how you just got . . . vibes, I guess you'd call it. Feelings about people. The strongest scents set off red flags about their neediness, their stalker potential. So maybe we do possess a glimmer of that sense it uses to 'see' us or 'smell' us." He smiled at the camera, and Dave was struck by how tired he looked, how worn—like old fabric rubbed smooth, its most distinctive features faded. Max took a sip before continuing.

"It collects identities and voices at will and uses them against you. It's the perfect weapon—the perfect disguise. Few things can hurt us more than the way we can hurt ourselves, am I right? Little else shakes our faith in ourselves so much as self-doubt, however off-kilter or misplaced. And few things are more dangerous than misconceptions about the world around—"

Max suddenly sucked in a sharp breath. His eyes widened as four or five quick footsteps drew closer to the mike and then receded. Dave leaned farther inward toward the television. Something was wrong.

Soft, sexless chuckling caused Max to grow stiff in his chair. There was a flash of static and the chuckling became soft blots of sound like wind blowing into a microphone. Then they stopped dead.

"It knows. It's here, I think. Outside," Max continued in a terrified whisper. "Watching. It's always watching, waiting." Another pause, followed by his own laughter, tinny and forced, which preceded his resolution: "It isn't going to torture me again. I won't let it. I—I won't be made a weapon against myself."

He took several large draughts of scotch and relaxed visibly on the tape, settling back into his chair. But his expression had changed. The terror spent, a strange, somehow more chilling tone of emptiness replaced it.

"I've told you all I know. All anybody knows. I daresay, that may be all anyone has ever known about the Hollower. And I can do no more." He sighed. Static skewed the picture on the screen for a moment and peppered out Max's image for the next, and for less than a second—barely even enough time for his brain to register it—Dave thought he saw a figure, a trench coat, a blond sweep of hair, a pale, featureless face. Then Max was back, the tape clear again.

"I left you something. When the time comes, I think you'll know how to use it. Think what it's for, what it shows people, and you'll know. I'm too tired now and

I can't bear it—I can't do what needs to be done, or what comes after. But you can. I know you can."

He leaned over and smothered the camera angle with shadow, and then the tape snapped off.

Dave rose and ejected the tape. It felt warm, almost alive in his hands, and he felt an immediate sense of relief when he broke contact by putting it down on the table. He picked up the mirror and his eye caught a folded article at the bottom of the box. Laying aside the glass, he picked up the paper. It was old, and he unfolded it gently.

Hyattstown, New Jersey had made the front page of the *Holston-Hyattstown Gazette* on October 5, 1952, when a man by the name of Krellbourne—Charles Krellbourne—was indicted on sixteen counts of murder. Over the course of nine months, he had strangled children ranging in age from eight to fourteen and left their bodies under blankets of leaves and dried grasses in shallow graves.

Max had taken care to underline certain passages with a red grease pen. Krellbourne stated to police that he'd attempted to remove the children's faces to find "the beast underneath." He claimed he'd seen through its deceptive incarnations, and had witnessed the beast's "true and faceless form." He spouted self-defense on the stand, but his official plea, entered by his public defender, was "not guilty by reason of insanity."

Dave wasn't sure what he thought was more horrible—what Krellbourne had done to those children, or that he might have been right in why he did it. But considering either for too long made his chest burn.

It destroys lives. It destroys every life it touches. Krell-bourne's, Max's, Sally's . . . mine.

Mrs. Claudia Saltzman had been absolutely right. It wanted them dead—all of them. And it didn't matter if no part of it ever touched this world. It didn't have to. It destroyed lives just by being in and near them.

The sudden, shrill ring of the phone trumpeted into the silence, and Dave flinched.

"Georgia?" he asked the phone, but it answered only with another blast of sound, louder and stronger than his own small voice. He grabbed the phone in the kitchen.

"Hello?"

"Sally's brother?"

Dave frowned. "Claudia? How did you—"

"There's someone here who wants to talk to you."

There was a rustling sound, and then, "Davey?"

Dave's heart flittered in his chest. "Sally. Oh, thank God! Where are you? Where have you been? Are you back at the hospital?"

A giggle. "No."

"No? Are you—is Mrs. Saltzman with you?"

"Mrs. Saltzman is one of you. I didn't know before now. I couldn't find her."

"Where are you? I'll come get you."

"You can't get me now. You can't take me back from here." She sounded delighted, almost gleeful.

"Sure I can, Sally. Tell me where you are, and I'll come get you, and everything will be all right. You're not in any trouble or anything. No one's mad. We just miss you, and want you to come home."

There was a sniffle from the other end of the phone, and a sudden change in tone from glee to childlike terror. "I'm scared. It's cold here. So very cold. I don't like the cold. . . ."

"I know. It's okay. I'll come get you. Just tell me where you are." A vague memory tugged at his heart, a recollection of frantic pounding on the front door and a frail form carried through it on the breath of the winter wind to collapse into his arms. Sally did hate cold.

"I'm scared. No one looks at me or talks to me. No one has a face. And every clock gives a different time." Her voice quivered, distorted as if filtered through something mechanical or something liquid.

He blinked hard to bring the kitchen back into focus. "Is . . . the Hollower with you?"

"Help me, Davey," she answered, on the verge of tears. "Please. I'm so cold. I don't think I'm alone."

"Damn it," Dave said into the phone. "I can't help you if you don't tell me where you are." Anger, fueled by worry, stiffened his fingers around the receiver as he pressed it close to his ear.

"I told you," Sally answered, but her voice melded into something deeper, something infinitely more sinister than Sally would ever be capable of producing in that slender, fragile throat. "I'm someplace where it wants you all dead, dead, dead as a doornail, dead as a coffin lid, dead as poor old Max, dead as Krellbourne's kiddies."

Dave pulled the phone momentarily away from his ear to stare at it. He felt cold, too, an unpleasant tingle across his whole body. He brought the receiver back to his ear and whispered, "Leave her alone."

"I'll play with her," it responded with delight in

its dual strands of voice, "until the tiny coils that hold her together simply snap."

Dave squeezed his eyes shut and whispered non-sense words to drown out the giggling until the operator's electronic disconnect message finally made its way to his ears.

Eight

Erik drove the landscaping truck home through the quiet streets of his neighborhood. He thought a single late-afternoon moment in Lakehaven, caught and framed by a windshield, would look like this: a row of boxy summer homes that lay quiet, collecting dust along the uneven shore of the lake. The gray-green outline of Schooley's mountain encircling most of the water, tapering into the stirred-up clouds. The 1971 Chevy Malibu, parked within view of Erik's house, radiating a liquid heat and white-gold shine. A ball cupped by the lawn, left untouched in the shadow of a large maple. A pair of roller skates that had made their escape toward the curb and hit the strip of grass between the sidewalk and the street, one standing upright, and the other lying flat in defeat next to it.

That moment saddened him. It seemed flimsy, a cheap knockoff representation of reality, too shiny and perfect to be either real or his.

The night before, he'd had a dream. The beginning found him and Casey on the shore of the lake, walking hand in hand through a warm sunset much like the one now. Mournful bird-cries echoed across the water. It was still warm on the shore in the early orange hours before twilight, and he smiled. Nothing ached, nothing felt lost to him. He was with Casey, and she was beautiful; the wind carried her hair playfully around her head, across her face, and carried the light scent of her perfume to him. She gazed at him with unwavering love and trust. With that certainty that only dream-selves have of events past and present, he knew things were better. Perfect, even.

He saw at times through his own eyes and at others as an omniscient observer. The sun sank slowly over the mountains and the sky took on a pale cast, a smooth and featureless white like the coming of fog, or a snowstorm. He and Casey looked up, surprised but not yet alarmed.

Small chunks of gray and colorless cloud-matter rained from above, carrying weight and substance with jarring little pings. They struck Casey from the clouds' gray underside, melting to rain, flattening first her hair to her head, then the cloth of her T-shirt to her breasts.

She started to back away. With growing horror, Erik watched as his girl smeared and dribbled into the ground as if she were made of ink. The visible drain of color from Casey's head down to her feet carried away with it that trusting look.

"How could you?" she mouthed with soundless hurt. *"How could you let it get me?"*

Her eyes grew wide as if she were suddenly caught in the grip of a deep and convulsive pain.

Her fingers, locking into claws, reached for him. Paralyzed by fear and confusion, Erik stood very still, his breath held in his lungs. He couldn't reach out to her, couldn't do anything now, because he knew it was too late. . . .

With a silent shriek, her body shriveled to a dry husk that fell at his feet. Wind carried sprinkles of crumbling skin up to the now trench-black clouds. Erik whimpered where he stood, unable to close his eyes against Casey's decay.

Her voice from far across the lake finally tore him from the pile of bones at his feet. He turned and found himself in the next instant in a residential area he didn't recognize. Schooley's was beyond his point of view, as was the lake. The deserted rows of bi-levels stood lightless and cool, their neat curtains drawn, their doors shut in grim distaste of his presence. A street sign farther down, too far in real life to see clearly but close enough in dream logic to be visible, read RIVER FALLS ROAD.

On the porch on one of the nearby houses, a semi-circle of wicker porch chairs had been arranged around a small card table. Mannequins with their faces rubbed off occupied each of the five seats. One reminded him very much of Casey—the hair, the body type—and the others were vaguely familiar, too. He thought he recognized one with coarse, bristling gray hair. It was the tattoo that looked familiar, stenciled on the plastic shoulder in black and gray, a Confederate soldier corpse astride a skeleton horse rearing on its hind legs.

They were posed as if engaged in spirited conversation with each other, but none of them moved. He took a few hesitant steps toward them and frowned.

Blood seeped from the seams at their wrists and neck. A white dust covered the table between them. He leaned toward it.

And the arm with the tattoo slammed down on the table.

Erik went to scream, but found he couldn't. No sound came out. Hands shaking, he brushed his fingers across his face. His lips were gone. He felt nothing but smooth, featureless skin. In a panic, he felt upward across a flat expanse where his nose should have been. And the porch blurred as the wind carried his eyes away.

He'd woken up from the dream that morning breathing hard and feeling sick. He hadn't felt right the whole day after.

It was the dream that he thought of as he pulled into the driveway. Everything in his life lately had that cast of flimsy reality and deviation from safe, solid normalcy. As he climbed out of his truck, he felt heavy. Tense and tired, as if he'd been standing on tiptoes for hours.

He found Casey in the bedroom sitting with her long legs tucked under her on the bed. She had a magazine open on her lap, but the look on her face suggested that she hadn't been reading it.

She was waiting for him. She looked up, started to rise, then reconsidered, when she saw him. "Hi."

"Hey." Erik stood in the doorway, uncertain whether to sit.

"Can we talk?"

He nodded, inched into the room, and sat across from her at the foot of the bed.

"I need to ask you something, and I need you to be straight with me." A pause, where she gently laid the magazine on the night table beside her. He noticed tears glistening in her eyes and found it hard to look at her. Her lower lip trembled slightly. She folded her arms beneath her breasts—not defensively, he thought. More like she wasn't sure what to do with them. More like she was trying to warm herself, or console herself. "Are you doing coke again?"

An ache began beneath the bridge of his nose, radiating outward toward his sinuses. A similar one started up in his chest, over his heart. He clenched and unclenched his fists—aches had begun there, too. "No, baby."

She returned a hurt expression, sucked in a breath, and let it out very slowly. "I really want to believe you. I do. I love you. I think I know you well enough to know when something's wrong. And, baby, something's wrong. I'm not blind. I'm not stupid. I can see something's bothering you." The hands slid back to her lap. "You swear it isn't another girl. You swear it isn't the drugs. But if you don't tell me what it is, then what else am I supposed to think?"

Erik's gaze dropped to the floor, focusing on the iridescent pink of her painted toenails. "I know. I know, and you're right, but it isn't easy to explain."

"If we're sharing a life together, then we ought to be sharing everything—good, bad, important, trivial, crazy. That's one of the things I'm here for." She scooted toward him, cupping the back of his neck with her hand. He looked into her eyes. Even with the gloss of tears and the soft charcoal smear of her eyeliner, her eyes were beautiful.

"Whatever it is," she whispered, "tell me. I'll understand."

The ache urged him. She would make it stop. She would understand. But—

"Casey, I can't—"

"Please." The word barely stood on its own. It seeped from her like a shallow breath, nearly drowned beneath the tears she fought to hold back.

Erik took a deep breath and let it go. "Okay. Okay." He closed his eyes, opened them, and took her hand. "The truth is weird, but if you want it . . . baby, if you want it, it's yours."

He continued when she nodded. "There's this . . . this guy, in a hat. Well, guy's not the right word. It— I think it can be both. Either. Or neither. I'm not sure. Anyway, this thing in a Bogart hat and black trench coat follows me sometimes. It has no face. No joke. Looks like someone took a giant eraser to its head and rubbed out anything remotely human."

Saying it out loud, and seeing her silent reaction in her expression, drove a stab of guilt into Erik's chest. "I told you—"

"I believe you. Go on."

Erik sighed. "It does things—bad things—to try to confuse me. Hurt me. I think it wants me dead."

"A psycho? If you've got some nut—"

"No, it's not like that. This thing isn't . . . a person. Not like what you'd think of as a person. It changes appearance and voices. It hiccups the world around it and—" He thought a moment, then settled on an analogy he thought fitting. "It's like when this thing is around, you're looking through warped glass. Everything you see through it is a distorted, inaccurate version of what it really is. Only, I think for that period of time, that distortion is the reality. I think if it could just convince me what it was showing me was real, those distortions would hurt me. Maybe kill me."

"I don't understand." She shifted on the bed.

"I call it Jones—you know, because it seemed like it was always trying to get me high. I couldn't tell you about it. Couldn't tell anyone. I thought . . . I thought I was failing you. Failing myself. I thought I was seeing this thing because I just couldn't cut being sober. And I couldn't face you like that. I didn't want you to think . . ." His voice trailed off. Didn't want her to think what? That he was a failure? A loser? Didn't want her to think that he'd rather get high than anything else in the world? That he'd risk losing her just for one more time?

He found he couldn't say those things out loud to her. He didn't have to. The hurt in Casey's eyes and the turn of her lips in grim understanding was enough for him. She never had been able to hide what she thought. It was always in her eyes.

"It isn't only me, though. The other night, I found out that at least two other people can see this thing, too. Probably more. And it's trying to do the same thing to them. It's trying to ruin our lives. It wants us dead and it'll do whatever it takes to lead us to that end."

"You realize how that sounds. I believe you," she added quickly. "I mean, I believe you're really seeing this . . . whatever it is—"

"Hollower. I'm told that's what it's called."

She frowned. "Hollower, then. I could maybe believe that you see it. But I'm having trouble swallowing why. I mean, come on, Erik. You're telling me this thing, this ghost or monster or alien or something, is trying to kill you. It's showing you hallucinations that can actually hurt you. It's lying to trick you, and for some reason, it's trying to get you high. You've got to understand that sounds paranoid. It sounds—"

She didn't finish her sentence, but he knew where she was going with it. *It sounds like something you'd say when you were high.* And he didn't have the strength to argue that. Because actually, it *did* sound like something he might have said when he was high.

"It's not," he said, his voice low and defeated. "Look, I know this is hard to believe and a hell of a mouthful to swallow. Could we just leave it at my need to explore my reasons for my shaken belief in my own sobriety? Can we think of it as at least a step forward that I'm aware of the problem this is causing and I need you to bear with me as I try to figure out how the fuck to fix it? Please?"

Tears blurred his vision, and with the hand not holding Casey's, he mashed them away. She pulled his head to her neck and stroked his hair, and he wrapped his arms around her. He suddenly wanted very much to be pressed close to her, their skins touching, to be inside her. He needed her not only near him but a part of him, and the need made him hard and hungry and shivering.

He kissed her neck. He hadn't realized how tense her body was, too, until she relaxed beneath his lips, beneath the fingertips that wanted to feel the heat of her and the breath that wanted to catch the scent of her and hold on to her forever. She let him ease her onto her back on the bed. They fumbled silently, somewhat awkwardly with clothes, but they exchanged soft, single words of comfort and

GET UP TO 4 FREE BOOKS!

You can have the best fiction delivered to your door for less than what you'd pay in a bookstore or online—only $4.25 a book! Sign up for our book clubs today, and we'll send you **FREE* BOOKS** just for trying it out...with **no obligation to buy, ever!**

LEISURE HORROR BOOK CLUB

With more award-winning horror authors than any other publisher, it's easy to see why CNN.com says "Leisure Books has been leading the way in paperback horror novels." Your shipments will include authors such as RICHARD LAYMON, DOUGLAS CLEGG, JACK KETCHUM, MARY ANN MITCHELL, and many more.

LEISURE THRILLER BOOK CLUB

If you love fast-paced page-turners, you won't want to miss any of the books in Leisure's thriller line. Filled with gripping tension and edge-of-your-seat excitement, these titles feature everything from psychological suspense to legal thrillers to police procedurals and more!

As a book club member you also receive the following special benefits:

- **30% OFF** all orders through our website & telecenter!
- **Exclusive access** to special discounts!
- **Convenient** home delivery and **10 days to return any books you don't want to keep.**

There is no minimum number of books to buy, and you may cancel membership at any time. See back to sign up!

*Please include $2.00 for shipping and handling.

YES! ☐

Sign me up for the Leisure Horror Book Club and send my TWO FREE BOOKS! If I choose to stay in the club, I will pay only $8.50* each month, a savings of $5.48!

YES! ☐

Sign me up for the Leisure Thriller Book Club and send my TWO FREE BOOKS! If I choose to stay in the club, I will pay only $8.50* each month, a savings of $5.48!

NAME: _____

ADDRESS: _____

_____

TELEPHONE: _____

E-MAIL: _____

☐ **I WANT TO PAY BY CREDIT CARD.**

☐ VISA ☐ MasterCard. ☐ DISCOVER

ACCOUNT #: _____

EXPIRATION DATE: _____

SIGNATURE: _____

Send this card along with $2.00 shipping & handling for each club you wish to join, to:

Horror/Thriller Book Clubs
1 Mechanic Street
Norwalk, CT 06850-3431

Or fax (must include credit card information!) to: 610.995.9274.
You can also sign up online at www.dorchesterpub.com.

*Plus $2.00 for shipping. Offer open to residents of the U.S. and Canada only.
Canadian residents please call 1.800.481.9191 for pricing information.

If under 18, a parent or guardian must sign. Terms, prices and conditions subject to change. Subscription subject to acceptance. Dorchester Publishing reserves the right to reject any order or cancel any subscription.

JOIN NOW!

encouragement, and giggled into each other's necks and hair.

As the flimsy gold of the dying afternoon gave way to cool, solid night, Erik found Casey again, and as he made love to her, he thought he would never let her go.

Dave arrived at the Olde Mill Tavern just after the sun set. Monday nights weren't usually too busy at the Tavern, and Dave hoped to find Cheryl relatively alone.

Erik had been right. Maybe there was safety in numbers.

Dave pushed open the door, and the warm glow of the bar's interior greeted him. He saw some of the regulars leaning over quiet dinner drinks, but didn't see Cheryl—or anyone else, for that matter—behind the bar. For a moment, he panicked.

Then she came out through the kitchen doors. Dave exhaled in relief. She scowled at him as he approached the bar, but before she could unleash whatever anger she had for him, he held up a hand and said, "You're right. And I'm sorry. Really, I'm sorry."

The glare softened. "How do you know what I was going to say?"

He chuckled. "Because I'm a dumb jerk about most things. Law of averages, really."

She smiled. "The usual?"

"If you can find it in your heart to forgive me."

She poured him a drink. "Don't be so hard on yourself. You're here now."

The smile faded from his face. "I'll tell you what you want to know. But not here."

"Then where? When?"

"Tonight after work?" He downed the shot of tequila.

"We close at midnight." She poured him another shot.

"I'll be back then. With Erik, if I can find him. He can see it, too." Dave knocked back the second shot, put fifteen dollars down on the bar, and rose.

"His name's McGavin—he's in the book."

Dave nodded. "I'll find him."

"What is it, Dave?" she said, barely above a whisper.

"It's called the Hollower. Good a name as any, I guess." He glanced around the nearly empty bar, then fixed her with a cool stare. "Trust your instincts. If anything happens tonight, get the hell out of here. Otherwise, I'll be back at midnight. I promise. And I'll tell you everything I know."

"Should I be scared?" She wiped the bar in little circles with the rag.

Dave thought of Sally in the dark, in the cold of wherever the Hollower had taken her. "Yeah. You should. But at least you won't have to be scared alone."

She looked up at him. "Thank you."

"Don't thank me yet. You're not going to like what I have to tell you." Dave headed for the door, then called over his shoulder, "Midnight?"

"I'll be waiting for you," she replied, tentative.

Dave pushed the door open and headed out to find one Erik McGavin.

Dave got back in his car and locked the doors. He didn't turn on the headlights or start the engine. Some part of him was vaguely aware of being watched. He stared through the windshield of his car to the woods across the road, waiting. It wouldn't want him to call Erik, he thought. They were each weaker apart.

Dave had had a girlfriend once, a blond with long legs and little inclination to ever wear a bra beneath her tank tops. She was light and sweet and dumb as a post. The most insightful gift she had ever given him was a cell phone that he never went anywhere without. He kept her number still in there, more as a nod of gratitude for the gift than any fond recollection of the deer-in-headlight eyes or the way her breasts bounced when she stamped her foot in disagreement. But he silently thanked her the time his car had broken down off Route 202, the times he was late for work and needed Georgia to cover him, and the times Sally had an emergency and needed him to come fix it. He had come to think of the cell phone as lucky.

He pulled it out now and prayed luck would hold out against the Hollower long enough. He got the information for an Erik McGavin in Lakehaven, New Jersey. Then he dialed the number. So far so good.

No movement from the trees, he noticed. Also good.

"Hello?" The voice on the other end sounded sleepy and distracted.

"Erik McGavin?" Dave scanned the trees across the street for signs of movement.

"Yeah? Who's this?"

"It's Dave Kohlar. From the Tavern?"

A pause, then, "Dave Kohlar?"

"I need to talk to you about the Hollower." Dave thought he saw a flash of white in the dense shadows of the woods, but in the next moment, it was gone. "If you tell me where you live, I'll come pick you up. I've got to meet Cheryl at midnight. I think

you're right. About it being safer with all of us together, I mean."

"What made you change your mind?" There was a
muffled grunt of effort, like Erik was doing something while the phone was pressed against his ear.
Getting dressed, maybe. Dave thought he heard a
snap of clothing and what might have been the *zifvt*
of a zipper being pulled.

"A lot has happened in the last day or so. I'll explain it all tonight. Thing is, I think you had something, about us standing a better chance together
than alone." His hand slid back and forth in small
arcs across the steering wheel and a pause stretched
across the phone between them.

Erik broke the silence with "It isn't ever going to
leave us alone, is it?"

"I don't think so."

"What time do you want to meet?"

Dave checked the clock on the dashboard. "It's almost ten thirty now. Can I pick you up at eleven?"

"Works for me." Erik gave him directions, which
he scribbled in pen on the only surface available in
the car—an old Dunkin' Donuts foam cup.

"Got it." He put the directions in the cup holder.

"Dave?"

"Yeah?" Dave switched ears.

"Thank you, man."

Dave didn't know why these people were grateful. He couldn't protect them. He wasn't even sure
what he hoped to accomplish by bringing them together. "You're welcome," he muttered. "See you at
eleven." Then he clicked off the phone.

He saw another flash of light in the trees and
frowned, peering out into the darkness. A moment

later, a deer stepped onto the road, and he let out a short breath.

Despite the glare of Dave's taillights as he pulled away, another flash of white went unseen, followed by a looming of black against the shadows, both so intense as to be almost iridescent.

The chattering of claws echoed softly across the lake.

DeMarco drummed the pencil against the side of the desk as she perused her notes on the Kohlar woman's case, chewed on the eraser, then drummed again.

Something wasn't clicking.

Three of her most recent files and two cold case files that instinct had compelled her to pull from the boxes in the basement lay spread out before her. Lakehaven Police Department had been for some time "in the process of converting the contents of the cold cases to electronic format for reference and storage," but truth be told, the project was an organizational nightmare and had stalled several times since '96. It had taken her a good three hours to find what she was looking for. As she sat with the reports and photographs and witness statements fanned out over the small space she'd cleared on her desk, she frowned.

How could the cases possibly be related?

DeMarco would have chalked up statements made by Mrs. Saltzman as mostly hazy, useless products of her condition, except that some of them rang familiar in her ear. The old woman indicated that a person unknown had taken Ms. Kohlar from

the hospital. She had also said this person could
"steal voices." Maybe someone who could do impressions, like a comedian or a ventriloquist. Not too
strange a detail, in itself. But it nagged her, reminded
her vaguely of Cheryl Duffy's case days before. That
woman mentioned someone lurking around her
house, someone who appeared to be able to throw
his voice and call her by name.

Then there was the face thing. Mrs. Saltzman said
this person who had kidnapped Ms. Kohlar had
taken her to "a place where they don't need faces."
Ms. Duffy insisted the figure she saw hadn't had a
face. Both seemed to believe this figure wished to do
harm. And yet subsequent investigations of the
premises had turned up no trace, no evidence of this
figure ever having been there at all.

It nagged at her, too, that Mrs. Saltzman believed
Dave Kohlar—she checked her notes—would understand these things or be familiar with them
somehow. The old woman thought he should have
known about this place where people didn't need
faces. It would have been easy to dismiss the assumption if it wasn't for his reaction, and his voice.

And the doctor—Stevens's name sparked some
recognition, although it had taken her most of the
car ride back to the station to place why. Stevens
had counseled Max Feinstein, too, and prescribed
narcotics.

All of it tenuously connected by leaps of instinct.
Except when she added the info from the Feinstein
suicide.

It had been ruled a suicide by the M.E., but De-
Marco hadn't needed Heddy Blickman to tell her
that. She and the other investigating officers

thought it odd at the time that there had been no note, but after talking with his ex-wife, DeMarco learned Feinstein attended group therapy sessions and took (or more accurately, according to the inventory of pills and the prescription date, did *not* take) heavy medication.

Max Feinstein saw Dr. Stevens, and he ended up taking out the back of his skull. Sally Kohlar saw Dr. Stevens and disappeared from a psychiatric ward of a hospital.

Was Stevens responsible somehow in either instance? Was that, under the guise of strict doctor-patient privilege, the reason why he hadn't wanted her to talk to the old woman? But then, if he was the mysterious figure in question, why hadn't Mrs. Saltzman recognized him? She appeared to know him well enough when they'd questioned her—in fact, seemed to hold the opinion of him that De-Marco herself did.

And further, why wouldn't Sally have recognized her own doctor, if that was the case? What could he have done to make Sally suddenly afraid of him, and what purpose would that serve if he was looking to get her out quickly and quietly, beneath the staff nurses' noses? In fact, why remove Sally from the facility at all?

So many questions. So many tenuous connections.

DeMarco realized at length that these connections were more or less secondary to the stranger one, the one that had been sitting on her desk a few mornings ago when she had come in. Brindman & Symmes, attorneys for the estate of Mr. Maxwell Feinstein, had sent her the original copy of a tape that had recently come into their possession. The police hadn't found it because it hadn't been marked as anything special, nor had it been with the other tapes. She suspected it was an oversight on the part of Rubelli's boys, and DeMarco was still fuming about it days later. But given his condition, even watching the tape hadn't meant much to the Feinstein case. He had mentioned some being, some kind of thing he called the Hollower.

But given the developments of the more recent cases, the things Feinstein said took on a whole new light.

"It collects identities and voices at will and uses them against you." That's what Feinstein said on the tape. This Hollower collected voices and used them. Just like Ms. Duffy claimed her bar intruder had done. Just like Mrs. Saltzman claimed Sally Kohlar's kidnapper had done. And DeMarco had a growing certainty that the "Dave" Feinstein addressed on the tape—the intended recipient of his suicide video—was, in fact, Mr. Dave Kohlar. Symmes had confirmed it over the phone.

The cases looked as if they were tied to Feinstein. A suicide, a disappearance, a possible stalking.

And the murders. The cold case murders.

Debbie Henshaw from Plainfield had been stabbed repeatedly in the chest and stomach, and most of the skin of her face had been removed. Her eyes had been gouged out as well, and the sockets filled with the ashes of burnt paper. That one had always bothered DeMarco. Her first homicide as a detective, but far from her first homicide, it had gotten under her skin, so to speak, because the vic was so young. DeMarco had seen a picture of the girl's face once she'd been identified, and the girl had a sweet look—innocent good-girl pretty. Freckles across a tiny nose. Someone's kid sister. Someone's high school sweetheart.

Someone carved one jagged word into the pale skin beneath her breasts: HOLLOW. At the time, De-Marco and her partner suspected it represented the killer's belief about Debbie's soul, her person, saying she was hollow inside, a shell without life and so there was no guilt or wrong in ending the shell's existence on this earth.

Now DeMarco wasn't so sure. Feinstein's faceless Hollower possessed awfully coincidental similarities. Even its name suggested uncanny coincidence.

The second case equally unsettled, in its own way. Not that any murder wasn't unsettling if she thought about it too long, but she didn't. She couldn't afford to. She wasn't getting paid to be derailed by sentiment.

In the second case, a neighbor found a woman named Savannah Carrington dead on her back patio with several shards of glass in her neck, arms, torso, and legs. Her death might have been ruled a suicide if not for the impossible odd angles of some of the shards. The police searched the premises and the yards of the surrounding properties and found nothing with a broken glass surface that might have accounted for her condition. However, small shards lay scattered about her and were also fished from her in-ground swimming pool. She slumped against the sliding glass door, her nightgown splattered with blood. More blood collected in sticky little puddles around her. The door against which her bloody cheek was pressed was intact; the glass hadn't come from there, either. In fact, it had provided a surface for her to write a message about the one part of her body that was unscathed.

My face. They thought she had written that after the killer had left, as she slowly bled to death in her backyard. Whoever killed Savannah Carrington (*"for Chrissakes, Detective, he didn't have a face"*) gave her the impression that for some reason he wanted to disfigure her.

DeMarco stared at the photo, at the dried drops of blood on the glass, at the wide-eyed glazed look of horror even death could not relax. She looked at the skinned head of Debbie Henshaw's corpse, and the blood-speckled wall behind the collapsed body of Max Feinstein. She thought of the ever-widening ripples of sadness, bitterness, loss, and mistrust that these deaths brought to family, friends, colleagues. In essence, all murder victims shared a common injustice. All grieving relatives shared a common pain. All of society shared a loss—of its members, its security and safety, its understanding of itself.

She sighed, rubbed her eyes, then let her gaze trail over the walls of the department. Most of the desk lights were off and only two other officers remained, poring over cases of their own. Behind one was a map of the Morris/Sussex County area.

She rose slowly. Scooping up the files, she made her way over to the map and found Feinstein's house. Then the Kohlar residence. Then the Duffy residence. Then the homes of the two cold case vics.

More ripples, with Feinstein's house in the center and the other properties forming rings around it spreading outward.

"Late night for you too, An?"

DeMarco smiled down at Bennie Mendez. "Hey,

Bennie. Yeah, late night for me. But I get my most genius deductions done after hours. Going to make a
phone call, then go home and rest this brilliant
mind."

He smiled up at her. "Your modesty rivals only
your beauty, Detective."

DeMarco laughed. "See you in the morning."

"Night, genius."

DeMarco turned and walked back to her desk.
Picking up the phone, she rang up the district attorney. "May? Anita here. I think I'm going to need a
warrant for the Feinstein place . . . Yup, I'll bring the
files over tomorrow morning . . . Right, right.
Thanks, May. I appreciate it. Night. . . . Yeah, you
too. See you tomorrow."

She closed the files and tucked them into a relatively neat stack, then grabbed her keys and called it
a night.

The last of the regulars had cleared out of the Tavern
by a quarter after eleven. Cheryl kept glancing at the
clock as she finished wiping down the bar. She
hoped someone, anyone—even Ray Gravelin, for
Chrissakes—would wait until closing time with her.
Dave wouldn't be there for another twenty-five minutes or so, and she really didn't want to be alone.

Ray stumbled out at a quarter to midnight, and
took the last of the barfly warmth and camaraderie
with him.

She remembered the voice at the bar, not quite
male and not quite female, but somehow a chilling
strain of each intertwined.

Cheryl realized that for a long time it had been
with her, watching her, close to her ear, a chill breath

on her neck not like any breath of this earth. It moved freely in her private places, in her safe spaces, and had for months. It invaded her life, her mind, her sense of security. It wasn't the first time.

"It was tall, broad like a man, but the way it moved . . ."

Cheryl crossed the bar to the dining area. She began to place the chairs upside down on the tables, her ear tuned to the silence of the bar, listening for disruptions in the after-hours hum of the bar's appliances.

As she upended the last of the chairs, it came to her soft and unobtrusive—the tinkling music of wind chimes.

She straightened and turned, and found she was no longer in the bar.

At least, not in the Olde Mill Tavern that she knew. The oblong shape of the bar rotted, its rough wood waterlogged and stinking now of lake things left to decompose—dead fish, decaying seaweed, baby doll arms floating in the shallow pools close to the shore . . .

Baby doll arms? That had been long ago, too far in the past. A past long gone. A past as hazy as the fog that settled low around the now-rotted hull where night after night she served drinks to leering men who talked to her breasts and then went home and tucked their little girls in and swore to protect them from men who might tempt them with dolls.

She blinked hard. When she opened her eyes, the bar remained, but she could see more of where she stood. She felt the warm grainy texture of sand between her toes and the slight tug of early sunburn across the backs of her bare shoulders. The white legs of the lifeguard stand reached up into the sun glare. From the crossbeam by one of them, the metal chimes knocked around in the midsummer breeze. All around her the sun was dazzling, but she saw a stretch of beach before her and heard the lapping of water against the gray-green wood of the dock a ways out.

Cheryl stepped backward and cool water splashed the backs of her legs. She cried out, turning in the water. The shimmer of sunlight hazed the world beyond the dock, a far shore lost now, if even a far shore existed out there.

She remembered this lake. Not a patch of beach in Lakehaven but a shore farther back, farther away. She remembered the ice cream man's truck came at three o'clock and if you stood perfectly still and no boys splashed loudly nearby, the little iridescent fish would swim right up to your ankles and dart between your legs.

She turned back to the shore, the rest of the Tavern faded away now into sun sparkle. The water around her calves was cold, colder. She tried to wade toward the warm sand again, but found she couldn't move. Cheryl looked down. A thin sheen of ice covered the water. A few little fish, keeled to one side and caught frozen, stared up at her with bulging eyes glazed in death. The skin of her legs grew pale, and the water hurt her instep, her toes, and her ankles. The sand slid beneath her feet, slimy and slippery.

"Hey, little girl. Do you like dolls?"

Her head shot up. She saw shiny shoes and black-clad legs. A glove floated obediently where a hand should be at the cuff of a sleeve crusted with cold. The glove held a doll.

The man stepped forward toward the water, which reached the shore by his shoes but seemed to shrink away from actually touching them.

This time Cheryl was afraid. This time she didn't *want* the doll, didn't want the man with the big towel in his trunk to look under her bathing suit.

She stood in the center of the ice, unable to move, unable to run, her own breath frost in her throat, her scream an icicle lodged deep, cutting off the air. Fear crystallized through her body.

Cheryl looked up into the glare of the sun, which had rubbed the features of the man's face right off his head. She kicked as best she could at the ice that bound her ankles. The skin of her shins split against the sharp edges of ice. The blood felt first hot, and then cold like lake water dripping down her legs.

The figure took a step closer. Tears threatened to break free from her lower lids and spill down her cheeks in panic.

"Are you alone, Cheryl?" The man spoke with the voice of the thing in the bar, the thing Dave had called the Hollower. The voice, androgynous and chilly, formed the words of the question as if they were foreign and took a great deal of effort to pronounce.

Cheryl felt the acceleration of heartbeats in her chest, pounding arctic pain against her breasts.

"What are you?" she whispered.

"I am ageless."

"Leave me alone." She closed her eyes, trying to press out the sight of the rotted bar, strewn across the sand like an old shipwreck, and of the Hollower holding the doll out to her and tracing her body with eyes it didn't really have.

"You are never alone. I will always be with you."

"No." The word barely made it past her lips, and until it answered, she wasn't sure if she'd even spoken out loud.

Its laugh echoed over the lake behind her, and also over the lake that some fleeting part of her mind knew to still be out there beyond the fog, a real lake and a real town of Lakehaven, not a phantasm of the past.

The Hollower stepped onto the ice toward her.

Erik was waiting on the front step of a pleasant-looking lake bungalow when Dave arrived. The boy's hands were shoved into faded jeans pockets, and he wore a leather jacket to brace himself from the wind blowing off the lake. He nodded a hello and jogged down to the car as Dave pulled up to the curb.

Once in the passenger seat, he said, "I'm not sure what to say. I'm glad you called. That's something."

"I wish I could tell you I had a plan for stopping this, but I don't." Dave turned at the end of the road toward the direction of the bar.

"But you do have information, right?"

Dave nodded. "Not much. A start. Maybe you and Cheryl will be able to come up with something I couldn't." A pause. "I think the Hollower is getting more aggressive, more intrusive. I think it's done toying with us."

Erik's breath came in excited little puffs of air. "I'd be lying if I said that didn't scare the shit out of me."

Dave snorted. "Yeah, you and me both, man." They settled into silence for a moment, and then he said, "It took my sister."

He felt Erik's wide-eyed gaze search his face. "You're serious? What do you mean, took her?"

"I think it . . . changes things. Bends reality, or the way we see reality. Warps our perception. It took her right in front of the night nurses, and no one ever saw a goddamned thing." Dave shrugged and turned left. "Took her right from the hospital."

"Hospital?"

Dave could tell from the tone that the question was born of genuine confusion. But he felt that ache in his chest, that familiar mix of embarrassment and guilt and defensiveness and sympathy. He slowed to a stop at a red light and glanced at Erik. "It's a long story. My sister is ill. She sees things. Hears things."

The glow of the traffic light flushed their faces through the windshield. Erik took in his words with a nod. "Heh. Yeah. Don't we all?"

The ache in Dave's chest eased. The light changed and he pulled forward again.

"Anyway, I talked to her roommate, who said she saw what happened. She told us the Hollower chased Sally—that's my sister—right down the hall of . . . of some other hospital that only she and Sally could see."

He wanted to go on, to say he thought it was somehow significant that the Hollower didn't notice or bother Mrs. Saltzman at all, before, during, or since, so far as he knew. But he wasn't quite sure what the significance of that was, or how, as a piece of the puzzle, it fit the picture he had so far.

"I'm not sure I understand." Erik frowned.

"I'm not sure I do, either. I think the old lady was saying the Hollower changed the hallway somehow, so Sally never saw the nurses and they never saw her. Like maybe it superimposed its own version of the hallway, a hallway from its dimension, on the one Sally was in. At any rate, the hospital told me the nurses' station was staffed all night, and no one saw Sally leave. The old lady said she never saw any nurses—not in that version of the hallway, at least.

"I've given it a lot of thought since then. I considered that maybe she was parroting back what Sally told her about the Hollower. I mean, I think it's a pretty safe assumption that if she was in the hospital with Sally in the first place, she probably sees and hears things that aren't there. But I got a phone call, too. From Sally, maybe. From the Hollower. I don't know which. But it has her. I'm sure about that. And I have to get her back."

He felt Erik's eyes on him again, expectant, full of a question he wasn't sure he should ask.

"I don't know if she's dead," Dave answered in a flat tone. "I really don't know anything, except if I hadn't been so fucking stupid and unwilling to actually do something about all this before, she might still be safe."

"You don't need to have all the answers. Ain't your fault, man."

Dave gave him a sad smile. "You know that for sure?"

"I know we go through life beating ourselves up about stuff that we really can't control, and never could." Something in the boy's tone made Dave steal a glance at his passenger, and he noticed Erik's expression darkened for a moment. "That's what destroys people. That's what eats away at them over the years. Guess that's what makes them empty. Hollow. Ready to be filled with all the bad luck and the accidents and those little slips of sanity that ruin everything."

"Susceptible to the Hollower, you mean?"

"Yeah. Yeah, exactly."

It made sense. Dave buried everything beneath other people's baggage, their useless springs and coils and junk of the past he had never been able to change. Obviously Max Feinstein had carried around some pretty heavy pieces of the past— carried them until he couldn't bear to hold them up anymore. He wondered what Erik beat himself up about, and Cheryl.

A thoughtful silence settled over the car like a soft snow, muting conversation. But when they rolled into the parking lot of the Tavern, he felt the change almost instantly—a tang in the air, a hum he felt in dull pricks on his skin, a nearly audible hum in his head.

"Something's wrong," Dave said, rolling to a stop in the closest space. He felt a greasy stirring of nausea in his stomach. "Where is she?"

Erik glanced around the parking lot. "That her car?"

Dave craned his neck to follow where Erik was looking and discovered an old Ford Taurus. "Yeah, I think so."

"So she's still here, then." Erik opened the door and got out. "Maybe she's finishing up inside."

Dave followed, but he knew something was happening. "No, something isn't right. Can't you feel it? Like being seasick."

"I was gonna say, 'like being hungover,' but yeah. Thought it was just me."

The two made their way to the door and Dave knocked. Several seconds stretched to a minute, then two, and Dave knocked again. "Cheryl?" He tried the door, but the knob wouldn't turn.

"Cheryl?" he called, loud enough, he hoped, to be

heard through the door. "You still in there?" He tried the knob again, threw his shoulder against it in case it had swollen and stuck, jiggled the knob again. Nothing.

"Door's locked," Dave said, frowning. "Maybe I should call her? Phone's in the glove box."

Erik nodded, and they got back in the car. Dave dialed up the number for the bar, a number his companion seemed faintly amused to discover he knew by heart. Immediately an electronic voice informed him, "I'm sorry, your call cannot be completed as dialed. Please check the number, or dial zero for assistance," in a pleasant simulation of human politeness.

"That *is* the number, damn it." Dave shook his head. "She's in trouble. She can't hear us."

Erik looked at the locked door and ran a hand through his hair. "Shit. What if it's in there with her?"

They became aware, by degrees, of a brightness coming from beneath the door. It looked to Dave like the sun had been captured and poured into the barroom. He and Erik exchanged a look. And then they heard laughter.

"Honk the horn."

Dave leaned on the horn.

There was a faint bleating sound, like a hurt animal, and at once, the illusion dissipated. Cheryl was back in the Tavern, back on the dusty tiled floors of the dining area, back amidst the forest of upturned chairs.

Blood from small cuts soaked through the shins of her jeans and dried crusty, adhering her socks to her ankles. Her feet felt frostbitten.

She made her way with slow and painful steps

across the bar and out the door, not bothering to shut the lights or lock up or even grab her purse. Outside, she sank to the step and curled her legs underneath her. For a long time, she breathed in the cool autumn air and let it go in grudging little puffs. All strength had left her.

She was vaguely aware of Dave jogging from the driver's side of his car to her, and of Erik McGavin getting out on the passenger side. When Dave touched her shoulder, he said something her mind couldn't quite wrap around. She looked up at him.

Then she started to cry.

Nine

On the way back to his apartment, Dave cast worried glances in Cheryl's direction every so often to make sure she was okay. Erik hovered over her from the backseat. She didn't seem to notice. Slumped against the car door, her arms wrapped around her body as if to keep warm, she stared out the window. Tears glinted in the moonlight.

Finally, she spoke, so low Dave missed it. She cleared her throat and tried again. "It tried to kill me tonight."

"Want to tell us what happened?" Erik patted her shoulder.

She didn't look at either of them. "When I was a girl, my brothers used to take me swimming at the lake near where we grew up. Place called Cutlass Cove. I used to love swimming there."

Dave noticed fresh tears brimming in her eyes.

"One day a man . . . gave me a doll. Asked me to come play with him. I was little, seven years old. He said I had a pretty bathing suit but it was all wet and

it wasn't good for pretty little girls to sit in wet
bathing suits. He had a big towel in the trunk of his
car and said if I let him dry me off, I could keep the
doll." She shook her head. "He touched me. Dried
me off. Just dried and touched and dried and
touched. For about twenty minutes. Then wrapped
me in the towel and sent me on my way. Police never
found him. My parents never talked about it. My
brothers never knew."

Neither Erik nor Dave said anything, but Dave
reached out and gently touched her hand.

"He changed everything," she whispered, and at
first Dave didn't know if Cheryl meant the man who
had molested her or the Hollower. Before he could
ask, she continued. "The bar, the whole room, everything was gone. I was standing in the lake—that
lake, and I was wearing a bathing suit—that wet
bathing suit. And it was there with a doll and it told
me"—the tears spilled down her cheeks now and
she sniffed—"that it would always be with me.
Dave, it's never going to leave me alone.

"I think it gets further and further in your head,
digs through the layers, and uproots the most buried
things." She wiped at the tears with the back of her
hand. "The things that can hurt you the worst."

"I'm sorry—"

She waved away his words. "Just tell us how to
kill it."

"I don't know how," he answered softly.

She looked at him. "Then tell us what you do
know."

Across the street, the Feinstein house stood dark
and still. Sean knew because he'd gotten up to check

a few times, expecting to see the monster across the street peering out at him from Mr. Feinstein's old bedroom.

He didn't. Maybe the Hollower was out for the night.

After his mother had popped her head in to kiss him good night, he lay for a long time, repeating the Warding Ritual with slow, deliberate motions, over and over.

It had lied to him. It would have killed him if it could have. Pumped his hand full of venom and the pediatrician he went to wouldn't have been able to explain Sean's death to his mom or anyone else.

Sean shivered and glanced at the window, tempted to sneak out of bed again and check on the house. He felt cold and kind of icky. No one had ever wanted him dead before. It made him feel sick and a little embarrassed, like how he imagined the kids might have felt in that video they'd watched in school about strangers who touched children or offered them *Magic: The Gathering* cards or PS2 games if they got into their cars or followed them into dark alleys.

He'd known a kid in school, a fifth grader the size of a small pony, who liked to threaten and sometimes knock to the ground anyone unlucky enough to get in his way. They called him Pach. They'd always called him Pach, although Sean couldn't remember why. Sometimes Pach told him he was going to kick Sean's ass. Sometimes he looked like he meant to. But no one—not even Pach—had ever wanted him dead.

Sean glanced at the window again. It had to be after midnight, but he wasn't going to get any sleep.

He climbed out of bed and tiptoed to his door. The reassuring blue glow of his mom's bedroom TV flickered irregularly over her sleeping form. She would probably wake up at some point to turn the TV off. In the meantime, though, the sound of Lifetime's reruns of old sitcoms made him feel less alone, even from across the hall.

His hands felt cold and kind of clammy, so he wiped them against the flannel of his pajama pants. His stomach lurched as he crept back to the window. If it was out there—or worse, if his dad was out there again—Sean was fairly sure he would be sick.

He looked out the window again and scanned the front lawn, the street between them, then his own lawn. Nothing there. The front door of Mr. Feinstein's house stood open, though. It hadn't been open before.

Sean sighed. It didn't matter, when he thought about it. In the Feinsteins' house, in the living room, in his own bedroom, even—the Hollower could be anywhere it wanted, anyone it wanted, at any time. He'd never be safe. He'd never be sure.

Not unless he killed it.

He'd been told the Warding Ritual could keep the monsters away. Part of him knew what his dad taught him was kids' stuff, like the Tooth Fairy—and maybe like Santa and the Easter Bunny (which he suspected but was unable and kind of unwilling to prove—some things he just didn't want to take the chance of messing up). But he'd wanted to believe then—still did, to an extent. In a way, it was like his dad was still looking out for him.

Another part of him, though, was beginning to understand that dads, alive and especially dead, couldn't protect their kids from everything. Some things found a way to get at you.

The videos they'd watched in school showed him and his classmates what kids could do to protect themselves when their moms and dads weren't around. Parents and teachers, that was their job—to teach kids how to stay safe, to be confident and prepared when adults couldn't be there to watch over them. He figured his dad had tried to do the same thing, with the Warding Ritual.

But it wouldn't have worked on those men in the videos. Their teacher told them human beings weren't monsters, even if they did bad things that scared even grown-ups. They were sick. In spite of his faith in what his father told him, he had known then that not everything could be turned away by circles around his face, Xs and spitting. There were things in the world more dangerous, more real than bug monsters under his bed. But if they weren't monsters, then an antimonster ritual was useless.

The Hollower was something different altogether, too. If he had to guess, he'd say it fell somewhere in between. It, like the bug monsters and the slithering sleevey things in his closet, was not a part of this earth but somehow moving through the smoke and mirrors and shadows of it. But the Hollower scared grown-ups, too, like that man he'd seen come running out of the Feinstein place. It was really in-his-face dangerous. And whether it was sick or mean or angry and crazy or whatever, it very much wanted him dead. It was most certainly a monster, but no kids' stuff Warding Ritual was going to scare it off.

Going to his mom or telling a teacher wouldn't work. Going to the police wouldn't work. And he didn't know if that man would ever come back—the only grown-up he knew of (besides Mr. Feinstein, he guessed) who had seen the monster. If he was going to fight the Hollower, he had to do it himself.

The curtains rustled in the bedroom window across the street, and Sean shivered. It occurred to him even when it had handed him the broken pieces of lamp, it never once brushed his hand with its fingers or stroked his hair or touched his cheek. He wondered what it would have done if he'd tried to kiss it good night, or give it a hug.

He wondered what would happen if he touched it.

Maybe physical contact was like poison to it. Of course, if just touching it would kill it, then why hadn't someone thought to do that already? Why hadn't someone tried to shoot it or stab it or smack it down with a crowbar?

Because it won't work, he told himself. Maybe weapons wouldn't do any good. Still, he didn't like the idea of going into the Feinsteins' place without *something* in his hands. Sean thought of getting a broom or a mop—something with a long handle that he could use to defend himself with. Maybe he'd bring a bat tomorrow, just in case.

He crossed back over to his bed and climbed in. The thought of facing the Hollower made his stomach churn. He wiped his palms on his blankets.

"What about big *monsters, Daddy? Will the Warding Ritual work on those?"*

"Well, son, big monsters is another kettle of fish altogether. For those, you need something extra special."

He wondered for a moment if *that* had been kid stuff, too.

Maybe not. Everything had a weakness. Monsters

had sunlight and silver bullets and magic spells and holy water. Kidnappers and molesters had soft, sensitive groins and eyes and throats. The Hollower had to have a weakness, too. He believed it as strongly as he did that there was a heaven, and that his dad was in it. Believed it more than Santa Claus or the Easter Bunny.

His father had also told him even the smallest of things have strengths. The balance of nature, he called it. And Sean believed that, too. Everything had strengths and weaknesses.

Tomorrow, one way or another, he'd go over to the Feinsteins' house and find out if his measured up to the Hollower's. Armed with a baseball bat and a feverish hope that his dad's "something special" would be enough—tomorrow, he'd try to kill a monster himself.

After settling Cheryl on a chair with her shoes kicked off, a blanket in her lap, and a hot cup of tea in her hands, Dave had shown them the tape. Erik, leaning forward on the edge of the couch, had suggested they watch it again and although Cheryl looked pale, she'd agreed. They let it run to static before Dave switched it off and ejected the tape. After the second time, Cheryl stared at the television. Dave had watched it again himself after the phone call from the Hollower. He'd let the tape run until it had gone black, thinking what he supposed Cheryl might have been thinking now. There was nothing else on the tape. Nothing else they could use to defend themselves with, no other hints or clues from Max Feinstein.

He watched her for a moment. The soft smudge of

her eyeliner beneath her eyes and the faded color of her lipstick gave her a diffused, dreamy look. Even exhausted, scared, and upset, she was beautiful, Dave thought.

"Wow." Erik let out a long breath. "With all due respect to the dead, how do we know this guy knew what he was talking about? How did he know so much?"

"I don't know. It makes sense, though, what he said." Dave crossed the room and handed Erik the newspaper articles. "And these suggest that Max is right. If he is, this thing has been destroying lives for a long time." He gave Erik a grim smile. "Lot of people bringing the Hollower right to them."

"What are we going to do?" Cheryl asked. A slender arm wrapped around her stomach, as if to keep its contents in check.

"We're going to find it. We're going to hunt it down and we're going to fight it. Because you're right, Cheryl. It's never going to leave us alone."

"We'll cave its faceless friggin' head in," Erik added.

"How? Where are we going to look? And what in God's name do we do when we find it? Guys, if Max Feinstein couldn't stop it—and he knew more than anyone else about it—and those people in those articles couldn't stop it, either, how are we going to?"

Erik looked away. Dave said nothing, but her gaze sought out his. Her eyes filled with tears at something evidently disappointing she found there.

He said finally, "We'll find a way."

"I'm scared." She pulled her knees up to her chest.

"Me too," Erik said.

"Me three. Look. I think we should meet up again

tomorrow night. It keeps coming to us. I think it's time we go find it ourselves. And I think I know where to start looking." Dave looked at the tape in his hands. "I think we should try Feinstein's house."

Erik rose. "Sounds like as good a place as any to me. In the meantime, though, I better go. Promised my girl I'd be home when I could."

"Okay, I'll drive you." Dave picked up his keys.

Cheryl tossed the blanket aside. "My stuff is still at the bar. My purse . . ."

"We can get it tonight, if you want, or wait until tomorrow. Either way, I'll go with you," Dave said.

"I don't think I'm quite ready to go back there tonight." She smiled at him. "But I definitely want you there when I go back."

Dave felt warmth spread outward from inside when she said that. He heard Erik chuckle behind him as he followed Cheryl out of the apartment.

They said little on the car ride back to Erik's, but it was a different kind of silence. They had formed a unified front. It wanted to isolate them and destroy them one by one, but whatever it tried next, they'd fight it together. Even without a plan in place, the comforting presence of the others made Dave feel less alone. The past, with all its little barbs in his memory, and all the places and people and things he'd let slip away, didn't seem as important now as what tomorrow would bring. He could die with his boots on, like the old cowboys used to say. A showdown at high noon was better than a slow death in the smoke and dark of a saloon, one drink at a time.

He pulled up in front of Erik's house.

"Tomorrow, then?" Erik opened the car door.

"I'll come get you at about seven."

Erik nodded. "Thanks."

Dave offered an awkward smile. "No problem."

"See you at seven tomorrow, then. Bye, Cheryl."

Erik got out and ran up to the house. Dave waited for him to disappear inside before pulling away.

Once they were back on the main road, he cleared his throat. "I know you had a tough night, and I was thinking that . . . well, you know, I figured maybe you wouldn't—or shouldn't—be alone, and well, if you wanted to, you know, crash at my house, you're definitely more than welcome."

From the corner of his eye, he saw her smiling.

"I'd like that very much. I'd really rather not be alone."

Once they'd returned to the apartment, he offered her an old sweatshirt and sweatpants. She emerged from his bedroom and gave him a funny smile. "What?"

He shook his head. "I was just thinking that even in sweats, you look great."

She looked away, embarrassed. "Thanks."

Dave felt warmth rise in his neck and face. "Um, anyway, you take the bed. I've got the couch here—"

"Oh no, Dave, I couldn't put you out like that."

Dave held up a hand. "I insist. Besides, I sleep on the couch all the time."

She gave him a skeptical look. "Are you sure?"

"Absolutely."

"Well, okay, then. Thanks." She passed back into the bedroom. After a moment, though, she popped her head back out again. "Dave?"

He looked up from fluffing a couch pillow. "Yeah?"

"Seriously. I appreciate this. I think I would have

gone out of my mind if I had to spend the night alone at my place."

The thought *You're welcome to sleep here any time you want* crossed his mind, but he squashed it. In truth, he'd imagined bringing Cheryl back to his place plenty of times, and much like most things he'd fantasized about, the real experience was something quite different. Instead, he said, "I'm glad to have you here. To be honest, I wasn't looking forward to spending the night alone, either."

She caught his gaze and held it for a moment. Her lips parted as if she wanted to say something else, but she stopped, and giggled. Dave found it endearing.

"Night." She closed the door behind her.

That night, he did dream of an alley, but the Hollower wasn't there. Cheryl was, and the way she kissed made for a pleasant sleep until the morning.

The following morning, DeMarco went for her warrant. She brought the Feinstein tape, and all the files she could find that bore a strong connection to the contents of it.

District Attorney May Davis's office was located on the third floor of the municipal building. Anita DeMarco had been there many times on business, and several times just to chat over coffee and ogle the handsome FedEx guy who delivered packages almost like clockwork every Monday afternoon. DeMarco didn't have many girlfriends, or many friends period, if one got down to the nitty-gritty of it. She didn't think she needed many, though. DeMarco was content. She dated sometimes—even went out with Bennie once in a while, although those dates consisted more of "staying in" and didn't require any real effort or emotional commitment. DeMarco was fine with that. She made pleasant small talk with the medical examiner when she saw her. A few of the guys down at the station joked and laughed with her, or invited her for beers after shifts sometimes. She had her sister in Colorado. And she had May Davis.

May had grown into her late forties with an easy kind of summery grace, poise, and natural beauty. Firm, flowery-smelling, and fairly young-looking, May embodied classy without being condescending, professional without being sterile, sexy without being overt. She was a presence.

May's office, DeMarco thought, served perfectly as an extension of her personality, a place not overrun by the power of the position, but sophisticated and inviting. DeMarco believed places soaked up the atmosphere of their inhabitants. Over time, wood weathered and paint chipped from the wear and tear of holding up families and businesses, holding in criminals, comforting the sick, the injured, the lonely. In May's office, freedom was bargained. Justice was measured. Lives changed. But the fine mahogany desk and leather-bound law books lining the shelves, the framed law degrees and pictures of her kids, took it all in stride. Behind her, a window looked out over the center of town. She kept the shades open all the time. Weather never seemed to affect May at all.

She looked up when DeMarco knocked on her half-open door, smiled warmly, and waved her in. "Anita, how are you?"

DeMarco nodded. "Not bad. Yourself?"

"Fine, fine." She gestured for DeMarco to sit in the

chair across from her desk. "Sit, sugar. I'd offer you coffee, but the pot's broken. . . ."

DeMarco waved that it was okay.

"Tell me how things are down at BPD."

"Ehhhh, the usual, I guess. Freaks, crazies, boozers, and wife beaters. And we've got all kinds of perps, too." She grinned, and May laughed. "Seriously, though, the guys are good. Keeping busy. Frankie had his operation—went fine. He's back and grousing already about the coffee. Nina had her baby. She told me after that gunshot wound a year ago, she thought no pain would scare her. Until her mama told her about giving birth, that is."

"It went well, though?"

"Smooth as silk. She had a baby girl, seven pounds, nine ounces. Named her Julianna Maria. She brought in pictures. My God, what a beautiful little girl."

"Oh, that's wonderful! I'm so glad mother and baby are well. And I'm glad to hear Frank is okay. I know he was worried about the surgery." She paused, then added, "How's Bennie?"

DeMarco rolled her eyes playfully. "Fine, I guess."

May arched a quizzical eyebrow. "Don't tell me the stallion's gone tame on you?"

"No, that part's still good. I just wonder sometimes if it's worth keeping something going that isn't going anywhere, you know?"

"Do you want it to go somewhere?" May had an uncanny ability to ask the most pointed, direct questions without being intrusive. Usually, she knew the answer anyway before she asked the question.

"I don't know. I think he does. He doesn't push. Doesn't even bring it up, really. But it's in his eyes,

sometimes, or the things he says when we're together."

May smiled. "I thought you didn't trust anything
a man said to you during or right after sex."

"I don't. It's what he says to me before." DeMarco
shifted in her seat. "Anyway, I could shoot the shit
here all day, May, but I should probably talk to you
about the warrant."

"Oh yes, for the Feinstein residence. Wasn't he the
suicide not too long ago? What're you looking for?"

"I've got a tape Feinstein made on the day of his
suicide. And I've also got two cold case homicides, a
disappearance, and a report of stalking that I have
reason to believe Mr. Feinstein knew something
about."

"Give me something I can take to the judge, sugar.
Sounds like cop hunch to me."

"Yeah, yeah, it is, partially." She put the files on
May's desk. "But these say it's more than a hunch."

May took the files and scanned them, the smile
fading slowly from her face. "I'm not sure I understand, An."

"It makes more sense after you've seen the tape."

"All right. I'm due for court in an hour, but I've got
some time around lunch. I'll watch it first thing."

DeMarco rose. "Thanks, May."

While her secretary made copies of the notes to
the files, May gave DeMarco the latest update about
her older sister's daughter Nadia in Ohio. "Evidently that young man she cares so deeply for has a
daughter." May shrugged. "It won't be an easy situation any way you turn it. But the young are ruled by
heart and instinct, am I right?"

DeMarco chuckled. "I wouldn't know. Bennie and I are usually ruled by something else entirely."

May smiled. "You live by instinct, friend, and you're ruled more by heart than you know." Her secretary came in and handed her the copies, which she put on her desk, and the originals, which she handed over to DeMarco. "Frankly, An, I wouldn't have you any other way."

Later that afternoon, DeMarco's phone rang. "Lakehaven Police Department. This is DeMarco."

"An, it's May."

"Hi there. Have you watched the tape?"

"Yes, and I've reviewed the copies of the notes to the files again. You've got yourself a warrant."

DeMarco made a silent victory fist. "Thanks."

"The coincidences are disturbing, to say the least." Her voice sounded clipped and tense. Not angry, but . . . something else.

"You okay?"

"Just tired, I guess. Tape got to me a bit. Did you see the part after? There are several minutes of static after Mr. Feinstein stops talking, and then—"

"A part after? No, I don't recall—I've seen the tape a few times and I never saw anything after Feinstein stopped talking."

A sound like a sigh, or maybe the intake of breath, came from the other side of the phone. "Watch it again—give the static a few minutes. It's . . . just please do me a favor and watch it again, okay?"

"Sure. Absolutely."

"I'll be in court until four thirty but I'll bring everything by right after, if that's okay."

"That's perfect. I'll see you then."

"Anita?"

"Yes?"

"Be careful in that house, okay?"

DeMarco frowned. She'd been in far more dangerous places than the empty house of a suicide victim before, and May knew that. "No problem. Hey, are you sure you're okay?"

"I'm fine. I'll see you around four thirty."

"I've told you all I know. All anybody knows. I daresay, that may be all anyone has ever known about the Hollower. And I can do no more." On the tape, Max Feinstein sighed. A moment of static followed, and then Feinstein's image cleared again.

"I left you something. When the time comes, I think you'll know how to use it. Think what it's for, what it shows people, and you'll know. I'm too tired now and I can't bear it—I can't do what needs to be done, or what comes after. But you can. I know you can." Feinstein leaned over, ostensibly to shut off the tape, and the picture went gray and scattered.

DeMarco watched through the static, leaning forward in the hard interrogation room chair, fists clenched in her lap. The static continued.

DeMarco waited five, six minutes before leaning back, surprised at the tension that dissipated from her hands, her teeth, when nothing else appeared on the tape. She watched the static for another couple of minutes, too satisfied—too relieved—to question right away what it might have been that May saw.

Static. There was nothing else there on the tape. She rose to shut it off.

Up close, her finger poised on the Stop button, she

heard the voices. That close to the television speakers, they sounded agitated, whispering to each other in a frenzy of words she couldn't make out. She could feel their meaning, though—the implication in the tone. She heard fear and pain and confusion.

She thought she heard her name.

DeMarco backed away from the set and sank back into her chair. The static wavered, and she thought she saw an inky sleeve, the skewed brim of a hat. The picture blurred, and the sound caught. A hiss drew out, thinning the voices into a shrill, stretched scream. Then both the sound and the static froze.

A moment later, the peppering pulled back to the corners of the set and DeMarco found herself looking at Feinstein's desk, the one from which he'd filmed his message for David Kohlar. A black-gloved hand passed across the lens and then moved away, and the view jostled a moment and then rose. The camera made a steady progression out into the hallway and bounced lightly up the stairs. At the top, it turned the corner and angled down as it crossed a threshold into a room. DeMarco thought she saw the toe of a black shoe.

Suddenly, the camera stopped. When it panned upward, DeMarco felt that tension return, tightening her jaw, her neck, her stomach.

From the doorway, the view passed a window and dipped down to a bed. What was left of Feinstein's head bled out onto the bedspread around his body. On the wall behind the bed, a blood-burst of red splattered the wall.

"Oh my God." DeMarco leaned nearly out of the seat, chewing her thumbnail thoughtfully. "Bastard's in the house." When the police had found the camera, it had been empty, sitting on the desk where Feinstein had left it. The tape hadn't been inside. Had the person (he/she/it) who videotaped this part gotten the tape out, filmed this, then put it back where Feinstein had left it?

The camera began to tremble, just enough to wiggle the picture, and DeMarco heard the dry rustle of a chuckle from behind. The black-gloved hand reached around the lens toward the blood splatter. The fingers waved and drew back, and for a minute, the blood writhed on the walls, pulling together in tribal-looking shapes and then squirming back into nondescript splashes.

The picture blacked out for a second and then flashed back to the desk, where it lowered slowly to the position in which Feinstein had left it.

Close to the camera—a whisper in the ear, really—a sexless voice full of mirth said, "That part was for you, not Dave. That part was just for you."

Immediately, the tape went black.

Ten

At the end of the dark period, the Hollower found two of them in the transportation object, and followed them without intrusion to the gathering-structure, a place where the beings put physical liquids inside them and dulled their crude senses even further. There, the female retrieved a false skin with a strap and a jingling set of metal. This far away, it couldn't remember the names, the *sounds* the beings used as names for those things, and it didn't much care. That information and more was always available when it went close to them, translatable from the ugly light and vile smells and sounds and awful heat of them, as outward as the false shells they covered parts of their solid, fleshy bodies with.

The black-hole spaces inside its own body tugged and pushed and stretched at its shell. It had hunted them long enough. It was time to move close enough for the kill.

Such grotesque skins had to contain such delicate meat.

It followed the male as he drove the female to another structure, then drove himself to yet a third, where it stayed until the shade came back. That structure was riddled with sound, diseased with noise. The being boxed into a corner of the structure came out to him when he arrived and yelled in anger.

It knew anger. It knew rage. It knew hate fueled by disgust. It recognized the thin overlap of its consciousness and theirs, like the brushing of walls between worlds. They ate lesser physical beings and it imagined there was overlap between senses cruder still in the most basic understandings of life and death. It had tried those lesser beings and found them for the most part not only unpalatable but barren, devoid of any real sustenance. They mostly lacked something their greater masters had in abundance—aberration of thought.

It had taken in millennia of thoughts and feelings constantly churning behind the beings' physicality, and nothing sustained so well as their aberrations. These were nearly powerful enough to change their physical senses, to alter the light and the sound, to recharacterize them. With these and only these did it find satisfaction, a quelling of the shifting spaces inside it, and moments of respite from the alien hostility of their world.

They had whole structures dedicated to containing beings with various aberrations. Often, though, other beings it couldn't always find gave them liquids or solids to put inside them and after, it couldn't find them, either. They also cut into each other sometimes and afterward, it would lose them. Not so, the ones who hadn't recognized the aberrations in themselves. True, the meat came in smaller quantities, but it made up for that by pursuing more of them.

It was delighted to find the other male crossing worlds, his body on top of an oblong and covered by a thin white skin. It knew that place they went to, the Point of Convergence between the dimensions. It found him there, and hurt him.

It pulled back a bit to scan for the little one. It found him in a structure surrounded by other little ones, pushing thin cylinders over flat surfaces bound together. It drew close enough to feel the full spray of their world head-on, and it collected the voices and faces and words it needed. It waited until the boy looked out the window, and it waved. The boy grew pale and looked away. It bent the school, and gave the boy a taste of what was to come when the night took over again.

When it had finished with the boy, it pulled back, back farther, back to the place just before the Convergence, right before the membrane to its home. There, its will draped in layers over the structure where the older male had snuffed his aberrations forever. In that place, it had taken in the older male's dying misfires of thought and feeling and maybe caught up a little of the essence that meant to carry itself to the Convergence.

In that structure it pulled close and armed itself with colors. It showed the woman awful colors. One they called red, which it splattered all over the house the way the fluid in the older man's head had splattered against the back wall. She cried for her brother. The woman was fragile, nearly broken. The sweetness of her welled up to the surface. It could crack her, if it tried hard enough.

She feared pain, the concept of which interested it—perhaps the only physical sensation that did not disgust it. Down in the basement, it talked to her through the furnace. It told her all the bad things it was going to do to her, all the ways it would make pain throughout her body. When the dark came, she was broken.

Then something changed. It pulled away when it felt them. They were together. Blurry. Angry. Scared. Not pinpoints but a mass. They had melded into a solid thought, a bouquet of feelings bound by a base idea. They were coming.

It would not need to collect them. They would deliver themselves up together.

It pulled back just a little more, to wait.

Dave Kohlar hadn't returned DeMarco's calls and since the car registered to him wasn't in the driveway when she drove by, she decided to do the Feinstein place first, then try him again after.

She glanced in the rearview mirror at the squad car behind her. Bennie and Rubelli hadn't seen the tape, but they had read the files, and agreed to serve as backup, in case the gloved hand and the possible killer that wielded it were still in the habit of visiting the Feinstein residence. She wasn't generally given over to getting the creeps, even in the face of confronting potentially dangerous people, but she was glad all the same to have them watching her back.

She felt better having Bennie there, especially. Some part of her brain recognized this in vague and discomforting terms, but it wouldn't quite gel in the forefront of her thoughts. She didn't need him. It was nice, was all. Nice that he was there.

She exhaled slowly, glanced in the mirror again, and shook her head. May would have called her out on that. *"Stallion sex, my left foot. You like him, An. More than you're willing to tell him."*

Maybe. She turned left and peered ahead into the darkness. Up in Lakehaven, some of the back roads got swallowed in the shadows of overhanging trees and outcroppings of rock for a curve or a dip or a small hill, and then emerged into the moonlight. She slowed down as she plunged into just such a pocket of shadow, careful of deer and unfamiliar bends and twists. Behind her in the rearview, Benjamin Mendez and Joe Rubelli followed her into the dip.

They didn't come back out again on the other side. As DeMarco pulled farther and farther from that patch of shadow, she glanced between the rearview and the windshield, expecting them to emerge any minute and pick up her back.

Behind her, the road lay like a silent tongue on the floor of a rocky mouth.

It had swallowed their squad car.

She slowed and picked up the radio. "Rubelli? Mendez? What the hell happened to you? Where are you?"

The radio crackled back but gave her no answer.

"Guys? Where are you?" Still nothing.

DeMarco frowned, checked the side view, then the rear view again. She rolled to a stop, waited a few minutes, then glanced at the clock. *Five more minutes. If those two ditched me . . .*

But Bennie wouldn't have done that. Something was wrong. She made a U-turn in the road. That small part of her more than professionally concerned for Bennie's well-being fully expected to be swallowed up, too, and spit out wherever the squad car had gone.

Their car broke down. They're stopped in that dark patch there, that's all. She came back through into the moonlight and turned around again. Her car rolled back into the dip. The headlights gave her little more than a foot or so, but she rolled straight through to the other side without rear-ending them.

DeMarco put the car into Park. Could she have missed them when she turned around? Possibly. What May Davis called her "cop hunch" didn't think so, but it was possible. She tried tracking them by pulling up their car on the computer. It was a bust. The computer told her they were a hundred yards or so behind her. She tried radioing into the station, but got static.

"Shit." Her voice sounded timid in her own ears, solitary in the darkness. "Shit."

She put the car in Drive and moved forward. With any luck, she'd find them at the River Falls Road residence. She glanced in the rearview mirror once more, her brow furrowed, and then turned her full attention on the road ahead.

"I don't understand what you're going to do, exactly. Who are these people again?" Casey leaned in the doorway and brushed a strand of hair from her eye, then crossed her arms beneath her chest.

Erik tugged on a pair of jeans and zipped them. Fragments of the dream he'd had about beating his father to death with a crowbar—and worse, that he hadn't been by himself when he'd done it, but watched by something—remained like a bad aftertaste. "That thing I told you about, the Hollower. We're going to stop it." He crossed to the closet and pulled a green T-shirt off the hanger. "We're going to kill it."

"Baby, you're scaring me. You're not going off to kill somebody, are you?"

"Not some-*body*. Some-*thing*. It's not a person, I swear to you. It's definitely not a person."

He paused in lacing up his boots. "You don't believe a word of this, do you?"

"I'm worried about you."

"You should be." He rose.

"I believe you," she said, coming into the room. "I believe you see this thing. I believe these . . . people you're meeting up with tonight see this thing. But—"

"You don't believe this thing is really there, is that it?"

She slipped her arms around his waist and rested her head on his chest. He put his arms around her, and wondered for a moment if it would be the last time he'd feel her.

"I don't know what to believe anymore. I really don't."

"Do you trust me?"

She looked up at him. "Yes. If you say this will make things better, then yes."

"Then that's all I need." He pulled her close to him, inhaling the scent of her hair.

"Promise me you'll be okay."

He kissed the top of her head. "I can't."

"Promise me something."

"I promise you I'll be careful." He thought a moment, then added, "And I'll do my best to stay out of trouble."

"Then that's all *I* need," she whispered, but he could feel the tears soak through his T-shirt.

Outside, he heard Dave's car pull up to the house.

"I've gotta go. I love you, baby." He pulled away from her, then grabbed his jacket without turning around and headed for the stairs. He couldn't look at her.

"I love you, too," she called from the bedroom.

He swallowed the lump in his throat and went out the door.

"You okay?" Dave asked as Erik slid into the backseat. From the look on the boy's face, he thought maybe there had been another run-in with the Hollower.

Erik shrugged. "My girl," he muttered, and from his tone, Dave thought it best not to press further.

They drove in silence toward Cheryl's house for a while before Erik said, "Not like I don't have buckets of faith in us or anything, but what we're planning to do—"

"We don't have a plan yet," Dave reminded him.

"But we have a goal. And we're up against some pretty big odds in achieving that goal."

"Yup." Dave kept his eyes on the road.

"It ain't a bad thing if we're scared, is it?"

"I wouldn't say so. Just my opinion, but I'd have to wonder about the sanity of any carload of fools who *weren't* afraid of staring down death like that."

Erik snickered in the backseat, and Dave cracked a smile.

"Yeah, they'd have to be real nut jobs, wouldn't they?"

"Hell yes."

Erik's smile faded. "Yeah."

Dave glanced at him in the rearview. "There isn't any other way. You made me see that."

Erik nodded.

When they pulled up to Cheryl's house, she was waiting outside. She hopped in on the passenger side and greeted them. She was shivering.

"Chilly?" Dave asked.

"Not really." She offered him a small smile, and he squeezed her hand.

There was a pause, and Erik said, "Hey, I've got a joke for you. Stop me if you've heard this one." Dave hadn't heard it—a dirty one about a drunk in a bar—and he laughed heartily at the punch line. Cheryl, who had heard that one and just about every other bar joke in her experience as a bartender, laughed anyway.

After that, the conversation warmed quickly. Dave had expected the car ride to the Feinstein place to be solemn and silent, but it wasn't. They talked about the Tavern, and the gossip that the locals told her in semidrunken hazes. They joked some more and laughed at one-liners and banter between them. And Dave and Cheryl flirted. He caught Erik's knowing smirk in the backseat from time to time. It felt comfortable. It felt *right* for them to be there, together. They were connected. Dave thought maybe they always had been.

The laughter died away when they turned onto River Falls Road. By the time Dave rolled to a stop in front of the Feinstein place, all conversation had ceased.

They sat for a moment, staring at the house, its front door closed, its curtains half drawn, its porch sighing into the foundation. Dave wondered what they'd do if the door was locked, then almost had to laugh at his own thought. The door wouldn't be locked, not if the Hollower was in there, waiting for them. It would be expecting them.

"It doesn't look so big," Erik said finally. "Not too many places to hide in there."

Dave nodded. "We'll find it."

"And we'll kill it," Erik said.

"Damn right, we will," Cheryl added.

No one made a move to get out of the car.

"I've got weapons in the trunk," Dave said. "Can't see that they'll do much good, but I thought we might feel better having them."

"Good idea," Cheryl said, giving his arm a squeeze.

Just then, movement in one of the upstairs windows caught Dave's attention. A moment later, the front door opened. They sucked in a collective breath. No one moved.

Nothing came out through the front door.

But it was in there, oh yes. Dave had no doubt about that at all. It was most certainly in there, waiting for them.

"Guess there's no time like the present, huh?" Erik opened the car door. Reluctantly, Dave and Cheryl followed suit.

They followed Dave around to the back of the car. The air blew cool around him, creeping beneath his jacket. He glanced around. No neighbors peered out. No one interested, maybe. No one to care about three strangers breaking into a dead man's house.

And then he thought of the nurses' station, fully staffed, and how no one had seen Sally leave and how the old woman hadn't seen any nurses. He shivered against the wind.

Dave popped the trunk. Inside, he'd put a butcher

knife, a crowbar, and a battery-powered nail gun, as well as three flashlights.

Cheryl giggled nervously. "Power tools—now, that's what I'm talking about."

"Take it—it's yours," Dave said, then nodded to Erik to help himself.

Erik grabbed the crowbar, turning it over in his hands. Softly, he said, "I wanna cave the bastard's head in."

Dave picked up the knife, then handed out the flashlights. "Ready?"

"Ready as we'll ever be," Erik said.

Cheryl nodded. "Let's kick some ass."

Dave suddenly remembered something, and popped the trunk again. "Almost forgot this." He reached in and grabbed Feinstein's mirror, then tucked its handle into a back pocket before closing the trunk lid. "Feinstein said we'd know what to do with it when the time came."

They followed Dave back around to the front of the car and stood a moment, facing the house. Dave took a deep breath and exhaled it. "We can beat this thing."

He wasn't sure he'd spoken it out loud, though, until a small voice behind him said, "I want to help."

No place would be safe, so long as the Hollower was still alive. It could get to Sean any time, any place.

It couldn't be put off any longer.

That night, Sean told his mother he was exhausted. He explained that he hadn't slept well the night before (which was the absolute truth) and that he wasn't all that hungry. He just wanted to go to bed. His mother hovered with a worried expression, questioning what he'd eaten, why he wasn't feeling well, what was bothering him, and why he was so willing to go to bed at a reasonable hour. He thought he did a good job of convincing her she had nothing to worry about, and went through the pretense of brushing his teeth, washing his face, and slipping into pajamas.

In bed, though, he found that his eyelids felt like they were on time-springs and his stomach felt all coiled up. He had to concentrate on relaxing his brow so that sleep wouldn't look forced when his mom came to kiss him good night. Beneath the covers his hands grew sweaty and he felt a warm, uncomfortable lump weighing in his chest.

This is it, Seany. Tonight's the night.

He heard his mom's footsteps in the hall and pretended to be asleep. His mom came and kissed him good night, ruffling his hair softly and making baby kisses on his temple. She did that when she thought he was asleep and wouldn't wiggle uncomfortably beneath the display of affection.

This time, it drove a pang of sadness through him. Sean had never felt so much in need of his mom as he did then. He hadn't felt so small in a long time. He wondered for a moment if it would be the last time he'd feel her touch his head or kiss him. He wouldn't allow the thought to stay, though. He swallowed it with the lump in his throat.

He waited for what seemed like hours, but was, by the digital clock on his night table, maybe twenty minutes at most. Then he slipped out of bed. He'd hidden jeans, a red T-shirt, and sneakers under the bed and he crouched and slid them out. Trying not to make a sound, he changed into his clothes. Then he wadded up the pajamas and put them under the covers of his bed, which he pulled over his pillow to make it look like he was tucked down under them. When he'd put on his sneakers, he reached under the bed once more for the baseball bat he'd brought up from the basement.

The entire time, his heart ticked into the darkness. He felt as well as heard each pulse.

With a quick glance across the hall at his mother's sleeping form, he crept to the window. The house across the street stood dark and quiet. The curtains in the upstairs bedroom did not stir. If the monster was there waiting for him, it didn't want to give away its location.

Sean was sure it was there, though.

He turned from the window and crept out into the hall. He fought the impulse to run; if he could catch it by surprise when he went into the house, maybe he could get a jump on it. But he had to be patient. He'd be outside and across the street soon enough, taking matters—taking his own life—into his hands. It took all his willpower to ease himself with careful steps toward the stairs.

He tiptoed past his mom's bedroom door. A floorboard creaked and his mom shifted on the bed. He squeezed his eyes shut and froze. If she caught him now, he'd never get out, and he'd have to spend a good hour explaining what he was doing back up again, fully dressed, with a baseball bat in his hands. He did have a cover story—he planned to tell her he'd heard a noise, and had gotten up to investigate—but he preferred not to have to use it, if possible.

He opened his eyes and turned his head in her direction. Part of him wanted to crawl into bed with her and stay there, safe from the monster across the street. He couldn't, though, and he knew it. The Hollower wasn't ever going to stop.

He watched her for a few moments and when he felt pretty sure that she was still asleep, he crept forward again, easing down the stairs. At the bottom, he exhaled a long, quiet breath. He crossed the front hall and unlocked the door, listening one last time. He heard nothing but the muted sounds of breathing, so he went out into the night, closing the door softly behind him.

Free of the house, Sean felt less pressure to be quiet. He jogged through the shadows across the street. Being outside at night without his mom knowing thrilled and kind of scared him. It made him feel grown-up. Like he really was man of the house. Like he could handle fighting off the Hollower.

A car sat outside the Feinstein place—the same car he'd seen not too long ago. His spirits lifted a little. The man who'd come running out of the Feinstein house the other day got out of the car, followed by another man and a woman, all of whom moved around to the back of the car. Then the man opened the trunk, and Sean thought he knew what the man was getting. He felt the bat in his hands, solid and secure. They were going inside Mr. Feinstein's house to fight it. They were going after the Hollower. The weight in his stomach eased, and he brightened, smiling.

And damn, he was glad to have the grown-ups there, too, even if they were strangers. He'd be safer with them. No one who was fighting a monster like the Hollower could be a bad person.

He heard the man say, "We can beat this thing," and that put to rest any lingering doubt he might have had.

Sean said, "I want to help," and the others turned around.

The kid with the baseball bat looked familiar. Dave recognized him from the day he went searching Feinstein's place at Sally's insistence. He looked smaller in the sea of darkness around him, the bat oversized and heavy-looking in his hands.

"What are you doing out here, kid? Your mom—"

"I'm going in with you to fight the Hollower." The boy's expression, serious without imparting that defiant rebellion so many kids wore nowadays, reinforced his words.

They exchanged glances.

"I don't know if that's a good idea, little dude," Erik said. "We've got some pretty dangerous work to do and—"

"And I'm coming with you. You can go ahead and threaten to tell my mom, but I'll tell her what you all are planning to do, too. You might as well count me in, because nothing you say is gonna make me go away. I want to kill it. And if you want the same thing, all the better. No one has to go alone." His voice quivered a little, as if being so assertive with adults was new to him. It probably was. He struck Dave as a good kid—a smart kid. In spite of what he said, Dave was pretty sure he wouldn't want to upset his mother. But other adults—especially cops, if his mother thought them trespassing—would bode ill for them.

His eyes, Dave thought, pretty much defeated all argument. He had seen it before, and knew exactly what he was getting into by vowing to fight it. Dave saw in those little-boy eyes the same tortured restlessness, the same resigned certainty, the same weary awareness that he'd seen in Cheryl's eyes, and Erik's.

"Look, it came after me today. In school. I saw it first out the window, and I thought if I looked away, if I pretended not to see it . . ." He shook his head. "But it didn't matter. It was already inside, changing things. Mister, I saw my teacher's face melt, like she was a candle and someone lit the top of her head. I saw her skull through her cheek and forehead and she kept talking about dinosaur bones. And worse, while she was talking, these bugs fell out of her mouth. I mean, she was up there crunching some of them between words while the rest spilled out the hole in her cheek and down the front of her blouse. They moved fast, too. Came across the tiles and up the legs of the desks and into everybody's laps. And then they dug into the kids."

The boy looked pale and kind of nauseated. Dave imagined a classroom fronted by a melting head yattering on about a lesson while black barbs dug into skinny arms and flat chests, probing for warm openings to fill and nest in. The picture in his head made him feel a little ill, too.

The boy continued. "The other kids didn't notice. They all kept taking notes and whisper-buzzing to each other and I saw one girl, Carly Friedman, pass a folded-up piece of paper to Amy Melnichek, and it had these antennae poking out from between the folds. And those girls hate bugs. They screamed one time when we had a giant spider in the classroom, and they pulled their feet up on the chairs.

"Anyway, they didn't come near me, the bugs. But it was worse, I think, seeing them crawling in and out of everybody else. It made me feel like puking. So I asked to go to the nurse, and the teacher nodded, and all these bugs fell out of her hair. I bolted."

He looked up at Dave, his little hands tight around the handle of the bat. "I can't do it again. I can't go back to school and sit in that classroom if something like that could happen even one more time. I've seen that thing, same as you, and it's seen me. It's not going to go away."

"Sweetie, you've seen it? You're sure?" Cheryl asked. "You know what it is." It was part question, part challenge. But Dave could tell by her face that she already knew. They all did. Nothing they said was going to dissuade this boy—in fact, Dave figured the boy had planned to come over here whether they had ever shown up or not.

"Yeah. And I know that man's seen it, too." Sean indicated Dave with the tip of the bat. His gaze traveled up to one of the upstairs windows. "It's definitely hiding out in there. I think it knows we're coming."

"You've seen it in there?" Erik asked.

The boy nodded. "In the room that used to be Mr. Feinstein's."

It unsettled Dave, the idea that the Hollower was using a dead man's bedroom and suicide chamber as a lair. It struck him as irreverent. Not surprising, but appalling nonetheless.

"It's dangerous," Cheryl said to Dave. "Dangerous for a boy."

Erik gave Dave a meaningful look. "No one should be alone, though. He's got a point. Safety in numbers, right, man? The kid's worse off now if we send him back."

Dave nodded. "I'm not thrilled about bringing a child into that house—"

"I'm eleven years old," the boy muttered in a touchy voice, frowning at him.

"Even so, I think Erik's right," Dave continued. "It's probably safer for him to stick with us."

The boy's frown softened. "Thank you," he said, and Dave could tell from his tone that he meant it. "I'm Sean."

"Dave, and this is Cheryl, and this is Erik."

"Nice to meetcha," Sean said. He smiled at Cheryl, and in a voice he'd borrowed from a grown man, he said, "And very pleased to make your acquaintance."

She giggled. "The pleasure is all mine, fine sir."

"Well," Dave said, turning toward the porch. "Should we go in?"

"Guess we should," Erik said.

They followed Dave onto the porch. The door opened easily into blackness. Dave gripped his knife and led them inside.

Eleven

Dust and dark had worked themselves into the interior of the Feinstein place, casting a filmy tint over everything that made Dave think of hazy nightmare places, half remembered. The living room, as he recollected, lay off to the left. The dining room and hall closet lay to the right. Ahead, at the end of the hall, another door faced them. Dave assumed it was the study where Feinstein had filmed his videotape.

Immediately before them, the staircase stretched upward into gloom.

"*Davey. . . .*" He remembered a throaty laugh and a metallic chatter echoing down from the top of those stairs. He cleared the discomfort that caught in his throat and turned to the others.

"How should we do this?" he asked. In spite of his best effort otherwise, his voice still carried in the utter stillness.

"I think we should stick together." Cheryl rested a protective hand on Sean's shoulder.

"Hell yeah," Erik replied. "Screw that splitting-up

sh—" He caught himself, in front of the boy. "Stuff.
Safety in numbers, man."

"Works for me." Dave moved forward. "Should
we try upstairs first? Sean, you said you saw it upstairs, right?"

Sean nodded. "In Mr. Feinstein's room."

They moved as one group toward the stairs, then
followed Dave single file, with Erik bringing up the
rear. Dave clicked on the flashlight with reluctance,
sure the beam of light would shatter any hope for an
element of surprise.

That ship sailed long before you walked into this place,
the voice inside told him. *It knows you're here.* He
gave a little wave of the flashlight beam. Nothing
much but a pale wall and a turn at the top, as well as
a closed door to the left.

At the landing, Dave moved forward and said,
"Okay, folks, stick together. We ought to be ready for
anything."

When no one answered, he turned around.

He was alone in the hallway.

At the top of the stairs, Cheryl, holding on to Sean's
shoulder, saw Dave move forward. She heard him
say, "Okay, folks, stick together," before there came a
faint chattering in her ear like teeth on a cold day,
and the flashlight snapped off.

As her eyes adjusted to the darkness, she realized
Dave wasn't in front of her anymore. She turned on
her own flashlight, splashing the upstairs hallway in
radical, panicked arcs. There was no sign of him.

"Cheryl, what happened to Dave?" Sean pulled
back against her, his baseball bat tight to his chest.

"I don't know, sweetie. Dave? Where did you go?

Dave?" She fought to keep her voice from cracking. Holding on to Sean, she took a few steps toward the nearest door, to their left. It was open slightly. Had it been before?

Cheryl hesitated at the door, her hand hovering above the knob. "Dave, are you in there? Erik, I think we lost—"

She turned and stopped midsentence. Erik was gone, too.

"Maybe they went into one of the rooms," Sean offered. He didn't sound like he believed it, though. He sounded like he was quite sure a gaping maw in the wall disguised as a door had opened up and swallowed them whole. Cheryl considered it a possibility.

She turned back to the door. She thought she heard someone call her name from inside, soft and urgent. "Come on. Let's check this one out. I think I heard one of them."

Erik heard Cheryl call Dave's name. He saw a brief arc of light followed by darkness, and thought he saw movement down the hall. He turned at the top of the stairs to follow them, and flipped on his flashlight. A small hall table stood outside one of the doors, an unplugged phone curled up like a sleeping cat on top of it. A linen closet door stood partially open beyond that. But he saw no sign of Cheryl, Dave, or the boy.

"Uh, guys? Cheryl? Dave, where the hell are you?"

Erik snorted. So much for sticking together. He moved past the linen closet. The door creaked open and he jumped as towels fell with a muted thump to the floor at his feet. He chuckled, turning down the flashlight on them.

They were crusty, stained with something that might have been blood. The chuckle died in his throat.

Erik moved forward again, the hand clutching the crowbar tightening into a fist. The door at the far end of the hall stood wide open, but movement from within drew his attention. Someone's shadow. Someone just out of his line of view.

"Dave?" He knew in his gut that it wasn't. The voice that answered him confirmed it.

"Erik? Is that you? C'mere, you little shit. Where the fuck you been all this time?" A belch followed that made his heart skitter. Hot liquid panic seared through his chest.

No. No, no, nononono. One, two, three, four, can't be. No way in hell. Can't be. Five, six, seven, the dead don't come back. . . .

Erik tucked first the flashlight, then the crowbar under one arm while he wiped the sweat off his palms. It wasn't him, *couldn't frigging possibly* be *him*, but Erik moved forward anyway, toward that awful stale-beer-and-smokes smell, that sweaty heat from the underarms of the black T-shirt, the rough elbows and the three-day stubble and the massive arms that had always seemed so, so intimidating and so inescapably strong.

His father sat in a beat-up pea-green easy chair, the only piece of furniture in the room besides a tiny television, which cast a spectral blue-gray glow across his wind-burned features. Gray hair bristled off his head. The dead Confederate soldier tattoo sized him up, its dead horse rearing over the movement of his father's biceps.

At his bare feet sat a case of Michelob, overturned

bottles the fallen soldiers of his evening's marauding. He'd won so many battles before finally losing that particular war.

The laugh track from the sitcom on the television made Erik flinch. He felt six years old again, busted for something that might or might not have been his fault. He eyed his father's belt, half smothered by the large stomach, with unease.

"You and those lowlifes out joyriding again?" his father asked without looking up from the TV. Sixteen, then, and not six. Little between him and his father had changed in those years between, except the belt had been replaced by the convenience of fists, or whatever else lay within handy arm's reach.

"No, sir," he mumbled, and wished he could sink into the floor.

Or . . . better yet, that he could be high. The old man was so much easier to tune out then.

"So, where you been? Out with that Kohlar boy? Or that little slut, what's her name—Duffy? You been hanging out with them, have ya?" Without taking his eyes off the screen, his father reached down between his legs and pulled out another beer. "Or maybe you've been out getting high, is that it?"

Erik swallowed several times and shook his head no, more to keep the world in focus than in answer to the question.

His father finally looked up. "Look, I know you stole money from me. Don't bother denying it, you little shit. The money's gone, and you took it. Either spent it on that bitch, or on drugs. Either way, I'm gonna take it out of that scrawny little frame you call a body if you don't cough it up right now."

"I don't have it," Erik whispered. He closed his

eyes. He'd paid his dues to the man. He was done answering to him. Had given that up when the old man died.

"You're lying. I don't like liars, Erik." His father had a way of saying things sometimes where the tone suggested more threat than any words he actually used. What his father liked and didn't like had always simply been a precursor to something more destructive. Sometimes he beat him up. Other times—and Erik often felt that these "life lessons," as his father called them, were worse—he scared the hell out of him. Simply drove any sense of security Erik had away not by the act, but the threat of it—the implication of a violence that wouldn't stop with a couple of punches to the stomach or a well-timed kidney shot. A camping trip turned hunting trip. Countless fixer-upper experiences with power tools. Driving lessons.

It occurred to Erik that, much like the Hollower, his father hadn't ever touched him during those life lessons. He hadn't needed to.

"You can't hurt me." Weak-sounding words leaked out of Erik, but in that moment, he felt that they could be true. He meant them in every sense. It couldn't touch him, this thing pretending to be his father. Not physically, and not inside his head. Not anymore. He wouldn't let it happen.

"Like hell I can't!" His old man set the bottle down on the floor next to the chair. "I'll bust your teeth down your throat. I'm not too old for that, and neither are you, asshole."

"You're not real."

He heard the sounds of his father fumbling with

his belt. "I'll show you how real I am." The leather cracked and he flinched, squeezing his eyes shut.

"You're not real," he whispered again, and when he opened his eyes, his father was staring at him nose to nose, the belt stretched between both meaty hands, his breath layers of stale beer and the ferment of pizza garlic.

Erik swore in the intake of breath but couldn't move. His father raised the belt over his head.

"You can't touch me." He clutched the crowbar. "But I'd sure as hell like to see you try."

"Yes, I can," the Hollower's multivoice answered from the father-thing. "In the places that really hurt."

Erik heard chuckling and a chattery sound from behind him. He turned, and the whole room changed. He was in his bedroom now, the one he shared with Casey. He blinked, disoriented. Was he home?

He saw the blood on the bed.

Creeping closer, he also saw a picture of Casey propped in the center of the bloody sheets. He remembered taking it at a picnic three or four years before. She wore a white tank top and the way the sun lit her skin and hair, she glowed. He loved that picture of her.

The glass holding it in was cracked, and the eyes and mouth had been scratched away by something sharp. A thin smear of blood streaked across her neck.

That same multivoice said over his shoulder, "While you're here, I'll be there, hurting her."

Erik turned again and bolted for the door. He emerged into another familiar room. Another bedroom, he remembered. His picture of Casey was tacked to one of the sparse white walls above a bed made up with pale green sheets. The room held the faint odor of stale sweat, different than his father's—cleaner, but tangy with frustration and strung-out nerves. He remembered the window behind his bed, reinforced with metal—no jumpers here, no, sir—and the scuffed tiled floor beneath his feet. He remembered it all, every detail he'd focused on as he counted his way through withdrawal. He'd both loathed and loved that tiny rehab room.

He moved toward the door. There had been one particularly bad night when he'd pounded on it, half on the verge of tears, begging them to just let him go already, while his roommate lay curled up against the wall on his own bed.

Erik pounded the door with his fist, tried the knob, and found it locked. "Shit. I swear, you son of a bitch, if you hurt her—"

He stopped when he heard the other bed behind him creak. He wasn't alone in the room.

Dave headed down the hallway, figuring maybe Sean had led them to Max Feinstein's bedroom. How they had gotten ahead of him, he could only hazard a guess. Beneath the gear-turning in his mind, though, he suspected he was alone precisely because the Hollower wanted him to be an easier target.

But to think that way would start a train of defeatist thought in his mind about the Hollower's abilities against his own, and he wasn't quite ready to give up yet. Wherever the others were, he hoped they were together, and safe. If he could draw the bastard's attention away from them by crashing the Hollower's new stomping ground alone, so be it.

A small table lay on its side on the floor. Next to it, the receiver of an unplugged phone rocked gently, its cord wiggling slightly with the movement. He had a strange compulsion to plug it back into the wall, jack and all, and when he did, he thought he heard muffled sound from the earpiece. He crouched and when he touched the phone, it stopped rocking. He brought the receiver to his ear and heard the shuddery breath of someone crying.

"Sally?"

"I—I used the towels. They're ruined. I used them to s-soak up the blood. There w-was s-s-so much. It sh-showed me blood."

"Sally, where are you?"

There was a click, and the receiver went dead in his hand. He dropped the phone and stood up. The door behind the fallen table was open now—wide open—and he could see a king-sized bed. An amorphous stain darkened the wall above the headboard.

Max Feinstein's room.

He stepped inside.

The room at the top of the stairs drew drafty breath in and out through unseen cracks in the walls. The dry flowered paper of its lungs, peeling away from the Sheetrock in some places, wavered in the slight breeze. Scuffs on the hardwood floor suggested that heavy pieces once furnished the room—a bed and dresser, maybe—but they had evidently since been moved. The vacancy of the room appeared out of place to Cheryl, as if, without life to sustain it, the house were falling to uneven decay.

She rubbed her arms. "Cold in here."

"What do you think happened to the others?"

Sean gazed around the empty room, bat clutched to his chest.

"Don't know, sweetie." Seeing his expression, she added, "I'm sure they're fine, though. Those two can handle themselves. They're fine."

Sean didn't answer. His gaze was fixed on the closet door, which stood open a crack.

"Sean?"

"I don't think that door was open when we came in," he murmured.

Cheryl crossed the empty room and took his hand. She knew the Hollower better than to offer the empty reassurance that it was just a closet, or that one of the drafts had urged the door open. Instead, she led Sean to the door and with the nose of the nail gun, nudged it open farther.

Before them, a long, smooth concrete tunnel lay twenty feet or so ahead, then branched sharply to the left and dissolved into darkness over what should have been the exterior of the side of the house. The tunnel went behind and through walls, taking up space that should have been wood and packed fiberglass and metal and electrical wires. It was round—a throat, an intestine, a soft vaginal place deep in the house that accepted bad things and expelled monstrosities in return. She tried to shake off those thoughts, heavy as they were with a cloying sense of sex and death, and found it hard to disconnect those associations.

"It might be a way back to the others," Sean said.

"Maybe," Cheryl said, giving his hand a light squeeze. "Or farther away from them. This is all wrong. It shouldn't be here—can't exist here, not the way this house is built. I don't think we should go down this way. I think we should go back out into the hallway and try to find them in another room."

Sean considered this for a moment, then nodded in agreement.

Cheryl closed the door to what should have been a closet and crossed back to the door through which they'd first entered. It was closed now. She wasn't all that surprised, she supposed. But it did startle her when she found the door locked—not the fact of it being locked, so much as the realization that they'd have to find another way.

Through the tunnel.

She looked back at Sean. His face was pale. A lock of hair stuck to the dewy sweat on his little forehead.

Cheryl crossed back and opened the closet door.

"Hold my hand," she said. "And whatever you do, don't let go."

"Believe me," he answered, "I won't."

Cheryl stepped through and immediately felt movement beneath her feet. Inside the concrete, it reeked less of claustrophobic sexuality, but that idea was replaced by a recollection of one of those fun-house tubes that rotated while people tried to walk through to the other side. It made her feel a little sick.

The tunnel seemed to bend to her perception then; the concrete turned slowly by the frayed edge of the shadows, and Cheryl's stomach turned with it in a seasick lurch. "Sean?"

"I'm right behind you," Sean said. If he had noticed the motion of the tunnel, he didn't mention it, but his shuddery breath made his voice tremble. A pause, then, "Are you scared?"

"Yes. You?"

"Yes."

"We can do this," she told him.

They plunged forward into the darkness.

When DeMarco pulled up in front of the Feinstein place on River Falls Road, the first thing she noticed was a car. Not Bennie's car, she realized with a twinge of panic. The plate number sounded familiar—Kohlar's? She tried to run it but she couldn't get anything to come up on the computer.

DeMarco frowned. There wasn't any good reason she could think of why the computer wouldn't work, but it kept blinking a prompt at her, patiently waiting for her to understand that she was alone out there.

She glanced at the car again. It was possible that Mrs. Feinstein, the widow, had returned to clean up or maybe go through some of her husband's old things. At this hour, though, DeMarco didn't think so. *Cop hunch*, May would have called it.

As she got out of the car, DeMarco felt for her gun in its holster. Cool metal beneath her fingertips steadied her a little. She surveyed the neighborhood. It was awfully quiet for evening. No one outside dragging the garbage cans to the curbs, no one tidying up the front yard or coming home from work. Come to think of it, it was awfully dark, too. How long had it taken her to get there?

A terrible idea struck her—what if she had been in that shadowed spot on the road for longer than she thought? What if it hadn't swallowed up just space and the cops who occupied it, but time, too? Or what if it hadn't really been the *guys* who'd been swallowed up and excreted into some overdark, overquiet alternate version of River Falls Road—

She closed her eyes and opened them. DeMarco had never been given over to wild flights of fancy, and couldn't fathom why such an idea might possess her now, except that (*"for Chrissakes, Detective, he didn't have a face"*) nothing about the case was normal or right. The whole situation had a fantastic quality to it. At the precinct, under the fluorescent lighting, the facts of her case files made her think of jigsaw pieces laid out on a table—pieces meant to fit eventually, tight and snug and proper. But out here, the house and the faceless maniac that maybe waited inside were ominiscent and menacing in the suburban night. It was almost as if she could hear its secrets through the walls.

"I used the towels. They're ruined. I used them to s-soak up the blood."

DeMarco drew her gun and moved forward toward the steps. From inside, she thought she heard crying.

Erik turned and winced. Immediately, he felt sick. The figure on the bed lay curled in the fetal position, its face to the wall. The bony back, each vertebra outlined by the thin graying T-shirt, shook as the figure cried. It wore a grungy New York Yankees cap turned backward. Erik could smell the sour tang of hair oils and dry-mouth and nights sweating out the tension from muscle pain.

The figure's scrawny arms covered its face so Erik couldn't see. That didn't matter. Erik had seen pictures of himself from back when he was getting high. He remembered well enough that he'd looked like hell.

And it was that version of him that lay on the bed.

He fought the gorge rising in his throat.

"Uh . . . ah, hello?"

The Erik-thing didn't answer. Erik reached for its shoulder, hesitated, moved in again. He jumped when the figure bolted upright and turned around.

It had his face—most of it. The eyes and mouth looked swollen and sealed with crusted blood. Where the nose should have been, there was blackness, and issuing from the hole with each convulsion of the body, white powder tufted into the air.

He could smell the cocaine, and he wanted it. He knew that the only thing keeping him from shaking the thing-version of himself for its snowfall of headcoke was the simple revulsion at the thought of actually touching it. He wasn't sure, though, how long revulsion would serve as a deterrent.

I could do it.

An ugly thought, but he felt no real guilt. No one around to care, no one able to get to him in this weird alternate version of the Feinstein house, even if someone did want to help. He could get high in peace, in private, and no one would have to know. A little coke to clear his head. He'd be stronger, faster, sharper. He wanted that.

He closed his eyes and saw Casey's face behind his eyelids. When he opened them, his alternate self was gone. The night table between the beds had been cleared for neat, long lines of white laid out in soft rows.

Everything would be better. Even dying high would be better than dying in a place he wasn't even sure was really there, with no one but that bitch sobriety to see him through at the end.

He thought of Casey again, and the way she felt in

his arms, and of Dave and Cheryl. Of the kid, Sean, who looked terrified and small with his baseball bat. But mostly, he thought of Casey, and the Hollower's threat to go after her.

Erik sat down on the edge of the bed where he could remember lying night after night, staring up at the ceiling and counting. He leaned in close to the night table, so close that he could stick out the tip of his tongue and taste the coke if he chose. So close. So close.

He inhaled a slow, deep breath, careful not to disturb the lines, then blew all the cocaine off the surface.

Somewhere above and beyond the ceiling, he heard a frustrated wail, and he smiled in spite of the lump in his throat.

Behind him, he heard a click and the familiar rusty squeak of his door opening. He got up and crossed to the doorway. Beyond it, a dimly lit stairwell, whose walls looked damp and almost shiny, led down to a door. Erik took a deep breath and headed down.

Cheryl held Sean's hand tightly as they moved through the tunnel. She had no idea how far ahead the tunnel went, or if it had an end at all. To her left, close to her ear, she heard steady dripping like water (*blood*) in a cave. She couldn't see much beyond irregular outlines that seemed to melt when she got close to them.

The tunnel had a dank, chemical smell, metallic in her throat. She became aware of the sudden absence of the dripping, and stopped to glance back. Cheryl hadn't heard the door behind them close and wasn't completely sure it had, but the dark stretched its legs out behind them, the empty room from which they'd come now lost.

Cheryl reached out in front of her with the nail gun. A flash of purple from below drew her attention. The floor had fallen away from a platform on which they now stood. Far beneath it, blackness swirled in blackness, drawing thin streams of red downward like a drain. Cheryl cried out, momentarily unsteady on the platform, and Sean squeezed her hand. She could feel its heat, the sweat of his palm, even the light, quick beat of his pulse in his wrist.

"Don't look down," he whispered. Cheryl nodded, even though she doubted he could see, and fixed her attention ahead of her. Reaching out the hand with the nail gun again, she inched forward.

The muzzle of the nail gun eventually brushed with something hard and she exhaled a surprised "Oh!" and accidentally discharged a nail with a small, sharp bang. She felt ahead and determined it to be a length of rough wood. Further search yielded a cold metal knob. She turned it and stepped into a closet. Sean packed in after her. A lightbulb like a bulging eye gazed down at them from the low ceiling, its rusty chain grazing her shoulder. A brass bar ran across the length of the closet about level with her neck, and musty, ragged clothes hung on old wooden hangers. The clothes retained the bulk of breathing chests and strong muscles. They hung tense with that careful, calculated stillness that masks and dolls seem to possess. She could imagine one of those moth-eaten sleeves reaching up and knotting tightly around her neck.

She felt between them, shivering as their fabrics brushed her arms, for a door on the other side. There was nothing there, nor to either side. She looked up. No trapdoor to the attic, either. She gave the back wall a solid kick and swore under her breath.

A sleeve reached up to touch her back, and she jumped.

"Just me," Sean said with an apologetic grin. "Are you okay?"

No. No, no, no, she thought. It couldn't be a dead end, not after all that. If they were in some god-damned maze between worlds, she was pretty sure that they would never manage to find their way back to the empty room. But she'd be damned if she would let them suffocate in some tiny closet quite literally in the middle of nowhere.

"Hm-mm." She couldn't bring herself to say yes.

"Now what?" Sean asked, breathless.

She choked on the disappointment. "I guess that wasn't the way out. We'll have to go back."

"I can't." His voice was hoarse. "I can't do it again, Cheryl."

She grasped the knob. "We have to, sweetie. We can't stay in this—"

She opened the door and stepped out into a hall-way she didn't recognize. Not the upstairs hallway, but someplace else.

Cheryl turned to Sean, who stood inside the closet doorway. "Well, at least we don't have to—"

The bulb winked out inside the closet. The door creaked once and swept inward to close Sean off from her. She thought fast and reacted faster, thrusting an arm in the doorway. She cried out from the impact of wood on her forearm, and squeezed her eyes shut as sharp pain ran up to her armpit. But she felt his shirt, his shoulder. She had him.

"Sean?" she said through gritted teeth. She felt his hand on her own.

"I'm here, but something's in here with me. Please get me out of here. Oh . . . oh God." He sounded very close to tears. She tried using her foot and shoulder to widen the opening, but the door wouldn't move.

"Please, Cheryl!" Sean's voice cracked on the other side of the door.

"I gotcha, don't worry." She clenched his shirt tighter and the pain in her forearm grew hot and bright behind her eyes. She tucked the nail gun between her knees and worked her good arm into the opening, then threw her weight against the door. It resisted her attempt, but budged enough to let Cheryl pull the boy through. The door slammed shut behind him.

He hugged her, and for several moments, she just held him. She didn't ask what he saw and he didn't tell her. She just hugged him and after a moment, she thought she heard little sobs, muffled by her clothes.

It felt nice, to be needed. To be the comforting one. The brave one.

When he pulled away, she saw his eyes were red, but he rubbed them with the heel of his hand before she could see tears.

"Where are we now?" He cast a suspicious glance around the hallway.

"I don't know. Looks like some kind of hospital."

"That can't be good."

"Probably not." Behind them, to the right, were a couple of closed doors, painted a pale eggshell color. Off to the left was an empty nurses' station, and beyond that, the door to the fire stairs. The entire hallway was dusted in white powder. It reminded Cheryl of snow.

She noticed a small plaque outside the door through which they'd just come. It read KOHLAR, SALLY in neat black lettering. Her grip around the nail gun tightened. Not good at all.

"Do you hear that?" Sean frowned, hugging the bat close to him.

"Hear what?" She strained but heard nothing.

"That," he whispered, his eyes wide, and then she heard it, too. A scrabbling sound, like a thousand tiny legs skittering over the hard floor. And the groan of wood under pressure.

From beneath the door at the far end of the hallway, black blood oozed onto the tiles, sending up puffs of white dust. At least, at first, that's what Cheryl saw. But then large individual drops of black began moving on their own. They caught the fluorescent lighting and shined.

Sean's bat fell to his side. "Oh God."

They poured into the hallway in an inky wave, kicking up a whitecap as they surged forward. Their contact with the powder increased the metallic smell, making it sharp in Cheryl's throat. Some drops jumped up onto the front of the nurses' station desk, leaving smoking furrows as they skittered along its length.

"Let's go," Cheryl said, but Sean stood transfixed to the floor, his horrified face taking it all in. "Now, Sean!" She tugged on his shirt and dragged him toward the fire stairs and pounced on the handle.

It wouldn't move. Inside her head, Cheryl screamed.

How could it be locked? She threw her good

shoulder into it, trying to force open the door. No luck. Her gaze darted to the nurses' station. Was there a key, maybe? A security button?

Sean held the bat out in front of him, ready to swipe through the first wave of attack. She grabbed his arm and led him over to the nurses' station. On the desk was a box with a series of buttons, but nothing marked security. There was one marked FIRE ALARM. She jabbed it.

A splintering sound like an ambulance siren filled the hallway with noise. The sprinklers turned on and snowed more powder down on top of them. The wave of black hesitated. The white piled up fast, burying the drops beneath it. Cheryl grabbed Sean and lunged back toward the fire door.

A long wail rose above the siren. She had *made it angry*. She wasn't sure where the thought had come from—it wasn't hers, really—but she knew it to be true.

The piles of white rustled from beneath. The drops were burrowing their way out again. She turned the handle and slammed herself into the door. It swung open and she and Sean spilled out onto the stairs. They raced down, two at a time to the landing, then down farther to the bottom. Only then did they stop and listen.

The stairwell echoed with their ragged breathing, but they were alone.

Sean offered her a grateful smile. They both turned to the door at the bottom of the stairs.

DeMarco opened the front door and stepped into the police station.

"What the . . . ?" She blinked, but there it was. Most of the other desks, even the night-shifters' desks, were unoccupied, their phones quiet, their desk lamps turned off for the night. The captain's door stood closed, the light off. Hers was on, though. So was Bennie's, and Joe Rubelli's. But she appeared to be alone in the room. Something was wrong. Very wrong.

"Hello? Anybody here?" No one answered.

Gun drawn, she crossed the room to her own desk. Everything on it appeared to be in order. She opened the top drawer. Extra paper clips, a granola bar, and some rubber bands, all as they should be. But this wasn't the police station. It couldn't be. What had happened to Feinstein's house?

She picked through the contents on top of her desk. Her case files lay stacked neatly in one corner, along with her morning coffee mug, her legal pad, telephone, computer . . .

The computer was on. She was sure she'd logged out and shut it off before she'd left.

An open writing document filled the screen. In a large black font that took up most of the page, someone had typed:

LOOK

BEHIND

YOU

She clicked the safety off her gun and turned slowly.

At Rubelli's desk, a body lay slumped over. Another at Bennie's, too. She recognized them from their builds, even hunched over, and swallowed the tightness in her throat.

Not Bennie. Please, not Bennie.

"Guys?" She moved toward Bennie's desk. A quick sweep of the room again told her no one else was there.

"Bennie? She looked down on him. From this close, she could see a couple of drops of blood already dried brown on his desk blotter.

"No, but I could be." The body sat up—jerked, DeMarco thought, like a puppet on a string—and tilted its head up at her.

She uttered a small cry and pointed her gun at it, backing away.

It had no mouth. No eyes or nose, either, but she suspected it could see and smell her as well as it had been able to talk, as if facial features were window dressings, and not actual conveyances for the senses. It did have a bullet hole, though—right where its forehead should have been. The skin around the small hole was stippled with gun powder. DeMarco felt a sharp pinprick in her chest.

No exit wound. There's no exit wound. There should be—

She clung to this thought, because underlying it was a more important one: this thing hadn't thought to form an exit hole in the back of its head because it hadn't copied a bullet wound from a real-life model. Which meant maybe Bennie Mendez was alive and kicking somewhere.

It seemed to hear her thoughts, and as if in defiance, blood dribbled out of the bullet hole and down the length of its face.

Behind it, at the other desk not too far away, the Rubelli-thing's body jerked upward. Scorch marks in the pasty flesh indicated where eyes would have been. It had a bullet hole in its chest. A crimson halo stained the front of its shirt and part of its tie.

"We found you," the Rubelli thing said. The sound came from the burn holes.

"Who are you?" DeMarco saw the Bennie-thing push its chair out from the corner of her eye, and she leveled the gun at its head.

"Don't you know?" It bled a little more from its bullet hole as it spoke. Its voice—Bennie's voice—sounded close to her ear, over her shoulder.

"I know who you aren't," she said.

When the Bennie-thing rose, she fired at its head. The bullet never made contact, though, because the thing dissolved into a pile of white powder on the chair. The bullet lodged itself in the wall behind the desk.

She turned and found the other one had closed half the distance between them. Each step pumped fresh blood through the bullet wound in the chest, too. The front of it shone in the dim light.

She fired at it and before the bullet could reach it, it snowed into a pile on the floor.

DeMarco ran a hand over her eyes and found them wet. *Pull it together, An.* She crossed the room, sidestepping the pile of dust on the floor, and opened the door to the waiting area—

—and found herself in Feinstein's basement, standing at the bottom of the stairs.

She assumed, at any rate, that it was the basement. Wiring hard-stapled to wooden beams ran across the ceiling. The washer and drier stood in one corner, and the casing of the water heater and the furnace stood in another. The floor beneath her feet crackled when she took a step, and she looked down. A sticky crimson stained the concrete.

The furnace belched and she jumped. The after-echo sounded like a word. . . .

And then she heard soft crying, like a child's, from somewhere farther in the basement. Ahead of her, the room took a ninety-degree turn to the right. She moved forward, the gun guiding her way, listening for the source of the crying. At the bend, it occurred to her there was something broken-record-like about the sound, its dips and swells following a pattern. She thought she even heard the muffled clip of a record skipping in its groove.

She kept going anyway. In the basement acoustics, her ears could deceive her. And besides, a record player still needed someone to turn it on.

The remainder of the basement around the bend proved a shorter distance. It ended in a door. She approached it with caution, weary now of doors and what could lay beyond them in the confines of the Feinstein house.

A sob broke out from under the door, and dissolved into whimpering and sniffles.

She leaned an ear closer. "Hello? Anyone in there? Hello?"

"Help me," a woman's voice said.

DeMarco tried the door but it was locked. "I can't get in. Are you hurt? Can you unlock the door?"

"It's unlocked," the voice replied.

"Well, then it might be stuck because I can't—" She turned the knob and the door eased open.

She stepped into a small storage room. Stacked boxes marked HOLIDAY DECORATIONS and WINTER COATS and GLADYS walled the room in on three sides.

DeMarco felt for a switch and flipped the light on. In the middle of the room, sitting on the floor with her legs tucked under her, was a frail blond woman. She hugged herself tightly with bony arms. Tears cupped in the skin beneath her eyes spilled over onto her cheeks.

She looked familiar—a photo from the missing persons case file.

"Ms. Kohlar? Everything's okay, ma'am. I'm a police officer. I'm going to get you out of here." She flipped the safety of the gun back on and put it in its holster. "Everything will be okay."

Sally Kohlar shook her head. "No, it won't. It's sensed you. Now it can find you like it finds us."

Twelve

Standing inside Feinstein's bedroom, Dave felt surprisingly at peace. He couldn't quite put a finger on it, but it seemed like the hub, a place from which all the rest of the rooms sprang. The rest of the house scared him with its alien hostility, but in that room, that objective control to the rest of the experiments remained constant. Ironically, the safest place in the house was right in the heart of it.

Until the Hollower returned.

By degrees, he realized he could hear other parts of the house—a television, a gunshot, what sounded like a fire alarm. His first instinct was to run toward the sounds, to try to find the others and help. After the first few steps he was seized with a strong sense that to interfere would cause the others harm, that he could cause them to get lost where they thought they were, or hurt by what they thought they saw. Or worse.

The idea wasn't his, though; the Hollower wanted him to think that. He bucked in doubt and made his way toward the door. Before he could get far, a space opened up in the floor before him and his arms pin-wheeled to keep him from falling through. Peering down, he saw Sally in some dark room—a closet, maybe, or somewhere in the basement. His heart thudded.

"Sally! Sally, up here!" he called, but she didn't seem to be able to hear him. "Sally!"

Sally for the others, a voice in his head said. *Sally if you just let me have them.*

Dave's hands clenched into fists. He made for the door again. When he opened it, he fully expected something with metallic claws to jump on him and tear open his throat.

He stepped out into the hall and made his way down to the first floor without incident. He checked the closet where he'd gone looking for the box. She wasn't there.

Dave turned to the study and was about to search there when the clock struck. He counted off the chimes, *one, two, three . . .*

And realized he hadn't seen a grandfather clock the last time he'd been there.

Six, seven . . .

He went toward the source of the chimes. The study? He opened the door to a large hall. At the far end was the clock.

Eleven, twelve, thirteen . . .

The polished mahogany casing stood tall and op-posing, hooded by a Gothic arch. Beneath the arch, its white face, set in a black frame of stars and nebu-lae, featured no numbers at all. The black iron hands pointed straight out at him.

Sixteen, seventeen, eighteen . . . He wondered if the chimes would ever stop.

They did, and that, to Dave, was worse. They didn't just ring and then fade to pleasant oblivion. They wound down, like a broken merry-go-round. As he got close enough, he heard wood splinter beneath the momentum of the heavy gold pendulum. It dislodged, crashed into the other side, pulled itself free again. The weights and their gold chains tangled in the gears, the force of their relentless turning prying loose cogs and shafts and gear wheels. They sprang away from the clock as if it were on fire, and he flinched when one grazed his cheek. When they landed, they turned into red meaty things—organs, chunks of flesh, tissue—and the chimes blurred into a long, loud wail of pain.

The clock was dying.

He backed away from it, then turned to find the room blazing with sunlight.

No, not a room. He was outside. In the front yard of his childhood home.

Dave felt queasy. He remembered that apple-blossom smell in the air, and the sunshine warmth on the back of his neck that made him hot as he realized what he'd done, and the tears cooled by the breeze.

Sally's little body lay on the ground at his feet. Her eyes were closed and she wasn't moving, except for her chest, which made shallow attempts at maintaining breath. Blood encircled her head like a halo. Dave looked at her through nine-year-old eyes, and remembered.

"Maaaaaaa!" A scream, terrified, frenzied—his voice, but not coming from his mouth.

His mom came running out of the house, saw Sally, and crumpled a little where she stood. "Sally!

Oh, my baby girl! Sally!" She came running, folded next to her daughter, and touched her neck.

"I'm sorry," Dave said, and the voice came out of time, a child's voice full of guilt and apology and abject fear.

"What did you do?" his mother growled, and looked up. He half expected her to have no face, but she did. Angry eyes, hateful mouth. "What did you do?"

"It was an accident," he said. That was what he'd said then, that it was an accident. He hadn't meant to push her.

But he had.

He hadn't meant for her to hit her head. It was the kind of thing he'd done to her a hundred times, a big brother's right to scrape off the annoying questions, the tiring demands that he play with her, the silly little girl observations about everything. He didn't want to hurt her, he'd only wanted to—

—get her away from him.

The lady next door came to watch him while his parents took Sally to the hospital. He couldn't sleep, though, until he'd mopped up the blood. He'd used towels. There was a lot of blood, for such a little head. It was late when they came home, three worn, pale faces, one tiny blond head with stitches.

His mother had grounded him for a week over Sally. She'd smacked his arm when she saw what he'd done to her towels.

"I'm sorry," he said again, with his own voice. He remembered, and felt cold inside his clothes.

"No, you're not. You want to be rid of her. You want to be free."

Dave shook his head. "That's not true." But part of it was. That part made him feel terrible.

"You're a bad brother, Dave. You've always been a bad brother. You let her fall apart." His mother rose, fixing a withering look on him. "You never wanted to take care of her."

"I'd do anything for her." Even now, his mom loomed impossibly tall. He shielded his eyes from the sun and looked up at her.

"Would you quit drinking? Worry more about her, maybe, than that floozy from the bar? Maybe show up for work on time and do your job so you can pay for better care? You think that doctor is doing her any good, or that silly support group? Maybe stop making promises to her you can't keep—are you ready to do that, Dave?"

As she spoke, she'd gotten closer and closer to him until she towered over him. "You've ruined her."

Dave felt his face grow hot, and his hands clenched into fists. All the years of guilt, the worrying, the frustration and anger, collected and smoldered in his hands and face.

His voice sank to a barely contained low. "No, I didn't. I love Sally. I take care of her as best I can."

"I should take her away from you."

"You can't have her."

The mother smiled. It was a terrible fault across the expanse of her face. "I already do." She nodded toward a place over his shoulder, and he wheeled around.

He was inside again, at the top of the stairs. He saw a flashlight beam arc its way across the landing at the bottom, but the source was out of his line of view.

Taking two at a time, he lunged downward. A figure stepped in front of him just as he hit the bottom and he nearly plowed it over.

"Man, I get that you're happy to see me, but you don't need to bowl me over." Erik laughed.

"Erik?"

"Yeah?"

"I mean, *really* Erik?"

He got Dave's meaning and punched him lightly in the arm. "Our friend doesn't seem to like physical contact, right? See, it's me. In the flesh."

Dave exhaled in relief. "Thank God." He pulled the boy into a hug. Erik laughed again.

"Have you seen Cheryl or the boy?"

"Right here," Cheryl's voice said. They turned and found her, holding on to Sean's hand.

"Found ya," Sean said.

Dave smiled at the sight of her. "Have to test if you're really you," he said, and hugged them both, relieved that they were okay. Then, smiling wider, he said, "Still not sure about you, Cheryl," and swept her up in a hug again. She giggled, and he felt her breath in his ear. It made him want to keep holding on to her, but after a moment longer, he let her go.

"So, what the hell just happened? I mean, one minute I'm following you guys, and the next minute, I'm having a conversation with my father." Erik exhaled an unsteady breath, and gave them a meaningful look. "My *dead* father. Every time I turned around, the Hollower was there, and I blew every chance to kill it. I'm sorry. I blew it." He held out a hand, palm down, and studied it. It shook.

"Yeah, we ran into it, too," Cheryl said, somewhat breathless. Her eyes crinkled in a worried squint, and she glanced once around the basement. "Well, not the Hollower exactly. But I guess it ran into us. Or over us. We didn't stand a real fighting chance, either."

Dave walked to the stairs and peered up. The door at the top smeared as if someone had taken a damp thumb to an ink picture. It looked surreal. Deadly, somehow. Certainly not the way to go. "None of us stand a chance alone," he said. "It's too easy, much too easy for it to change up reality and fade back and watch it all happen."

"It split us up for a reason," Erik said. "I figure, we stick together and if the Hollower wants us, it'll have to show its face, so to speak, and come get us."

"I think we should look for it around here," Cheryl said, looking to Dave.

Erik shrugged. "I think she's right. Basement's got kind of a lairish thing happening."

"It seems we might have more to go on here than I found in Max's room. This place feels—"

"Unstable," Cheryl finished.

"Yeah," Dave said. "Unstable." Maybe he'd been wrong about Max's bedroom. Maybe it wasn't the hub of the Hollower's activity but simply the room most grounded in humanity. Maybe it struck him as an eye in the storm of the house not because it was the first place the Hollower retired to, but the last place it touched in its torment of Max, and likely, only after the man died.

In that basement, the feeling was different than in the bedroom. There beneath the house, the solidity of wall and floor gave way to material thrumming with alien life. The very *sureness* of a wall or floor was missing. To get lost in such a place was to mistake a slab of concrete for a safe place to lean, or to take a step and keep falling through to the center of the world.

The Hollower's world.

He thought of the vision of Sally, and felt impatient to move forward.

"Anyone see a light switch around here?" Dave felt toward the nearest wall, but found nothing. He didn't much expect to. The Hollower didn't need to see, and wouldn't want to make it any easier for them.

"Nothing up there," Erik called from the middle of the stairs, then jogged back down. "There isn't even much of a door anymore."

"I saw that," Dave replied with a grim nod. "Nice touch."

From over by the far wall, Cheryl and Sean shook their heads.

"Okay, I guess we forge ahead with the flashlights."

Their flashlight beams skittered about ahead of them, but didn't illuminate much more than a few feet. Their footsteps echoed and as they walked on, Dave got the distinct impression that beyond where the flashlights could penetrate, the walls were drawing back and the distance ahead of them stretching beyond the width of the house.

But then they turned at a bend in the hall and came abruptly upon a wooden door. In the weak light, the irregular patches of chipped paint looked like bloodstains. From beneath the door he heard muted sounds of voices.

Dave held up a hand for them to wait, and they stopped, silent and huddled, behind him.

He turned his head and whispered, "There are people in there."

"People." Erik's whisper implied doubt.

Cheryl touched him lightly on the shoulder. "Maybe Sally?" Dave met her gaze for a moment, and she gave his shoulder a squeeze.

He turned back toward the door. "Let's find out." He was aware of the cold metal of the knob before he was conscious of the fact that it was turning in his hand. The door opened.

And the muzzle of a gun pointed directly at the tip of his nose. He felt his stomach bottom out.

The detective from the hospital stood in the doorway. When recognition dawned in her eyes, she lowered the gun.

Her name came to him after a second. "Detective DeMarco?"

"Mr. Kohlar. Ms. Duffy, hello there." She paused, looking from one to the other, and finally to Sean. She looked unsure what to say next. After a moment, she opted for, "I've found your sister."

Dave's heart leaped in his chest. "Is she okay?"

DeMarco stepped back to let them pass, and he moved into the room on heavy legs. The others crowded in after him.

Sally sat with her feet tucked under her on the floor and her arms wrapped around her. She rocked gently to a rhythm only she could feel. Dave felt a rush of both relief and lingering fear. She looked okay, but the slack-jawed expression made him worried.

"Sally?" The question sounded so loud in his ears, so pregnant with the things he needed to know.

She kept rocking, but closed her eyes.

Dave crouched next to her. "It's Dave. Can you hear me?" He felt a lump forming in his throat, which made pleading with her difficult. "Please. Please talk to me."

She turned her head and gave him a blank stare. "It's here, in this basement," she whispered. "The furnace. It says the most awful things."

Then he saw the gash on his sister's ankle, the dried blood that had collected over and at the top of her shoe, and looked up at DeMarco, his eyes burning with the beginnings of tears. "What happened?"

The detective reholstered her gun. "I wish I could tell you, but that's all she'll say. I was hoping *you* could tell *me*." When none of them answered, she added, "Look, I'll spare you the breaking and entering bit, since I have a pretty good idea why you're here. I'll also spare you the interrogation, since I would bet a paycheck that none of you brought Ms. Kohlar here yourselves. And I also figure that whatever condition Ms. Kohlar suffers from, none of you were the ones who made it worse since she's been gone. But someone did. Someone made it a whole lot worse. Someone you're all here looking for. But what I don't get," she said finally, "I mean, what I've been spending the better part of the last half hour trying to wrap my brain around, is what the hell this Hollower really is. And how does it mess up the world the way it does? Because that's enough to break *anyone*."

Dave gaped at her. Erik exchanged a glance with Cheryl and said, "You . . . how did you . . . ?"

"Call it a cop hunch. Or an instinct for connecting jagged pieces of a puzzle. And a very nasty run-in somewhere I couldn't have been with people I couldn't have seen. Well, people, such as they were." A dark expression passed over her face for a moment, and then she looked down at Sean. "Sweetheart, I'm willing to bet your mother doesn't know you're in a dead man's house this late at night. You do know that a sensible, respectable cop would march you right back home and into your mother's custody, and probably spend a good hour ranting about what a terribly stupid and dangerous idea it was for you to have come here in the first place."

Sean started to protest but DeMarco held up a hand. "As it is, the sensible, respectable thing isn't going to work here."

"What do you mean?" Dave rose.

"I almost lost your sister once—when I went to step out into the hall. I heard the sound of footsteps. Yours, I suppose, but I didn't know that then. I meant to check out the situation." She cast a wary glance at the door. "But the second I set one foot through, the hallway out there changed. I happened to have a hand on the door frame still, and managed to pull myself back into the room and close the door. That wasn't the first time part of the house changed. And frankly, I don't believe it will be the last. I can't in good conscience risk letting the house swallow any of you up if I can help it. So it's an all-or-nothing situation for me. Assuming I could find the front door again, I'd either have to escort all of you from the premises at the same time, or risk losing those I left behind, possibly forever. Of course, if I did force you all to leave together—"

"You'd have to shoot us first," Dave said. "We're not leaving until we take down that thing, or it takes us down." He heard the finality in his words, and his resolution felt good. Being sure felt good.

DeMarco gave him a resigned smile. "And I figured as much. Given what I've seen the last few days, I can't much say I blame you. But I'd be lying if I didn't say I was scared as hell for you. And me too."

Dave could see it then, the exhaustion creeping around the edge of her features, the tension in her mouth, the carefully reined-in terror in her eyes. And he felt more comfortable, more safe with her than he had felt in a long time with anyone. She felt real and honest, and those things made her endearing.

She took a step toward the boy. "All that being said, kid, you stick with me, okay?"

The boy glanced up at Cheryl, and at her gentle nod, replied in kind to the detective.

"So, I think if I'm to help you, I should know who you all are. I'm Anita."

"Call me Dave."

The cop acknowledged it with a nod.

"And Cheryl."

"Sean," the boy said in turn, and gesturing, added, "And that's Erik."

Erik offered an awkward grin and a half wave. Dave suspected that with his drug history, cops probably made Erik nervous.

As if to confirm that, DeMarco smiled and said, "Erik, yes."

"How's Detective Mendez?"

That same darkness passed over DeMarco's face, and she answered in a tight voice, "Was fine, last time I saw him. He moved out of Narcotics two years ago."

"Was he . . . one of the people you thought you saw?" Cheryl's expression was a strange mix of confusion and realization, as if she had a working picture of something almost too awful to look at fully with her mind's eye.

"Beg pardon?"

"We've been fending off the Hollower's mind games for months. Warps in our everyday lives.

Wrong places, a wrong face. But before, you said 'people.' You said 'people you couldn't have seen.'"

DeMarco looked genuinely sympathetic. "I can't imagine what that must have been like. I can certainly understand your resolve now."

"You said 'people,'" Cheryl repeated.

"Not sure we follow," Erik said.

Cheryl looked down at Sally. "None of us have ever seen more than one figure at a time, have we? None of us have ever seen 'people.' We've seen one—the Hollower—pretending to be someone else." She looked up at Dave and there were tears in her eyes. "God, what do you think more than one means?"

The others were silent. Sean drew close to Cheryl, who put an arm around him.

DeMarco stepped toward the door. "Could simply mean it's strong enough now to split off into other figures. I have no idea what the limits of its capabilities are, if it has any at all. But given that it's invited me into your little circle, and given that obvious escalations have drawn you here, I think it's probably safe to assume that this thing is kicking up its tactics a notch. We have no real reason yet to believe this splintering of figures is anything more than a new trick."

Dave noticed that in spite of everything he'd seen in her face of worry and fatigue, DeMarco still had a way of commanding authority, as if she could bend the Hollower's world back to her will. He looked back down at his sister, and for the moment he felt stronger, more capable of protecting her. "We can't stay here all night. We'll have to try to leave this room. Together. With Sally."

DeMarco cocked an eyebrow at him.

"We seem to have done okay so far when we stuck together. Not as much change as when it split us up. Maybe it has more trouble moving the earth under us when there are more feet firmly planted on it." Dave shrugged.

"If you try to leave now," Sally muttered from the floor, "it will paint you with pain and suffering." She looked up at Dave. "It hurt me."

Dave tried very hard not to read any notes of accusation in her last statement. The logical part of him asserted that she wasn't blaming him, but the rest of him had trouble backing it up.

"You need to get up, hon. We have to go." He reached an arm down to her to help her up.

"You can't. If you snip me from the ground I'll wither and die."

It occurred to Dave that she meant what she said literally, that maybe somehow she was only still alive in this room, and outside it, she'd disintegrate to a pile of dust and he really would lose her forever.

And he decided in the next moment the idea was irrelevant. If taking her out of the room meant taking the risk, so be it. There was no life in that room, no real life, and no peace in leaving her behind.

"Sally," he said, maybe more sternly than he intended. "Get up. We're going."

She obeyed without a word, rising unsteadily on shaky feet, favoring the bad ankle but refusing his help, refusing even to let him touch her.

"You want me to die." The voice was a light breeze past his ear. He wasn't sure whether she'd breathed it in his direction or he'd heard it in his head, but he watched miserably as she stumbled past him, her

feet heavy and her body drugged and clumsy. He tried to touch her arm again and she yanked it away.

She didn't want his help. She didn't want him to protect her—or else, she finally believed he couldn't anyway.

Sally stopped when she saw DeMarco and took her hand, like a child. From the corner of his eye, Dave noticed the others watching him for a reaction, but he didn't acknowledge it. Erik had tucked the crowbar into his belt, and had taken both Sean's and Cheryl's free hands while they held on to their respective weapons with the other. Cheryl offered Dave her arm to link his own through. He tucked his knife into a belt loop and took it. DeMarco offered her other hand, and he took that, too.

The detective led them into the hall.

Thirteen

When Erik, bringing up the rear, crossed the threshold back into the basement hallway, nothing happened. Not at first.

Dave had expected the walls to melt, the floor to drop out from beneath them, the gloom to ooze up into something massive and hungry and very deadly. But the solid foundation of the Feinstein house stretched out exactly as it had before.

Maybe there really was something to what Erik had said about safety in numbers.

They pressed forward as one on careful, quiet feet, not speaking, as if to make too much noise would summon the Hollower to them. Which was pointless—it knew where they were, if it wanted them.

Come to think of it, Dave wondered, *why hasn't the Hollower come after us? If it does know where we are, why hasn't it confronted us yet?*

The answer came so quickly he couldn't quite be sure if the thought was really his. *It's waiting. It has every intention of confronting us, but on its own terms. Its own turf.*

Dave looked around the basement. There wasn't too much to see; the dark around them ate at the edges of the flashlight glow. The dank smell of concrete holding out the cold, wet mold and moss and dirt was humid, palpable in the air and on their skin. Dave felt Cheryl shivering through his arm.

They passed beneath a curved arch of wood beams and continued down a long, straight passage.

The hall changed. No turn now. Here we go again.

The air grew heavier, a terrible silky, almost slimy density that slid in and out of his lungs. He found breathing it both difficult and repulsive.

All at once, the flashlights tucked into belt-loops or clumsily clutched between them died out, leaving them in total darkness. Moments later, a chittering sound like nails on a chalkboard came from somewhere a ways off.

Dave froze, the chain of hands to either side of him taut and suddenly cold.

"Oh my God," Sean whispered. "It's coming."

"Where is it?" Cheryl squeezed his hand.

Erik said, "Sounded like it came from back here. Behind us."

"Let's move." DeMarco tugged his hand. "Let's keep going."

They moved forward again as one. Dave held his breath until it grew painful in his chest. He couldn't hear anything other than their breathing and their footsteps.

The basement passage sloped down, an endless black yawn ahead of them, and Dave wondered if the house had finally swallowed them up. The possibility that they might spend days walking deeper and deeper into the belly of a basement that didn't exist in his world, walking until they dropped from exhaustion and thirst, inked its way into his thoughts. He felt cold all over, and was quite sure his hands were clammy in the grip of his partners.

"I'd kill for a window," Erik said. "Just a little moonlight or something."

A drawn-out *scrrrreeeech* followed by a few quick chirps sent an electric chill through the chain of hands. Their muttering worry came all at once.

"If we run—"

"We can't see—"

"—is coming."

"—scared."

They moved faster, stumbling blind on unsure feet. Cheryl tripped and nearly brought them all down, but Dave managed to pull her to her feet before she broke the chain and spilled onto what Dave could only suspect was a floor. He was sure that if his hold had been broken, he would have lost not only Cheryl, but everyone behind her. The gloom would have surged up like a black tide and washed them away.

Sally giggled. Dave thought it was an awful sound.

"Oh, shit." Erik's disembodied voice stopped them once more.

"What?" Dave turned around, and then he saw it, too.

A faint silvery light, and within it, movement— rapid, fluid movement, of many legs and arms scrambling to get at them. From the light—from *behind* the light somewhere—they heard noise. The sounds made Dave think of great metallic jaws chewing wads of metallic things. *Like gears* was what came into his head, *like huge, rusty gears and cogs tumbling down a long metal throat*. On the heels of this thought were simple panicked impressions; it was getting closer, it was swallowing them whole, it would crush their bones and tear away skin beneath the metal teeth and endlessly whirring, turning, churning gears.

"It's the Hollower," Sean whispered.

They broke into a clumsy run, uncoordinated on six pairs of feet, but loping away from the Hollower as best they could. The light picked up speed and grew brighter, blotting out the moving shadows behind it and whatever cast them. Cheryl squeezed Dave's hand tightly, and he thought he heard her say his name beneath the roar of scraping metal.

The light overtook them, blinding them for a moment. They stood still. The light was worse to Dave than the darkness. And then it blew past and returned to flashlit brightness again, and utter silence reigned in Max Feinstein's basement in the room where Dave first rediscovered his friends.

"Everybody okay?" DeMarco was the first to let go of Dave's hand. The others reluctantly followed suit, nodding.

"Okay here," Erik said. He didn't sound sure, though.

"Me too." Cheryl uttered a nervous little laugh.

"Are we back?" Dave glanced around the room. "I mean, really back?"

"Looks that way," DeMarco said.

Sean's cheeks looked ruddy and his eyes shone. There was an emptiness about his expression that concerned Dave. It struck him as . . . hollow. The boy's voice reflected the same. "We can't kill this thing. We can't do anything to stop it. It's too strong."

Cheryl crouched down beside him. "Sweetie, it isn't over yet. We still have a chance, okay? We made it this far, didn't we?"

"And we're no closer to killing it than we were when we got here." Sean kicked at a spot on the floor. "My dad—"

His words clipped off in his mouth.

They'd all heard it. A faint laugh, close enough to be among them, but from no discernible direction. They drew their weapons.

Suddenly Dave felt movement in his hand, as if the knife squirmed against his palm. He glanced down as the blade pulled against his skin. It curved upward, and shiny black poured down over the metallic surface from the tip. Then it reformed into a scorpion stinger. The scorpion tried to gain footing in his palm.

Dave flinched and threw it hard against the wall. The handle grew tiny, spindly legs and skittered away. Behind him, Sean gasped.

Dave turned to see the baseball bat become a python. Sean threw it away from his body. DeMarco drew her gun, but she didn't need to. When the snake hit the floor, it broke into a trail of dust.

"What the—?" The curve of Erik's crowbar separated into teeth, the shiny silver body drawing back to strike. He ripped it from his pants and threw it away. It, too, turned to dust upon impact with the floor.

For several moments, no one spoke. Then Erik said, "Well, then. Guess we won't be needing those."

"Oh, fuck." That came from Sean. The others turned in his direction when he said it—surprised, Dave supposed, at how grown-up words sounded in such a small voice. Sean was looking up, and they followed his gaze.

Dave felt his chest hitch.

The Hollower stood right there among them, solemn and unmoving. Its gloves lay folded in front of it, frosted black clothes nearly blending into the background. Only its head stood out, pale like a full moon hanging in the night air of the basement.

Dave had never seen it so close before. From where he stood, he could see the blank slate of a face that was not as empty as it appeared. Countless tiny fractal threads in the white seemed quite capable of expression, subtle suggestion, even question. The slightest movements of the threads changed everything.

It regarded them then, unperturbed by their number, the threads rustling slightly and giving the impression of watchfulness.

DeMarco drew her gun.

It tilted its head in her direction. Its real voice, layered with female and male strains and unpleasantly musical, surrounded them. There was venom in the deadly flicker of it in their ears. *"You can't hurt me with that. You know that."* It shook its head. *"Guns hurt people."*

DeMarco's gun held steady—so steady, Dave thought, that only someone who was really looking would have noticed how much effort DeMarco put forth to keep it from shaking.

"People like Bennie."

"Bastard," DeMarco said, and fired. There was a

gunshot that made the others flinch, but instead of a bullet, the gun dribbled blood from its muzzle that pattered on the floor.

Sally crouched down and splashed her fingers in it.

"Don't," Dave said, swooping down and pulling her to her feet.

She laughed, reaching behind him. He half turned to see what she was doing. She grabbed Feinstein's mirror from him and with the blood on her fingers, thumbed two dots and a crooked swiggle like a drunken happy face on the glass surface.

What had Max said? *"Think what it's for, what it shows people, and you'll know."* Sally understood somehow. She knew.

The ripple in the layers of the Hollower's head conveyed confusion at first, then anger, and then something Dave thought looked very much like dread.

Sally stepped around DeMarco and held the mirror up to the Hollower, and it growled. The sound filled the basement, vibrating the concrete beneath their feet. Sean covered his ears.

A sharp turn of its head toward DeMarco's gun caused it to fire again. The bullet tore through the back of the mirror, shattering the glass. DeMarco looked thrown by the suddenness of it, and fought to reclaim control of her weapon.

Unperturbed, Sally dropped the mirror frame, and bent to pick up a shard of glass. Dave stepped up to stop her, but Erik grabbed his arm. Dave was about to say something to him, to pull free and take the glass from his sister before she cut herself. But then Sally lunged forward, a blond blur, lashing out at the luminous pale canvas in front of her.

The Hollower staggered back. The thin horizontal black slice she'd made across the bottom half of its head quivered. With a wet ripping sound, the faceless expanse started to dissolve in places. That's how it looked to Dave, like some kind of acid was eating through from the inside. Cheryl cried out. DeMarco put a protective arm across Sean's chest. The slice pulled apart to a jagged tear. The Hollower groaned like a metal door. The sound came from the slack, gaping mouth. It stretched, elongating into a scream. Punctures in the top hemisphere puckered and then sank into empty sockets. Other fainter rips and tears delineated nose, ears, cheeks. Its mouth stretched open in a wail, its sockets pinched into a scowl. The whiteness of its face fought to fill those rips in, to seal them up and smooth them over. Its head became a tumult of movement.

Its body changed, too. It expanded upward, straining at the fibers of the trench coat. Dave thought it was reclaiming its real shape—its homeworld shape. It towered over them, filling up most of the space at the base of the basement stairs.

DeMarco ushered Cheryl and Sean behind her. Erik gaped at the monster that was quite literally unfolding and expanding beneath its trench coat before them.

Dave's gaze slid from the Hollower to the staircase. There was a little room there at the base stair, and the change would give them enough time to run for it.

The Hollower shot up by about two feet and threw off the trench coat. Its body swept up behind its head and then curved down like a grotesque swan to pale white stumps of thighs split four ways. From these, it rested on two pairs of long, lean scissor blades. Great discs of bone slid in and out of the curve of its back. Along the sides of its ribs, whips of segmented bony spikes dangled like chains. They rose up with indignant flips every time it wrenched its body. The whips braided into arms and it tore off layer after layer of its face-in-flux until it reached a pure, unbroken white.

"Oh, for Christ's sake," Erik muttered.

Cheryl covered her mouth.

Dave was so in awe of it—so horrified, but if truth be told, fascinated, too—that the comparison of Sally's small stature to the massive bulk of the thing took several moments to register. It drew whips above her head.

"Sally!' He made a move to grab her. The Hollower buried a whip into the cement floor by her feet. Another reached behind her and pulverized the floor between him and his sister. He stopped short and gazed up at the Hollower.

Something was different. Beyond the obvious changes to its appearance, something else was different. It looked less a superimposed thing, devoid of color and size and seams that matched this world. This version of it was solid, physical in a way it hadn't been even minutes before.

Dave stepped back. "Anita, try your gun now."

DeMarco gave him a funny look. "Won't work, Dave. You saw—"

"Try it now. It's changed. I think you can shoot it."

The detective regarded him for a few moments, seeming to consider what he said. She turned her attention back to the Hollower, studied it a moment, then raised her gun and fired over Sally's head.

This time, she fired bullets. The first grazed a disc of bone with a metallic ping and was redirected to a place in the ceiling. The second, though, hit the Hollower dead in the chest in a dusty spray of white. It roared, turning on DeMarco. What looked like a dark burn hole bore out a chunk of its body straight through between two swimming blades. But after a moment, the hole sealed, leaving an ashy black smudge where the bullet had passed through.

It tried to smack the gun out of her hand with a whip. She held firm, but when it disengaged from her wrist, a barb took a small chunk of skin off the back of her hand. DeMarco yelped in pain.

She fired again, this time at its head. The bullet burrowed like a burning ember through where its right eye should have been, and its body trembled in pain and rage.

"Run," Dave said. When no one moved, he shouted, "Run!"

He grabbed Sally's arm and tugged her away from the Hollower and toward the stairs. The others followed his lead, dodging angry whips as they slipped past it. One connected with Erik's arm and tore out a small chunk of his triceps. He bit his lip and slapped a hand over the wound. Dave saw the blood dribbling from between his fingers as he shepherded Erik and the others up the stairs. The Hollower's raging bellows below spurred them on. At the top, DeMarco threw open the door.

Instead of spilling out onto the first floor of Feinstein's house, they found themselves in an enormous backyard. They stopped on a shiny black marble patio that spanned about twenty by forty feet. Beyond it was another thirty to thirty-five feet of lawn. To their left, resting on the marble titles, was an obsidian oblong that vaguely resembled a bench, and another oblong on four small blocks that might have been a table. *Or an altar*, Dave thought, *and a high seat*. Small curlicue carvings made complex patterns across the shiny top surface of the table-altar. Laid out across the symbols were metallic instruments—tools, maybe, or utensils—formed into shapes not meant for human hands or human uses.

A ragged picket fence about eight feet high, its posts leaning at odd angles like a drunken lineup, fenced them in on three sides, while the house sealed them off from behind. There was no gate that Dave could see, but the odd tilt of the posts left gaps wide enough for a head. Beyond, as far as he could tell, there were nebulous clouds of silvery dust in an expanse of blue black. The same continued above them. Occasional massive chunks of silver- and green-veined marble hammered into odd geometric shapes blocked out the view as they drifted by.

Before them, the blades of grass grew long and sharp, dusted with a frost that glinted silver in the light of unseen moons. The grass writhed with movement. To Dave, it looked like fat drops of black ink surging up from the grass, separating and pooling together. In the center of the yard, the ink spidered small streams all over what Dave thought at first was a large doll in a pink-flowered bathing suit, lying on its back. The black oozed over the entire expanse of its head and covered it. The force of the inky drops rocked the little figure. He squinted and leaned in, and realized that what he mistook for a crack in the porcelain hand was actually a line of dried blood. The ink worked over part of the chest, separating, melding together, threading outward, and the chest finally caved. They devoured the cloth and skin around it and from inside the chest cavity, and gold coils sprang out and dissipated like smoke in the air.

Erik gazed upward, shaking the excess blood off his hand and curling up the corner of his T-shirt to press against the wound. "What the hell is this place?"

"Home," Sally muttered inside a breath. "Both and neither. The topsy-turvy. The underside of night."

"I think the Hollower leaked into Feinstein's backyard," DeMarco said. She followed with a small laugh, but she looked pale. The gun hung limp at her side.

"What do we do now?" Sean took Cheryl's hand. They both looked solemn, tired, their lips dry and their eyes unblinking as they fixed on the figure in the center of the yard. "I don't think we can cross through the grass."

"Let's see." Dave grabbed one of the strange instruments from the table and tossed it onto the lawn.

It made a light thump in the grass where it landed. Immediately, the black inky mass paused, as if a collective consciousness noticed something new on its territory, and the black drew away from the figure and surged forward toward the tool, washing over it completely.

Cheryl cried out. The figure (Dave could see what they saw, that it wasn't a doll at all) lay unmoving. Its dark hair hung in limp clumps from a bloody scalp. The face—what was left of it—stared glassy-eyed, the mouth caught in a misshapen O of terror.

Most of the left cheek had been dissolved. There was skull bone beneath.

Dave grabbed two more instruments and threw them in opposite directions. When they landed, two parts of the black split off and one each went in the direction of an instrument.

When the divided portions of the ink were finished, they pulled back from the instruments and merged in the middle of the lawn. Dave could see the corrosion of the metal even from where they stood. The inkiness, whatever it was, had dissolved it.

He exchanged glances with Cheryl. "It can hear or smell, maybe. Or feel vibrations in the ground. Either way, the grass is out."

"Are we safe here? What happens if it swarms the patio?" Cheryl gave him a worried look.

Sally flopped down on the tiles. "Don't feed the bears." She ran a gentle finger along one of the blades of grass, and drew it away covered in blood. Dave pulled her to her feet. Three red drops fell into the grass and another two fell on the tiles. The ink swam through the grass and enveloped the blood there. Dave pulled Sally away from the edge of the grass, his heart picking up speed.

The inkiness didn't acknowledge the blood on the tiles at all. It merged with the rest of the black out in the center of the lawn.

"Guess that answers my question." Cheryl tried to smile, but it looked more like she was trying not to cry.

"No door to the house."

They turned to Erik, who was feeling along the outer wall. "Whatever we came through, it's gone now. And it looks like the fence disappears around the side of the house. Not on this side, but down that end." He pointed. "But there's a big strip of grass between the fence and the house, maybe too big, seeing as how that stuff moves so fast. I don't see anything we can lay across like a bridge down the far end there, but if we could scale the length of the fence, I saw a gate on the other side." He jerked a thumb at the corner of the house behind him as he walked back to them. It met the fence exactly.

"Sounds dangerous," Cheryl said.

"We don't have much of a choice." DeMarco holstered her gun. "We can't stay here. No sense in us all going. Let me go first, and I'll holler back if it's safe to follow."

"But how will we get Sally across? I don't think she's in much shape for climbing."

"We'll have to get her to try." DeMarco walked over to the fence. Dave followed until they were just out of earshot of the others.

"I think I should go," Dave said. He heard his voice saying words but he felt detached, like he was hearing a dream version of himself.

DeMarco cocked an eyebrow. "Spare me the machismo, Dave. I appreciate the thought, but—"

"I'm too restless. I can't wait here. Frankly, they're all making me too jittery. I'd welcome the time alone."

"You really want to go?"

"Yeah." Dave forced an easy smile.

"On one condition," she replied, staring hard into his eyes.

"What?"

"Tell me what you're thinking. Don't lie to me, Dave. I'm a cop. I'll know."

Dave sighed. He glanced back at the others, who stood more or less transfixed by the ink. It had gone back to working the flesh off the little figure in the yard. Sally stood close to the edge of the grass. Only her gaze was on him. She looked angry. *Jilted*, was what came to mind. *Abandoned, maybe.*

"She doesn't trust me," he said to DeMarco, dropping his voice to a conspiratorial tone. "I was supposed to protect her, and I let it get her and hurt her. And I can't live with that. I'm tired of living with having let her down. I can't stay here and wait. I need to do something to get her out of here, instead of making these stupid, useless attempts at running and dodging. Then, maybe—"

"You can fix her?"

Pain jackknifed in his chest. "She can't be fixed. But she could be comfortable. Safe."

DeMarco looked hesitant. Her eyes never left his face.

"I need to do this." It came out harsh, desperate. He softened his voice. "Please. I need to do this."

"Can you even climb?"

"No, but I can't fight, either." He nodded toward the house. "If the Hollower isn't out here somewhere already, it's on its way. And when it comes, I need someone to protect Sally. You're trained to protect people."

"Dave—"

"Protect them," Dave pleaded with her. He hoped his eyes, his whole face conveyed it.

"Okay."

He exhaled. "Thank you. If this works, I can't imagine anyone better equipped to get my sister around that fence than you."

"Your faith overwhelms me." A small grin found her mouth.

He smiled. This time it did feel easy, and genuine. "I feel it's probably well placed."

"I hope so. Listen, I think you should go grab one of those . . . tools, or whatever they are, off that big stone slab. I'd feel better if you were armed with something, at least."

"Okay, will do."

DeMarco followed him back to the obsidian table and examined the objects. They seemed to be made of metal, each with a smooth silver handle and a bar of metal twisted and bent into random snaking designs. When he touched one, it caught and reflected green light. Another gave off slips of blue in the silver. He settled on one that reflected burgundy. Its shape reminded him of those straws he'd had as a kid—Crazy Straws, or Twisty Straws, he thought they were called. Its tip spiraled about four inches to a sharp point. He picked it up. It hummed, vibrating in his hand.

Then he turned to DeMarco. "I'm ready."

DeMarco put a hand on his arm. A sweet gesture—soft and gentle—and it touched him. "Be careful."

In the next moment, she turned on an authoritative heel and called to the others. "Dave's made a good argument for going. I'm staying here with you. With the gun."

Cheryl's eyes widened, and then she frowned. "What? Wait. Why, Dave?" She followed him to the fence.

He had trouble looking her in the eye, but from

the side glances, he could tell by her face that she was afraid.

"Dave, wait." She took his arm, forcing him to turn and look at her. "Why you?"

He sighed. "Cheryl, believe me, I'm not a brave man. Not a strong one, and obviously not a smart one. But Sally . . ." He looked over Cheryl's shoulder at his sister. "I've lost her. I'm no good to her if I can't get her out of here."

"You're no good to any of us if you fall off that fence and whatever's eating away metal objects on that lawn eats you, too. You have no idea what's beyond that fence, or beyond the gate. We need you here. I need you."

Dave felt warm in his chest, and for a moment, he considered telling DeMarco to forget it. Then in his mind, he saw Sally (*"You want me to die"*) tottering forward onto the lawn, the black swarming over her, eating into her face. He didn't want her to die, but God, how he'd wished every once in a while that he didn't have to worry about her. Wished he could put her on a shelf somewhere safe to collect dust so he could be free of responsibility.

And all he'd managed in thinking that was a life of guilt and shackles anyway. And that tied him down more than anything else.

If he went, he'd know he tried to take care of her—really take care of her. Maybe then he'd feel free.

"I have to, Cheryl. It's hard to explain, but I'm no good to anyone if I'm buried under my own failure as a brother."

"You're not a failure. But I can see you're going, whether I like it or not."

He looked at her then, really looked at her. She was beautiful. For a moment, he was amazed by how much he'd let slip away from him—work, friends, family. Love.

He pulled her to him and kissed her. It was neither a gentle nor a fierce kiss, but it was passionate all the same. He put every fear into it, and every word to her unspoken, every date he'd never asked her for, every thought unfulfilled of taking her to bed. Every shy, humble, vulnerable, totally honest sentiment toward her.

And she kissed him back, as if all this time, all he'd had to do was ask.

When they pulled apart, he noticed DeMarco smirking at him, arms crossed beneath her chest. Erik wore a big goofy grin. Dave's face and neck felt hot, but he smiled back. Cheryl followed the look over her shoulder and giggled.

To Dave she said, "You will come back to us," then walked away. It left no room for debate, or for any other possible outcome.

He looked out on the lawn. The black oozed upward, bobbing on the grass. It seemed to be watching him. Waiting. He wondered if it could flow right up the pickets of the fence, right over his foot and ankle and sink into the muscles of his calf.

"Only one way to find out," he muttered to himself, too low for anyone to hear.

Tucking the handle of the strange tool into his belt loop, he eyed the fence.

Not so tough, that fence. He could climb it. No worries.

The wood was weathered and pockmarked, hairy

with splinters. He put a palm to the picket directly in front of him, which canted wildly to the left. It felt rough, as he expected. He pushed on it, then leaned on it. It didn't budge.

Good, he thought. *So far so good, at least. One damned picket at a time. No worries.*

He looked back at the others. They were watching him with hopeful, expectant, anxious eyes. All of them except Sally. She was looking out across the lawn.

Dave turned back to the fence and, taking a deep breath, hoisted his foot to the V where the picket in front of him met with the one next to it. He pushed down, put a little weight on it, but it didn't move. Taking hold of the edges of the wood, he climbed on.

So far so good. Good little fence.

The next space between pieces of wood was narrower, but Dave managed to switch his left foot for his right, and wedge the freed foot sideways into the space. The fence wiggled a little, and Dave sucked in a tiny breath. After a moment, when he felt confident he could move again, he leaned his head out to check for the next open space.

It pointed down, wider than the last, two pickets away. If he stretched, he could reach—maybe. He chanced a look back at the others and his hand slipped off the wood.

For one panicked moment, he felt himself slipping, saw himself landing on his back and the inkiness swallowing him whole. Then he caught the wood again with his hand and pulled himself close. The wood felt rough against his cheek.

With slow and deliberate movement, he carefully replaced right foot with left again. Then he stretched his right leg out as far as he could. His toe found the next foothold between the two pickets. He looked ahead. The back fence looked so far away.

Ahead of him, beyond the pickets, a long, low wail filled the black. Through knotholes and in the dips of open space between his hands, he saw an endless blue black, and through it, metallic bars twisted into asymmetrical shapes floated. One bumped the wood right next to his head and he flinched.

Take one side at a time, he reasoned with himself. *Just make one side for me, Davey-boy, and we'll talk about the next one.*

Behind him, he heard floating words of encouragement. Erik, Cheryl, DeMarco, Sean. They were counting on him.

Sally was counting on him.

Left foot to right foot. Rook to Knight 4. The next V was a picket away.

He made his way down the length of the fence that way, right foot to the foothold, left foot to replace it, right foot to the new foothold, move the hands.

At the corner, Dave took another deep breath and leaned out to gain purchase along the first perpendicular picket. He stretched his hands, each in turn, with spasmodic little waves. They were cramping from clutching the wood. The arches and blades of his feet were starting to hurt, too, but he could ignore that.

Two sides left. Two sides. Seventy feet, maybe. Seventy feet of fence.

The next open space was down low, close to the grass. Dave looked to the one after. It stood higher up, out of the reach of the blackness on the lawn. If he tried, he might be able to make that one.

He stretched a foot out. His toe caught again but slipped, and the momentum nearly pulled him off balance.

Dave took a few moments to breathe, to switch gears to plan B.

The space was awfully low. The inkiness pooled a few feet away. It was aware of him. It spread thin, separating into small, shiny black drops, and this for some reason seemed more awful, more deadly to Dave. He half expected them to splash up, pelting him with deadly acidic juice in tiny pinprick burns all over his face and body.

Not going to think about that. He could dip down and up. He could do that, a quick dip. His right foot slid into the space and the black ebbed forward. He put his left foot down on top of his right foot, missing the cue, blowing the coordination.

"Shit." His right foot jammed. He moved his left foot out of the way, back to higher ground. But when he went to remove his other foot, he met with resistance.

"Oh, come on, for Chrissakes—" He leaned his weight on the secure purchase and yanked on his right foot. His shoe gave a little. The blackness pooled beneath the picket. He could hear it now, humming, a crowd of tiny voices contributing to a collective mind-buzz.

He gave one more sharp tug and pulled his foot free. The picket groaned and shifted outward toward the endless night. Dave closed his eyes and prayed *pleaseohpleaseohplease don't let me die* and waited until the picket settled again. Then he opened his eyes.

He could almost hear . . . words? No, thoughts. Sentiments.

They'd waited too long and he'd pulled free. He sensed hunger, anger, hate. The Hollower's thoughts in microcosm. Drops of its blood, sentient and plotting. This last idea terrified him. It wasn't completely his thought, and it surprised him. He hadn't figured the Hollower even to have blood, given the way it took the bullets from DeMarco's gun, but the idea that it had maybe had parts that functioned separately and with their own agenda scared the hell out of him.

He made a little hop and landed with his left foot in the low space and his right in the next one over. This time, the mass on the lawn didn't hesitate. Drops of black splashed up onto his pants as he used his right leg to pull his left out of harm's way. After a moment, he winced, then cried out as they ate into the spaces behind his ankle, his calf, a spot just below his knee. He felt twenty or thirty needlelike jabs beneath his pants, and then tiny trickles of blood dribbling down his leg.

Gritting his teeth, Dave inched down the length of the back fence. Each time he put his injured leg down, tiny pricks of pain shot up toward his thigh. He stopped, took a few breaths, continued on. At the corner, he swung gently out to the final stretch of fence.

One more. One more side. One more. The gate was within sight, massive weathered wood with thick gray posts and a large gold plate with a keyhole. Thirty, thirty-five feet, maybe. He could make it. He could get Sally out.

Dave ignored the voice in his head. It wanted to know what happened next if what was on the other side of the gate was worse than back there on the lawn. Instead of thinking on an answer, he chanced a look behind him. Way over on the patio, the others watched.

Erik cupped his mouth with his hands and called, "Good job, Dave. Keep going. You're cool, man. Cool and collected."

"You're doing great, Dave!" Cheryl yelled. "I'm proud of you."

DeMarco gave him a thumbs-up, and Sean waved. All present and accounted for.

Except Sally.

Dave felt nauseated and a little dizzy. Despite the cramps, his fingers dug into the wood. Where was Sally?

He mouthed the words—he must have—because Cheryl frowned at him.

"We can't hear you," DeMarco said.

"Whe—" The breath failed him. He tried again. "Where's Sally?"

"What do you mean? She's right—" DeMarco stopped midgesture, because Sally wasn't right there.

Dave spotted her around the same time the others did.

Maybe six feet or so out from the patio, she stood on the lawn.

Fourteen

"Get her," Erik heard Dave yell. "Get her!"

"Oh my God." DeMarco tugged his arm. "C'mon, let's get her the hell off of there."

He saw Dave's sister standing still toward the far side of the lawn opposite Dave. Turned three-quarters away from them, her head was bowed so the blond hair dangled over her shoulder and obscured her face. Erik searched the ground around her. Blood highlighted the tips of the grass where the long blades had brushed against her legs.

He saw movement from the corner of his eye and turned his head.

The mass moved in slow surges toward Sally, covering a few inches at a time as it snuck up on her.

"Oh, hell."

"Sally? Sally!" Cheryl's voice rose, thinned by panic. "Please get off the lawn!"

"Get off the lawn!" Sean echoed. "You can't stay out there."

Erik jogged over to the edge of the patio and

leaned forward, trying to grab her arm, her clothes, something. His injured arm—the blood had dried mostly and adhered his sleeve to his triceps—tugged painfully as he stretched it out to Sally.

He felt his balance thrown and his good arm pinwheeled for a moment, and then he caught himself. His heart thudded in his chest.

"Damn it, she's out of reach," he told DeMarco.

She frowned, keeping a wary eye on the blackness. It had closed half the distance between Dave and Sally.

"We have to get her." DeMarco pulled out her gun.

"Drag her back, if we have to." Erik wiped sweaty palms on his jeans. His wound had started to seep blood again, and small throbs of pain coursed down the length of his arm.

"Count of three?"

Erik shrugged. "Just say 'go.' "

DeMarco paused for a beat, then said, "Go."

They jogged out onto the lawn. Immediately, the blades of grass *whicked* as if caught in a wind and sliced into their shins and calves. Some blades reached the bottom of his knees. He stopped a moment, and the blades and terrible cutting stopped, too.

Of course. Neat little psychological trick, right there.

The blackness, having sensed not one but three large chunks of meaty prey, flowed forward on a hungry tide.

"Come on," DeMarco said with barely concealed impatience. She fired at the tide and it stopped, backsplashing away from them.

Sally was within arm's reach. The black oozed forward.

"Grab her." DeMarco fired again, two shots, arresting the flow.

Erik put a hand on Sally's arm, but she wrenched it away.

"Sally—"

"Go away."

"Oh, hell no, sister. No time for this bullshit." He bent at the knee, feeling blades of grass sink through his jeans and tiger-stripe his thighs. Then he scooped up Sally.

She was light—too light. Too soft. It was like picking up a doll. She wriggled a little, and he felt it where the Hollower had taken a chunk of his arm, but she was not nearly strong enough to make a difference to his balance. He held tight anyway.

"Anita, let's go."

She nodded, fired once more at the oncoming black, and ran back through the grass, wincing. She was shorter than Erik, and the blades cut higher—thighs, even hips. By the time she reached the patio, her pants sported long, crimson crisscrosses along both legs.

Erik lagged behind. Sally kicked her feet, pounding little fists against his chest, but he ignored it. The grass wrapped itself around his ankles, and each step required a pull, followed by a painful gash and the burn of open wound.

He looked at the edge of the patio—the cool tiles, the smooth tiles—and stopped. The grass eased its hold. Behind him, he could hear a low hum, like a thousand tiny voices. In the pause, even Sally grew quiet, her legs limp, her fists curled up against her chest.

Erik waited another second. Then he dove for the patio. The grass tried to tighten around his legs again, but it was a second too late. He stepped onto the tiles and away from the lawn and when he turned, he saw blades still reaching, still making blind swipes at the air where he'd been. He put Sally down, staying close for several moments to make sure she wouldn't bolt for the lawn again. She didn't.

Cheryl was there, hugging him suddenly.

"Good job, Erik." Her voice sounded heavy, and when she pulled away, he saw tears in her eyes.

They turned to Dave, who still hung off a picket across from the edge of the house. His pale face looked relieved, nonetheless. He called out, "Thank you!" Erik thought he mouthed something else—could have been a prayer, could have been more thanks—before turning, with some degree of reluctance, Erik thought, back to the fence.

When Dave faced the wood again, he let the tears go. He cried for the absurdity of having to hang on to a goddamned fence, and for nearly having lost Sally to a bloody lawn. He cried that she was so broken. He cried for having been so much a coward and a failure that once again, instead of saving her, he was as far away as possible, and he cried because it was better that way, with him strung up on old wood, caught between two dimensions. Better because the ex-junkie and the cop were the bravest, most beautiful people he knew right then, and he was glad that he'd convinced DeMarco to let him leave Sally in their care.

He cried because they were going to die in that yard, every one of them, because their sole plan of escape rested on him. Their entire plan since the beginning had rested on him, and he hadn't had a clue any step of the way.

And when the silent tears were done, he sniffed, wiped his eyes with the back of his sleeve, and inched forward again. The picket behind him creaked, then groaned. When it fell, the rush of wind nearly tore him off his spot on the fence. He held on, eyes squeezed shut, until he heard the thud of wood smacking tile. Then he chanced another look behind him. The others came running. Erik held Sally's hand, tugging her gently along.

DeMarco grinned at him. "You're better than we thought," she said. "Nice bridge."

The break was a foot or so off the lawn, creating a slight incline from the tiles to the fence. But its weight rested sturdy on that fence. The others could cross there, and continue out the gate. That is, if Dave could open it.

"Heh. I'm a regular mastermind up here." He gave them a grim smile, and jerked his head toward the gate. "Almost there."

"Good luck, Dave," Sean said.

"Thanks."

Dave turned his attention back. The gate was all that mattered now. Three more pickets. Left foot, right foot, left foot. Two more. Cramped hand. Burned calf. Left foot right foot left foot. One more.

The gate had no noticeable cracks or crevices, other than the keyhole.

He remembered the odd tool in his belt loop, and wondered. Letting go of the wood with one hand, he reached for it and worked it free. He had the crazy notion then (*why call it crazy?*) that all of those strange tools laid out on that slab of obsidian were keys, and that whatever lay on the other side of the gate depended entirely on which key one used.

Dave hoped to God he'd chosen the right one.

Behind him, DeMarco had one foot on the fallen picket, ready to help him if he needed it. The others crowded close behind her.

"Hold hands," he told her.

"Sorry?"

"Hold their hands. I think . . . I think things are going to change."

DeMarco didn't question him further. She took Erik's hand and Sean's, who took Cheryl's. Sally looked up at him, tilting her head to the left.

"Are we going home, Davey?"

He nodded between breaths. The strength of holding himself up on the fence was starting to get to him. "We're going to try."

"Our home, or its home?"

"Don't know, hon. I don't know."

Dave pointed the tip of the key—he was nearly sure now that a key was exactly what it was—and it slid in, glinting burgundy off the gold plate.

Nothing happened. Dave gave it a slight turn, and it clicked.

He looked at them, all but Sally paused in anticipation, eyes expectant, each clutching a hand, chests rising and falling, lips chewed and an air of silent prayer hanging overhead.

Dave wondered for a minute where the Hollower had gone, and why it hadn't come out after them while they were in the backyard. It occurred to him that maybe it was there, though, all along. Maybe it was the little figure disguised, watching, waiting for them to fall prey to the lawn, waiting for them to scale the fence and sail off into the space between worlds.

It occurred to him to that maybe by their drawing

the Hollower into the physical world, all the deviations and changes and overlaps and wrinkles of reality it had caused, once fluid and subject to the Hollower's whim, took on physicality, too. In whole or in part, its skewed perceptions had dried and hardened into nightmarescapes. When Dave opened that gate, he'd be unleashing whatever else had taken form from its mind.

Dave was terrified.

He thought he heard DeMarco say, "Do it" as he turned back to the gate. *Do it, one quick shove, fast and forceful like ripping off a Band-Aid.*

With a grunt, he pushed the gate open, and a giant shark-mouth rushed forward, obscuring all else, roaring humid heat and the stench of rotting meat, and its long black gullet swallowed them all whole.

For what felt like a long time, it lost them in the maelstrom of hate. It was being pinched and stretched into parts scrabbling for dominance, clawing each other in a race to the same goal. It was spread apart and snapped together, and the dark and empty spaces inside, in between, blinded it to everything else, even to the sense of them.

They had done this. They had hurt it. Its hold on the reins of both worlds slipped. It could not have meat biting back. It would not tolerate their survival.

The voids inside it roared. It screamed with them, and fought against them.

And then it was whole again. Hungry. Angry.

The Hollower had regained some control.

As suddenly as they had been swallowed up, they found the long throat and the smell of decay and the thunderous din ceased. Dave found himself face-down on a lawn—the front lawn, maybe—with his arms flung over his head. He dropped his hands to leverage himself up and picked up his head. He moved slowly, aware of the blades of grass. Out front they were smaller, but that didn't mean they were any less dangerous.

He pushed himself up on his knees, listened for the angry hum of blackness, and heard nothing. He patted the grass to his right. It felt soft, cool, and a little dewy. Probably safe. The Hollower was done with that particular game, for now.

In front of him lay the metallic key he'd used to open the gate, and without really thinking too much about it, he picked it up and tucked it into his belt loop. Then he got up and looked around.

Cheryl lay half on top of Sean as if to protect him from falling debris, her arms curled around his head and back. DeMarco lay somewhat crumpled and awkward on the porch steps. Erik lay on the drive-way. A trickle of blood had run from his nose and down the cheek turned to the pavement. His eyes were closed.

No one moved. For one horrible moment, Dave thought maybe he was the only one left alive.

Then Erik groaned and stirred, followed by De-Marco, who winced and rubbed her shoulder as she sat up on the step.

"Everyone okay?" She got up to help Cheryl, who was shaking Sean gently. The boy's eyes fluttered open. He had a small bruise on his cheek, below his right eye. Dave got up on shaky legs. He didn't see Sally anywhere.

His chest felt tight. His throat, made drier by

heavy breaths, issued a weak cough when he tried to call her name. He jumped when he felt a hand on his shoulder.

When he turned, he saw Sally standing behind him. She offered him a small smile, and he pulled her into a hug.

"Thank God."

Cheryl squeezed his arm. "She was over by the gate."

Dave followed where Cheryl pointed to the side of the Feinstein house, to a normal-looking gate at the end of a normal-looking wooden fence to the back-yard. In fact, when he let go of Sally and took a good look around the neighborhood, everything looked as it should. His car was parked on the street where he'd left it and another car, ostensibly DeMarco's, was parked behind it. The other houses stood still, their doors locked, their curtains drawn, their lights out for the night. Garbage cans lined the curb, and they rattled soft rhythms in the wind.

"Looks like we're back." Dave wasn't sure how, but there they were. "Back where we started."

"I don't get it," Cheryl said. "Why did it let us go?"

"Maybe it gave up." Erik ventured a grin.

"Maybe." DeMarco gave Dave a skeptical look.

Dave was inclined to agree with DeMarco's doubt. He was pretty sure they hadn't killed it. He wasn't even sure if they'd hurt it that badly. So why *had* it let them go?

"Something's wrong." Sean's gaze fixed on the house across the street—his house.

"What is it?" DeMarco put a hand on Sean's shoulder.

"That's not my house."

"What do you mean?"

Sean shook his head. "It's . . . wrong. I don't know." He looked down one end of the street, then the other. "This isn't my street. I think . . . I think if we were to go all the way to the end of the street on either side, we'd find dead ends. Or daylight. Or corners of the real world. But not this night, not this place. This isn't my street."

Cheryl gave a suspicious glance around the neighborhood. "How can you tell, sweetie? It looks okay to us."

Sean pointed. "See my window up there, on the right? Left of that shutter there should be a scuff in the paint from where I hit a baseball and it bounced off the house. The way the moon's hitting the house, you oughta be able to see it. And see Mrs. Parks's whatchamacallit? The thing with the plants on it?"

"Trellis," Cheryl offered.

"Yeah, trellis. There's nothing wrong with hers. She keeps it clean and grows ivy on it. That one's chipped, and it's missing that piece of wood there. And that isn't like the kind of ivy she grows. Isn't like any kind of ivy at all, at least none I've ever seen."

Dave squinted, looking hard at the trellis between Sean's house and the house next to it. It looked a little shabby, true, but nothing weathering wouldn't have caused. But then, it was Sean's neighborhood. He'd probably spent every nice summer day out in that street playing with his friends, soaking up the colors and fibers of his stomping ground. He probably did know every scuffed shingle and every painted trellis. And the kid had a point about the ivy. Now that Dave looked at it, it looked black, snaking through the diamond-shaped openings. It seemed alive with movement—breathing, pulsing, slithering, its leaves curling and uncurling.

"And over there," Sean added after a time. "Mr. Porticallo's house, four down on the right. He's always had an oak tree on his front lawn with one low-hanging branch. When I was eight, he used to let me and my friends climb it all the time."

Dave saw the lawn that Sean meant. There was a maple tree to either side. No oak.

Sean shook his head. "It's like the Hollower wants us to see that it changed just enough of this street to still own it." He made a little fist, his face knotted in anger. "It didn't let us go. It's messing with us."

"He's right," DeMarco said, strolling over to her car. "This isn't mine. Well, not all of it, anyway. The side mirror is broken. And the license plate—it's off by two numbers." She crossed around to the trunk, and tried her keys. They didn't fit in the lock. "Figures. I have a shotgun back there."

"Speaking of numbers," Erik added, "anyone notice that all of the houses—all that we can see, anyway—are numbered sixty-eight? Like Feinstein's place, sixty-eight River Falls Road?"

A breeze picked up, rattling the garbage cans even louder. It threaded through the trees and became dry laughter. It nipped at their clothes and hair, teasing them, and beneath its rustle, they heard words close to their ears, the murmur of a betraying lover before plunging the knife in.

"Found you," the wind said. "Found you, found you, found you . . ."

"It's here." Sally shivered.

Dave followed her gaze up to the roof of the Feinstein house.

The Hollower crouched above them, its blade-legs digging into the shingles and its facelessness wrinkled in fury. Its chains whipped back and forth like the tails of cats. Up there, it looked impossibly large.

"I'm scared," Cheryl said.

"You too?" Sean looked up at her.

Dave said, "We all are." Seeing the boy's face, he added, "It's going to be okay."

"I hope so," Erik muttered from the other side of them.

Dave hoped so, too.

The Hollower scissor-clipped to the edge, then nailed itself with its own whips—symmetrical blows to the front of its hips. When it tore the barbed whips out again, the skin split, and shiny silver crablike claws broke through. They looked to Dave to be mounted on jointed stalks. When it pinched the air in front of it, the chittering of the hard substances scraping together echoed in the suburban canyon between the houses.

Dave knew that sound. He'd heard it in dreams, and in the woods around the Tavern. He felt a little sick to his stomach.

Above them, the Hollower shivered. Then it leaped off the roof.

Fifteen

Cheryl cried out when the Hollower landed a few feet from her and Sean. But then something changed in her face. She ushered the boy behind her, standing firm between him and the beast, her chest rising and falling in quick, shallow breaths. Dave saw her hands clench into fists.

It occurred to him then that she meant to kill it, or die trying. Essentially, they had all made a pact to do that very thing, by agreeing to come to the house. Without weapons, without a plan, without any conceivable means of destroying the Hollower, they intended to stand up and fight or fall on that front lawn together.

And Dave felt something change in him, too. A kind of calm settled over him—not one that dispelled fear or tension, but one that simply let him think clearly, without panic dissolving the corners of his confidence.

Its head twitched back and forth. Beneath the blade feet, frenzied sprays of dirt and grass kicked

up. Dave felt the cool blast of its rage, but also something else—a kind of intensity bordering on desperation. The Hollower meant to kill them, too. He had
no doubt of that. But from the way the Hollower's
head seemed to focus above and around but not
quite on him and the others, Dave got the impression something was wrong with it. It looked as if it
sensed the bulk of them, but maybe not each of their
individual presences. He wondered if they really
had hurt it.

It swung a whip knee-height in his vicinity, and
Dave jumped over it. It swung back and he ducked.
The momentum of the swing landed the whip
against one of the porch posts. It yanked back, free-
ing the whip in a spray of splintered wood.

From somewhere behind Dave, DeMarco fired at
its head. The first bullet hit it at about the temple.
Tiny veins of black spidered out from the hole. It
howled, turned in her direction, and the veins
stopped, then receded. The second bullet nailed it in
what would have been the forehead. It bellowed
again in pain and anger, but absorbed the bullet.

It backhanded a whip toward DeMarco, and connected with her wrists. The whip wrapped around
both of them, binding her hands together. The Hollower flung out a wave across the whip and on the
other end, DeMarco cried out in pain. Then it
yanked her off balance, and she stumbled forward
onto the grass. Her feet scrabbled in the grass, but
every time she made a move to roll over or get up,
the Hollower yanked her off balance.

It raised another whip above DeMarco's spine,
and she floundered.

Suddenly, Cheryl dropped from the porch and

dove underneath the Hollower. She plunged a splintered wooden porch spindle deep into its chest, then bolted away from it. The whip intended for DeMarco's back fell with a heavy thud they could feel in their feet, making a small crater in the lawn.

The Hollower made a few attempts to pull out the wood with its claw, but it seemed unable to get the proper leverage to keep the blades from sliding off. It untangled its whip from DeMarco's wrists and tugged the wood from its body with a long, parchment-dry rustle. Its scream shook the trees and echoed between the houses. The claw snapped the wood in two.

Dave glanced at the detective, who had rolled over and out of the way. He could see bleeding rings around the outsides of her wrists.

The Hollower tore another whip's barb out of the ground in a little flying tuft of grass and dirt. It swung the whip out in a wide arc. Cheryl bent backward out of range, lost her footing, and crab-crawled out of the way, toward Sean. He stood frozen, eyeing the monster. His lips moved, but Dave couldn't hear what he was saying.

It smacked at Dave, landing a barb in his thigh, and Dave cried out. In a panic, he yanked his leg away, and the pain sizzled down the length of his body. Blood welled up immediately, soaking his pants.

Dave limped closer to Sean and the Hollower followed. Its hate felt tangible now, a chill that crisped the grass around its legs and crackled like static in the air around it.

"It's real," Sean muttered.

It watched him, too, wary of the child for the first

time. It snaked a whip out near Sean's shoes, but
didn't close in. Sean didn't move.

"Kid, I think you better get out of the way." From
the corner of Dave's eye, he could see the others
drawing in, afraid to make a sudden move. Sean
stood stone still, his little chest rising and falling
with shallow breaths, his lips tight as he mumbled
through his teeth.

"My dad told me you fight big monsters differently. You need something special. Some lose their
power when you stop believing. But you can't help
believing in something when it's standing right in
front of you. That won't work here." His voice
sounded hoarse. "He said bravery works, but I'm
scared. I don't think silver bullets or crosses or garlic
will make a difference to this thing. I don't think it
has a groin. Holy water, sunlight—it's all useless. It's
not like killing monsters in video games." At that
point he did look specifically at DeMarco, then Erik.
They were bleeding, both of them, and Dave suspected that Sean understood just how deadly the
Hollower was.

It growled low. A shiver shook its frame as it
scissor-stepped toward Sean.

"What are you getting at, baby?" Cheryl moved
next to the boy.

"Everything has a weakness, doesn't it?" Tears
formed in Sean's eyes.

"Sean, maybe you should back aw—"

"My dad thought so," Sean continued, oblivious
of Dave's words, "but he never saw anything like
this, I don't think. I saw what it did in the house. Its
strength is going after our weaknesses." His voice
was flat, hypnotically monotone, as he spoke.

He glared at the Hollower and said, "But I don't think it can use our weaknesses against us anymore. Not now. Not all fleshy like that."

Sally poked him in the arm and when he jumped, she giggled. "It hates us. Hates this world. We chill it. Blind it. Starve it."

Sean nodded. "Being like us is its weakness."

The Hollower's head spasmed, its claws grinding like angry brakes, its whips snapping above its head. It leaned toward them and screamed, and all around it, the property changed.

High above their heads, starbursts of blood swelled and then popped, raining chunky bits of gore down onto the lawn. The blood soaked into their clothes, matted their hair, and the stink of old meat got into their noses and throats.

Feinstein's house trembled, and each vibration carried a sustained groan into the air. Pieces of vinyl siding rotted and quickly fell in meaty thumps around its base. Dave saw a complex machine of steel beam framework, gears, springs, and pendulums. Smooth, pale human limbs tumbled bedroom-height from one gear to another, mashed to pulp by the time they reached the ground. The porch creaked and its floorboards moved slowly to the right, now an assembly line to carry out what was left from the gears, mostly in smears of red and black. The trees around the house sloughed off their bark to expose torsos stretched long, the branches reaching up as grotesque arms that fractalized into fingers and then into—what, toes? They swept high overhead and Dave couldn't be sure.

Dave and the others huddled closer together, backing away from the Hollower as one. It shook with rage, its whips striking the air like snakes. It was carpet-bombing them with its ideas. Dave suspected since it couldn't tap into their insecurities, it was bending the world to its own mind's hatred of all things body. *A kind of autocannibalism*, he thought, and grimaced.

A spike of bone erupted near Sean's feet, and Cheryl dove and tackled him, rolling out of the way with him just as a larger one burst through the lawn and up toward the sky. Dave grabbed her arm and pulled her up. There was a low rumble by her ankle and he tugged her and the boy out of the way as a whale-size rib arced up out of the ground.

Sally tugged on his sleeve and he turned around. Behind them, tightly arranged cage-bars of bone, each topped with a skull, had them closed off from the curb. Beyond the bones, Dave could see the street exposed like open tissue, flinching as the breeze blew over it. Across the street, Sean's house, also flayed to expose machinery, churned what looked like hamburger meat out of one of the upstairs windows.

Both his car and DeMarco's reeked of rot; the Hollower had made them slabs of carcass, skinned and twisted into vaguely animal shape and left to buzz by the curb.

Dave took a step back and slipped on something rubbery and full of lumps. He looked down and saw an upturned face, its nose mashed against his toe, its eyes closed, and by reflex he shrank away from it.

"Oh, Christ." Erik nudged DeMarco, who looked decidedly pale and uncoplike at that moment. "They're scalps. Scalps and hair. The whole fucking lawn."

Cheryl cringed and a soft "ewww" leaked out from between her lips.

The grass had been replaced by countless caps of black hair that knotted beneath their feet. Whether there were heads or just skin beneath the strands, Dave didn't want to know.

Sean looked up at him. The tears still cupped his eyes, but he looked determined not to cry. He whispered, "My dad never told me what to do about this, either."

Dave squeezed his shoulder. "Mine, neither. We'll figure something out, though. I promise."

"We can't stay here with the bones to our backs," DeMarco said. "Dave, we can't—Dave!"

He followed her gaze and the muzzle of the gun that, by reflex, was pointed at the threat.

The Hollower was cutting a swath through the hair to get them.

"Run!"

They bolted sideways, along the length of the bones, which kept speed with them as they rose from the hair. From the periphery of his vision, Dave noticed the occasional bone spearing a scalp and launching it upward.

"Keep going! Keep going!" he shouted, and they ran while the bones fenced them in, finally dodging inward toward the center of the lawn. The Hollower seemed to catch glimmers of them, then lose them. Then it turned on them suddenly and they skidded to a stop.

It lashed out, swiping at Erik. A whip connected with his knee, and Dave heard a pop. Erik fell on the lawn. He clutched his knee and whimpered, but didn't stay long on the ground. Cheryl shouted to

Erik. DeMarco grabbed his hand and she and Cheryl yanked him to his feet.

The Hollower backhanded Cheryl with a claw. She flew back a few feet and landed with an "oof" on the hair, a foot or so shy of a sharp spindle of bone. The Hollower lurched in her direction and landed a barb squarely on her shoulder. Her eyes grew wide, but she didn't scream until it ripped the barb out. She rolled over on her side, tears wetting her cheeks, and pushed herself up.

Four whips shot out, each encircling one of Sally's limbs; they wrapped around both wrists and both ankles. She screamed, but the scream was cut short. A fifth looped around her neck and pulled tight.

The whips groaned as the Hollower stretched Sally's arms and legs. Her mouth worked open and closed, but little more than choked whimpers made it out of her throat. Where the whips bound her wrists, blood oozed out from beneath and trickled down the length of her outstretched arms. She flinched as one of the whips tightened on the ankle of the leg where she'd injured her calf. It squeezed blood from that wound, too. She jerked as she tried to pull her arms and legs into herself, out of the grip of the Hollower.

"Sally!" Dave ran toward them. The Hollower's head snapped in his direction, and he stopped short, feeling cold all under his skin.

DeMarco shot it once in the head, but it shook off the bullet and the white swallowed up the hole.

The Hollower pulled Sally taut, stretching her arms and spreading her legs. Her face twisted in pain. She glanced once at Dave, her eyes pleading, her skin very pale. Blood flowed heavily now from around the sides of the whips on her wrists. It spilled down her neck and down inside the front of her blouse, where it soaked through in uneven dark spots.

Dave became suddenly aware of the weight of the backyard key in the palm of his hand. He couldn't remember how he got it again, or if he'd ever put it down in the first place.

"Everything has a weakness," Sean had said. A soft spot, a vulnerable underbelly to everything, if a person knew how to pierce it.

The whips pulled a little more, and this time the groaning sound came from within Sally. Her head lolled. The Hollower raised a claw.

Without a word, Dave charged forward.

He felt it when he drove the sharp end of the key through what should have been a face—he felt the texture of the Hollower's head, the terribly wrong softness that killed the first few layers of skin on his fist and split his knuckles. He felt a small imploding from inside it somewhere and beneath that, like a vacuum behind cheesecloth, he felt a sucking against his hand. He let go of the handle. A claw knocked the wind out of his chest, and he went stumbling back. Already, the pain in his hand was growing numb.

The Hollower did not cry out, but its whole body trembled. Its head shook like it was trying to clear its mind, or bring the world back into focus. With spasmodic jerks, it wobbled on its long and now unsure scissor legs. Its whips fell away from Sally, who crumpled on the grass. Then they thudded into the earth in unison, its claws chattering irregularly in some spastic SOS.

Dave hooked his arms under Sally's armpits and dragged her away from the Hollower. Her eyes were closed, but she whimpered in her throat, and in between whimpers, she mumbled words. He couldn't make out all of it, but he caught enough: "It hurt me," and "I'm scared of it, Davey."

Around the key in its head, the wound distorted, tugged and snapped back against the metal. Beneath its chest, the taffy pull of its insides made movement beneath the pale and fluttering chest.

The claws picked up a fevered pace, opening and closing so fast they almost blurred. Then they slumped at its sides and the chest lurched up as if the force inside it pushed it toward the sky. The swan curve of its neck lashed back and forth, and the blades fell out of its back and clattered on the ground.

It sank toward the earth, slumping a little, twitching its head, its body wracked by shudders it could not control.

Its last breath, if it could have been said to even have a breath, sounded like thunder, cracking against the sky. Then it collapsed on the grass. From beneath, the blades bit into its skin, embedded like shrapnel.

For a long time, no one said anything. Dave concentrated on the throbbing in his thigh, the pain keeping him alert and aware, keeping him from sinking to the ground. He put a protective arm around Cheryl, and another around Sally. The former, breathless, maintained her ground but leaned against him, her bloodstained hand pressing the wound on her shoulder. The latter trembled slightly, slack in the crook of his elbow.

To his right, DeMarco squeezed Sean's hand. Erik leaned against her on the other side, bruised, bloody, his eyelids heavy.

All around them, subtle changes rippled through the neighborhood: houses regrafted with vinyl siding, scalps balding to reveal grass beneath hair, bones sinking into the earth, maples to oaks, trellises whole and blooming with ivy, scuffs on house siding, cars restored to usable condition. The shower of gore dried up and disappeared from their clothes and hair, and the stench of dead meat dissipated.

They were back.

Before them, the Hollower lay, but not quite still—not yet. Inside, something still stretched and expanded the shell of the body, and it began to emit a low wail like an air-raid siren far, far off in the distance. The sound seemed sad to Dave, the leaking out of a life of anger and hate and nothing else to be remembered by. The end of a predator known only through the eyes of prey.

The wailing continued long after the movement beneath its surface grew still and the whole of the monster sank a little in the grass.

"Is it dead?" Erik limped forward. "Maybe we should—"

He flinched when a black bolt of what looked like lightning schismed the air above the Hollower, stopping just short of its body. The bolt—more of an inversion, Dave thought, or some kind of rip—crackled with energy, tearing open the air of River Falls Road. It quickly grew to about six feet in height, then pulled apart, gaping like a mouth turned on its side.

The wailing inside the dying thing ceased.

And through the rip stepped three Hollowers,

each blank-faced, gloved, and trench-coated, hats
tipped low on hairless heads, black-clad legs step-
ping carefully down into the grass around their
dead comrade, their feetless shoes not really touching any part of the earth at all. Behind them, the fis-
sure between worlds sizzled and hummed.

In unison, they looked up at Dave and his friends,
and the luminous white committee of facelessness
seethed with hate.

Two bent low, one at the head and the other at the
legs. For several long moments, their gloves passed
over the body as if they were swishing the air above
it to clear it for a better view. With each pass, they
made muted sounds that reminded Dave vaguely of
whales—mournful, angry sounds that got into the
meat of him and stuck there.

Their arms slid beneath the body and lifted it up.
They didn't look quite like they were touching it, but
rather, the air between it and their arms rippled and
blurred and that carried its weight. The third Hollower stood watching, almost daring Dave and the
others to try and stop them. It tilted its head, and
raised an arm, its fingers spread in a wave. But then
the fingers curled into a fist it held away from its
body, and from the black balled glove, blood pattered into the grass. When it opened its fist again,
palm out, he saw clean black leather. Behind it, the
other two Hollowers disappeared with their fallen
back into the black rip.

The last watched them without eyes for several
moments, and Dave heard a whisper, sexless, powerful, but somehow of a different timbre than their
original Hollower.

In his ear, it said, "Found you." Then it stepped through the rip, which promptly zippered up and disappeared with a pop, until it was as if nothing had ever been there at all.

Sixteen

Dave felt dizzy for a minute, leaning against the women on both sides of him. He wasn't sure if that Hollower simply meant to echo the last thing the dead one had said to them, or if maybe—

His brain swallowed the second thought. He wouldn't consider it, wouldn't entertain the possibility.

Sean ran to Cheryl and buried his face in her stomach. He laughed and it dissolved, as laughter sometimes does, into tears of relief.

"Let me walk you home, baby," she cooed at him, and he nodded into her top. Taking his hand, she started with him across the street. Erik, DeMarco, and Dave with Sally in tow followed to the far curb, but Cheryl brought him up to the door.

The boy put a hand on the knob, glanced back once at her, then peered around her to the others. "Thank you." To her he repeated it specifically: "Thank you, Cheryl."

It looked as if he wanted to say more, but couldn't

think of anything that better said what his "thank you" encompassed. Cheryl gave him a hug, then waved as he disappeared through the door.

When she turned back to them, there were tears in her eyes, but she was smiling.

"We did it," she whispered. She walked up to Dave and kissed him, and nothing had ever felt so good, so complete to him. He slipped his free arm around her waist, wanting to hold on to her forever. He thought that maybe he could—not because he was a great protector or a brilliant man or even a brave one, but because he earnestly cared about her, and he thought she knew he would try, at least, to be everything else to her that he'd never thought he could be to anyone.

When the kiss ended, and the others, with embarrassed grins, nodded toward the car, he held her hand as they crossed the street.

At the detective's car, Erik limped over to De-Marco, who was returning her gun to its holster, and stuck out a hand.

"You take care of yourself, Erik." She pulled him into a hug instead, and although he winced in pain, he smiled.

"Don't think I can do much more damage than this, eh? Hey, tell Detective Mendez I said hi when you see him, okay?"

DeMarco pulled away from him, looking pained for a moment, but then she said, "You got it."

To Dave and Cheryl, she said, "We should take Sally to the hospital."

Dave nodded, and caught the detective's eye. She winked at him, then leaned in and said, "She's lucky to have a big brother like you."

He didn't know if he had ever been a good big brother or not, but he thought that maybe it had never been about fixing her, or keeping her from falling apart. Maybe it had always simply been about keeping her comfortable and safe, and not beating himself up because he couldn't do more.

He smiled. "Thank you, Detective."

"How about you, Anita—are you okay?"

DeMarco waved Cheryl's question away. "I'm fine. I'm a tough broad."

"And your cases?"

DeMarco grinned at Cheryl as she opened her car door. "You folks are gonna cost me a hell of a lot of confusing paperwork. But I'll survive." She got in the car, then leaned out her window, waiting for them to pull away to follow them out of the development.

Dave put Sally in the passenger seat. She sank against the fabric and smiled up at him, but her eyes were vacant. He wasn't sure she even recognized who he was. Erik got in behind her, and Cheryl next to him, and Dave drove them all away from River Falls Road.

They dropped Erik off first, at home. He said he'd go to the hospital later, but right then, the most important thing was that he get home. He only wanted to see his girlfriend. Not just see her but *feel* her, to make sure she was okay. Dave could understand that.

She likely had been waiting by the window, since she came running out to greet him before he'd even managed to hobble too far from the car. She hugged him, almost hugged through him, and he hugged her back.

He waved good-bye as Dave, Cheryl, and De-

Marco pulled away from the curb, but neither he nor his girl let go, nor even looked up. Dave suspected it would be a long time before either of them did.

DeMarco discovered her police radio worked on the way to the hospital, when it crackled to life, startling her out of worried thoughts about Bennie.

It was his voice, though, that came through.

"DeMarco, where the hell are you?"

She frowned, picking up the radio to respond. "Bennie?"

"Yeah. Where've you been for the last few hours? We were at sixty-eight River Run Road, then radioed the station, then went back to the station, then went to sixty-eight River *Falls* Road, then radioed in again—"

"Bennie, is it you?"

A pause, then, "Yeah, An, it's me. You sound funny. You okay? What happened to you?" His voice, gentle, sounded concerned.

She eyed the car ahead of her, full of weary bodies and tired spirits. "Nothing. Nothing, I'm fine."

"Did you check out the Feinstein place? Everything okay?"

"Fine. Yeah. I found the Kohlar woman wandering around inside. Her brother and I are taking her to the hospital now."

"Wanna tell me about it?" Cop hunch. He knew something was up—something unprotocol, something off-kilter. She could hear it in his voice.

"Yeah, I do, actually. Later. Later, I want to tell you a lot of things. You gonna be around?"

"Sure." He sounded pleased. "For you, Annie, I'm always around."

She smiled. "Good. 'Cause I like you around."

In the background, she heard Rubelli's voice singsong an "oooooooh" reminiscent of grade school teases.

"Shut up, man," Bennie said, but she could hear laughter through the radio. To her, he said, "See you later?"

"Looking forward to it." Then she clicked off with him, and radioed the station.

Inside, she felt warm and giggly. May was right about her feelings for Bennie Mendez, but then, May was always right.

Epilogue

There were police reports to be filed, and medical papers to fill out, and insurance issues to be taken care of. Sally's ankle had to be bandaged, as well as DeMarco's wrist, and both Cheryl and Dave needed stitches. DeMarco fielded the hospital's questions. And when all of that was said and done, when a few weeks stretched into a few months and the dreams faded from the night's rotation, Dave started to relax.

He sat on the porch swing with Sally, enjoying the sunset. It was Friday afternoon, and he'd taken the day off from work to come see her. He went to see Sally regularly in the assisted living community that Dr. Fiorello suggested. Sally trusted the new doctor, and seemed to like him much better than she had Dr. Stevens. And Dave liked Oak Hill. The community was quiet, pleasant, a comforting series of cool white-stone buildings encasing a hilly green lawn on which most of the residents met for picnic lunches, chess or checkers, or occasionally, to paint pictures or play games. Dave thought Sally was content there. The whole place kept an easy, soothing rhythm that appealed to her gears-out-of-whack.

"You okay? You warm enough?" He adjusted the blanket over Sally's lap, and she giggled, waving him away.

"I'm okay, Davey." Sometimes she knew his name.

"Okay, then." He stood. "I've gotta go now, hon. I'll come see you Sunday, okay?"

She stared off across the rolling lawn between the buildings. She'd already forgotten he was there.

"See ya, Sals." He kissed the top of her head, then walked down the steps and around the corner to where Cheryl was waiting.

Cheryl smiled when she saw him, and linked her arm through his. "How is she?"

Dave shrugged. "Comfortable. Safe."

Those things—comfort, safety—had finally settled into the cracks and grooves of his life, and he was glad for it.

He saw Erik sometimes; the boy had eventually gone for stitches in his arm and some bandages for his other injuries, and was healing up nicely. When they ran into each other at the Tavern, they made light, easy conversation—Erik and Casey's wedding plans, movies, the latest Yankee game, a bar joke that Erik had heard at N.A. Sometimes, after a shift, even Detective DeMarco would stop in for a drink. And Cheryl would come by with her cloth and wipe the bar down and put a Diet Pepsi in front of each of them, and the conversation would be both comfortable and safe. The Hollower hung between them, keeping them from ever really enjoying the silences of friendship, but they were content to talk around it, and to fill the spaces with anything else.

They didn't talk about the Hollower directly. Not there.

Sometimes, after sex, though, Cheryl would snuggle close to Dave, and with the window open and the cool breeze blowing over their bodies, it would come up then, but only in vague terms, and only murmured in passing. Once, Cheryl asked if he thought it would come back. She meant the third Hollower. He was fairly sure about that.

"No," he told her. It didn't matter whether he believed it or not, or whether she believed him. It was the only answer to give her.

Dave figured it was a mistake to waste time worrying about something he couldn't fix. They'd cross that bridge if—God forbid—they ever came to it. In the meantime, things were good. Much better than they'd ever been, in fact. And he was proud of that.

As they walked back toward the Oak Hill Assisted Living parking lot, Dave noticed a sixty-something woman sitting on a wooden bench that was painted a kind of sea-foam green and set next to the concrete path. The woman looked up at them. She wore a pink blouse and white linen slacks, with sandals. Her curly ash-blond hair was pulled up in a short ponytail tight to her head.

She made him think of how Sally would be years from then—content, well dressed, well fed, well cared for. It wasn't often, he'd noticed in his thirties, that he looked forward to approaching old age with satisfaction and even a kind of anticipated relief, but seeing the woman there, he caught a glimpse of the future, of comfortable benches and warm sun and he wanted that. With Cheryl, he wanted that. For Sally, he wanted it.

Dave waved at the woman on the bench. Then, with a mischievous grin, he took off at a half jog toward the car. Cheryl laughed to keep up with him, and the sound buoyed him. Dave had an amazing feeling of being free.

The woman on the bench waved back a few seconds after they had already passed, and the wave closed into a fist. A slight, soft breeze picked up, teasing her hair, blowing away her eyes, nose, and mouth like dust right off her face. When the crude conveyances of human sense were gone, the smooth expanse of white followed the retreating forms with interest.

They got into a transportation object—a car; it knew the word now—and it waited until they were gone, far along the road and into their lives, before settling back onto the bench.

The ones in this dimension had never appealed to it. Their horrible physicality disgusted it. But these few were different. They did not have much meat, but the empty, stretching, pulling voids inside it and the fathomless anger drove its hunger for them anyway.

It would find them, when it needed to. Now was not the time, but soon.

"Remember you," its voice said, trying out words. It imitated their laughter.

Soon.

It frosted the air around it with its hate.

GHOUL

BRIAN KEENE

June 1984. Timmy Graco is looking forward to summer
vacation, taking it easy and hanging out with his buddies.
Instead his summer will be filled with terror and a life-and-
death battle against a nightmarish creature that few will
believe even exists. Timmy learns that the person who's been
unearthing fresh graves in the cemetery isn't a person at all.
It's a thing. And it's after Timmy and his friends. If Timmy
hopes to live to see September, he'll have to escape the…

GHOUL